BREAK
MY
RULES

BY ROXY SLOANE

The Oxford Legacy Series
Cross My Heart
Break My Rules
Seal My Fate

The Flawless Series
Flawless Desire
Flawless Ruin
Flawless Prize

The Ruthless Series
His Ruthless Heart
These Ruthless Games
Our Ruthless Vow

The Priceless Revenge Series
Dig Two Graves
One Dark Secret
No More Lies

The Kingpin Series
Kingpin
His Queen

The Seduction Series
The Seduction
The Bargain
The Invitation
The Release
The Submission
The Secret
The Exposé
The Reveal

The Temptation Series
One Temptation
Two Rules

Standalones
Explicit

BREAK MY RULES

THE OXFORD LEGACY

ROXY SLOANE

AVON

An Imprint of HarperCollins*Publishers*

BREAK MY RULES. Copyright © 2023 by AAHM, Inc./Roxy Sloane. Excerpt from SEAL MY FATE © 2023 by AAHM, Inc./Roxy Sloane. All rights reserved. Printed in the United States of America. No part of this book may be used or reproduced in any manner whatsoever without written permission except in the case of brief quotations embodied in critical articles and reviews. For information, address HarperCollins Publishers, 195 Broadway, New York, NY 10007.

HarperCollins books may be purchased for educational, business, or sales promotional use. For information, please email the Special Markets Department at SPsales@harpercollins.com.

Originally published as *Break My Rules* in the United States in 2023 by AAHM, Inc./Roxy Sloane.

FIRST AVON TRADE EDITION PUBLISHED 2024.

Interior text design by Diahann Sturge-Campbell

Rose illustrations © vectortatu/Stock.Adobe.com

Library of Congress Cataloging-in-Publication Data has been applied for.

ISBN 978-0-06-341842-4

24 25 26 27 28 LBC 5 4 3 2 1

For all the readers with revenge on their minds . . .

BREAK MY RULES

Chapter One
TESSA

I can't breathe.

I stay, frozen in place on my knees by the lakeshore. Saint is sprawled before me on the ground, finally naked, tense with lustful anticipation. Just a moment ago, I was caught up in the same thrilling rush, eager to strip him bare and drive him crazy, but now . . .

Now my heart is like lead in my chest as I stare at the small tattoo he has inked on his thigh. A crown with a serpent snaked around it. It's small but distinctive, and I would know it anywhere.

It's the same tattoo that my sister described. The only detail she could remember from a terrible assault that left her spiraling into the depths of depression—and made her take her own life. I've been looking for that tattoo—and that monster of a man—since the moment I arrived in Oxford. I thought I'd find it at the secret society party I infiltrated tonight, and I was right. Just not how I imagined.

Because here it is: inked on Anthony St. Clair. *Saint.* The man I've been falling for, the only one I trusted, the man who's introduced me to the heights of wild, reckless pleasure.

The man who just held me tenderly as I sobbed, and told me that I needed to move on from my self-destructive quest for revenge.

It's him.

No.

This isn't happening. I can't believe it.

"Tessa?" Saint lifts his head, his piercing blue eyes still dark with desire. He gives me a lazy, seductive smile, the same smile that's melted me a dozen times over. "I thought I told you to stop being such a damn tease."

I gasp for air, reeling. How have I not seen it until now? But every encounter we've had has been spontaneous, so passionate, I never realized I hadn't seen him fully naked before. The dim lights of the Midnight party . . . When I was blindfolded in the club . . . Even our first time having sex, he took me hard up against the wall—from behind.

And I loved every minute of it.

"I'm sorry . . ." I blurt, sick to my stomach. I don't know what the hell to do right now. I only know that I have to get away from him. "I can't . . ."

In an instant, the desire on Saint's handsome face is replaced with concern. "Tessa?" He sits up, reaching for me. I flinch back.

"It's just, I guess I'm still kind of emotional, from before," I babble, trying to avoid his gaze. "I thought this was what I needed, but . . ."

"Shh, it's OK," Saint says, easily pulling his clothes back on. He smiles at me, so reassuring. "We can just sit here and talk for a while longer, or whatever you want."

What I want is to rewind the last five minutes, so I never saw the tattoo.

Or go back further, to before I even met him. So I wouldn't have wound up falling for the one man who destroyed my sister's life. When I think of how I laughed with him, confided in him . . .

Fucked him.

Oh God.

I lurch to my feet, unsteady. The woods that only moments ago seemed secluded and romantic now are dangerously quiet. We're all alone out here, with nobody around. I felt so safe with Saint, but now . . .

Now I can't trust anything.

"Let's get back to the party," I say quickly. I don't want to let him know I've figured it out. Not until I have some kind of plan.

"Are you sure?" Saint frowns, and it takes everything I have to force a smile.

"It'll be good for me, some distraction. Fun," I insist. "I don't want to sit around crying anymore tonight."

Not with the man who could have caused every single one of my tears.

"Alright then." Saint gives me another affectionate smile. "Your wish is my command."

He straightens up the rest of his clothes and takes my hand. Every instinct in my body wants to recoil in disgust, but I force myself to act normal. Somehow, I manage to walk with him, side by side, back through the woods and to the lights of the party like nothing is wrong. And with every step, my head is spinning.

How could it be Saint?

All those secrets I bared to him . . . I opened up about everything. I shared Wren's pain over her attack—and my own heartbreaking grief over losing her. He told me that the man who did that to her was a monster. Evil.

Was he laughing at me all along?

Was this some kind of sick game to lull me into trusting him?

It doesn't make sense.

Finally, after what seems like an eternity, the house comes into view. The party we left is raging now, with music playing loudly, and all of the Blackthorn Society members dancing and drinking, all pretense at good manners lost to the debauchery. I can't believe I thought I'd find some dark conspiracy here, when it's nothing but a bunch of privileged aristocrats having a good time.

And the true threat was closer than I ever knew.

I shoot a sidelong glance at Saint as he leads me to the terrace. He looks the same as he always has: devastatingly handsome, with tousled dark hair and stormy blue eyes, and a smile that could tempt me to forget all my inhibitions.

Once, I called him a fallen angel. Now, I wonder if he's the devil himself.

"I need a drink!" I declare loudly, dropping Saint's hand. "Be a darling and find me something sparkly? And some snacks too. I'm going to find a bathroom. I'll be right back."

I catch a flash of concern on his face at my abrupt mood change, but he smiles and nods. "Sweet or savory treats?"

"Surprise me!"

I leave him by the bar and slip through the crowd, back into the huge main house. There's a bathroom down the hallway, but I head straight for the front doors instead, my heart pounding like I'm staging a jailbreak. Any minute, I expect to hear Saint's voice, or find him blocking my path, but I keep my head down, ignoring the partygoers all around me until I finally burst outside.

The front drive is busy now, cars still arriving and dropping people off. Of course, the after-party, I realize. Saint told me that once the official secret society business was over, fresh blood would sneak in to enjoy the fun. It's how my sister would have wound up here, at a party just like this one. Where she was taken and held captive in a cell somewhere, while an unknown man did things that she was grateful to never remember.

It couldn't be Saint.

Swallowing back the bile in my throat, I make a beeline for a cab that's just dropped off a group of glamorous women. "Can I get a ride back to Oxford?" I ask desperately.

The driver raises his eyebrows, no doubt calculating the massive fare. "No problem, luv. Hop on in."

I all but lunge for the back seat, keeping my head low as I hold my breath and watch the doors for Saint. But he doesn't come after me. The driver eases past the rows of gleaming, expensive cars and heads down the driveway, leaving the bright lights and music of the party behind.

I don't relax, not for a moment. Not until we're miles away, speeding through the dark countryside, and I can finally give in to bewildered tears.

"You alright?" The driver glances in the rearview mirror as I try to stifle my sobs.

"Uh-huh." I make a muffled sound. "Sorry, I just . . . Bad breakup," I manage to mutter, and he gives me a sympathetic nod.

"Sorry to hear it, luv. Don't you worry. You'll feel better in the morning."

But as the questions whirl in my mind, I can't imagine feeling better ever again. I replay everything that happened tonight, searching for answers, but it just doesn't add up.

I thought I knew him. I thought he cared about me.

Surely it all wasn't a lie?

Who are you, Saint?

* * *

BACK IN OXFORD, I direct the cab driver to my old student apartment. I moved out just days before—

No, Saint moved me out, I realize as I trudge up the stairs and unlock the door. He packed me up and moved all my things over to his townhouse. He said it wasn't safe here, that he wanted to protect me.

All along, was he the one I needed protection from?

To my relief, my old roommates, Jia and Kris, are out tonight, and the apartment is silent. I head straight for my bedroom and sink down on the mattress, looking around the empty room in shock.

What do I do now?

My phone buzzes in my bag, and I pull it out, seeing a dozen missed calls and texts from Saint that arrived during the drive back to Oxford.

Where are you?

Did you leave the party?

Are you OK? We can't find you anywhere.

Tessa, I'm worried. Please,
tell me what's going on.

The messages get increasingly anxious, and I feel a traitorous pang of guilt, just imagining his confusion to find me suddenly gone.

But he doesn't deserve my guilt, I remind myself as I turn my phone off entirely. He doesn't deserve anything from me, except my anger, and revulsion, and rage for what he's done.

Except . . . I don't feel it.

I can't feel anything except numb shock and disbelief.

I lie back on the bed and stare at the ceiling in a daze, trying to reconcile the man I know with the monster I've been chasing. It doesn't make sense to me that he could lie to my face, over and over again. That he could be guilty of such terrible crimes against my sister—but make me think that he really cared about me. Be so tender and supportive, passionate and fun.

As the memories taunt me, my tears come again, hot sobs of anguish and betrayal as I lie there, broken.

How could I have been so wrong about him?

Chapter Two
TESSA

I spend the weekend locked away in my room, ignoring his messages and struggling to make sense of it all. It's not just the shock and horror of discovering that Saint might be the one behind Wren's attack; I'm surprised by the force of my heartache, too. I guess I didn't even realize just how deeply I was falling for Saint, until I realized that it was all a lie.

Now I'm careening between hating him and missing him. Cursing his name and wanting desperately to believe there's some other explanation. Maybe someone else has the tattoo . . . Maybe he hasn't been lying to me . . .

By the time Monday morning comes, I'm exhausted from the battle raging inside me. I stumble out of my bedroom and down the hall. My roommate's voices come from the kitchen in hushed, gossipy tones.

"Do you know what happened? She's been bawling her eyes out all weekend."

"She wouldn't say. Just that they broke up."

"You mean, he dumped her ass, just like we knew he would."

"She's a wreck. Clearly, she didn't see it coming."

"What? She figured she'd fall madly in love and live happily ever after with the duke?" There are snorts of laughter. "We tried to warn her. Those rich bastards never really care."

"Shh, I think she's coming. Just don't say we told her so."

I swallow hard and brace myself, opening the door loudly. "Morning."

"Good morning!" Right away, Kris and Jia leap to attention, giving me wide-eyed looks of sympathy.

"How are you feeling?" Jia coos. "Do you want some coffee? Did you get any sleep?"

"A little. And coffee would be great, thanks." I manage to force a smile as I pour myself a bowl of cereal and perch at the table. I know they're being two-faced, pretending to care when they were just laughing about my heartbreak, but I'll take it.

I'd rather them thinking I'm some naïve woman who just got dumped than have to explain the truth.

"So, what are you up to today?" Kris asks brightly.

"Study, I guess," I reply, downcast. "My academic advisor gave me a talking-to last week, said I need to turn things around if I don't want to lose my fellowship."

Although why I'll stay in Oxford now, I'm not even sure.

"Well, at least you have plenty of time," Jia says smugly. "No more distractions."

Like Saint.

"Right." I nod, numb.

"Why don't you take first dibs on the shower?" Kris says, giving me a meaningful look. "There should be plenty of hot water."

"Thanks," I say, even though it's clear that wasn't so much a kind offer as a sign of just how bad I look right now, after two days sobbing without so much as glancing at a mirror.

I don't know if I'm crying because of Saint's betrayal, or because I still can't believe that the man I'm falling for could be capable of such crimes.

"We're getting drinks at the college bar tonight," Jia adds. "It's karaoke. You should come!"

"I don't know . . ." I wince.

"You'll feel better, getting out and about," she promises. "You shouldn't waste your time crying over that asshole anyway."

"Wanker," Kris agrees. "You're better off without him."

"Just forget all about it," Jia adds. "You know he's already moved onto the next flavor of the week!"

Kris gives her a look.

"What? Sorry," she adds to me, insincere. "But we did try to warn you. Those rich bastards are all the same. At least you know who he really is now. Just chalk it up to experience and move on."

If only it was that easy.

"Thanks." I give my roommates a brief, insincere smile. "You're right."

"Shit, we've got to go," Kris says, grabbing his bag. Jia flashes me another smug grin.

"Take care. And remember that shower!"

The door slams behind them, and I'm left in the apartment.

Alone.

I take a deep breath. I want nothing more than to hide away under the covers again, but what I told them is true: I'm already on shaky ground with my less-than-stellar academic perfor- mance. I have no idea what my future holds here in Oxford, or if I even want to stay now, knowing what I do. But I can't bear another day alone, obsessing over Saint's betrayal, so I take that shower they were so insistent on, luxuriating under the water until I feel halfway human. It's a gray, overcast day, so I dress in my coziest sweatpants and college sweater, wrap up warmly, and head out to the Ashford College library.

"Hi, Tessa." My favorite clerk, Maeve, is on duty and greets me as I step through the carved wooden doors. The library is con- verted from an old church, with soaring ceilings, wood beams, and stained-glass windows. "I have those books you ordered," she adds, collecting them from the packed shelf behind her. "There's a waiting list a mile long for them, so let me know when you're done."

"Thanks," I say, taking the stack.

"Are you feeling OK?" she asks, frowning, and I realize I should have spent a little more time with the concealer to hide my red-rimmed eyes.

"Fine!" I lie. "Just allergies. I'll get these back to you as soon as possible!"

I head upstairs, to my regular study carrel in the far corner, and settle in for the day. When I decided to come to Oxford to hunt down the truth about what happened to Wren, I realized just showing up as a random tourist wouldn't get me the answers I needed. I had to come here, to Ashford College, where Wren had taken her research fellowship, and investigate from the inside as a student myself to retrace her steps.

I've never been much of an academic. I scraped through my undergrad and then went to work at arts nonprofits around Philadelphia. I hadn't cracked a book in years, but I managed to find a scholarship for people from "nontraditional" education backgrounds to study here at Ashford for a year. Aka, people who hadn't been turning in perfect grades since birth. I managed to fake my way through the application process and get enough glowing references to win the spot, but now that I'm actually here, trying to keep up with all my lectures and tutorials . . .

It's a full-time job to stay above water, even at the best of times.

And this definitely isn't one of those times.

I check my schedule for the week. I have a bunch of lectures, and two essays due. One of them is for Saint's class on libertine and radical literature. I gulp. There's no way I'm attending that session—just imagining being in the same room as him fills me with a panicked ache—but if I don't submit an essay, I know there'll be trouble from my supervisor. "Libertines and the Church" is the topic of the week, so with a sigh, I pull out the list of articles and essays I need to review, take the first dusty book, and start to read.

* * *

LUCKILY, THE DENSE texts are difficult enough to require every drop of my concentration. I struggle through the reading and outline a half-hearted essay on the subject before moving on to my next assignment. And the next. Before I know it, the whole day has passed, with only a short break to grab a sandwich from the commissary before returning to study again.

By the time my head aches too much to focus, it's dark out, and the library is almost empty. I stretch, yawning, and pack up my things. Maeve has long since clocked off, so I leave the books in the return bin, hoist my backpack, and let myself out, to the cool night air breezing through the quad.

"There you are." Saint's voice makes me stop in my tracks. He's hurrying from another building, looking anxious. "Tessa, thank God. I've been looking everywhere for you."

I freeze. *Fuck.*

"Saint . . ." My voice shakes as I take him in. He's looking ragged and unkempt, with two-day stubble on his jaw and a rumpled button-down under his open peacoat.

My heart aches, just looking at him.

"What happened?" he demands, coming to a stop in front of me. "Fuck, Tessa, you just disappeared from the party. I was looking everywhere for you, until someone said they saw you leave. Why didn't you tell me?" he asks, raking a hand through his hair.

"I'm sorry, I just needed some space," I say carefully, glancing around. But it's late, and the quad is empty and dark, with only the glow of the old-fashioned lamps to light us.

I shiver.

"Space?" Saint repeats, looking angry. "Tessa, do you have any idea how worried I've been? You won't talk to me. You won't answer my calls. What the fuck is going on?"

I swallow hard, trying to think clearly, despite the conflicted emotions storming in my chest. "I've thought about it, and this thing between us, I think it's best if we ended it," I tell him. It's the story I told my roommates. Maybe it's my best way out of this—at least until I can figure out what the hell I'm going to do.

Saint stares at me like he's been struck. "You want to end this . . . ?" he repeats. "Tessa, what are you talking about? What happened?"

I avoid his gaze. "It's just not going to work between us," I say firmly. "We're too different. You're from a whole other world. We were only supposed to be a fun fling," I add, "and then things spiraled, and we moved way too fast. The Blackthorn Society party just made me realize—it's best for us to end it now, before anyone gets hurt." I hitch my bag and start walking, but Saint moves to block my path.

"Tessa, talk to me," he says, looking anguished. "You know that bullshit doesn't matter to me. Tell me the truth. What's making you say this?"

"It's just how I feel," I lie, trying to step around him. "We want different things. You're the hot professor, remember? You won't have any trouble keeping your bed warm."

"That's what you think of me?" Saint demands, looking hurt. "After everything we've shared?"

Again, I feel that treacherous pang of guilt. Seeing him wounded by my words, searching to make sense of this explanation, I feel my resolve slip.

I need to get away from him, before my defenses crumble for good.

"I don't want to talk about it," I state clearly. "Please, stop calling. Just leave me alone."

I walk away.

"Tessa!" Saint yells after me. "Tessa, wait!"

He catches up, grabbing my arm to stop me. I instinctively recoil, adrenaline surging as I yank away. "Don't touch me!" I scream.

Saint releases me instantly, staring in disbelief. "You're *scared* of me?" he says, realization dawning in his eyes.

Realization—and hurt.

"I don't know what's happened, but please, Tessa, talk to me," Saint urges. "Let me help you. Whatever's going on, we can figure this out."

I shake my head, more confused than ever. His innocent facade isn't slipping for a moment. Either he's one hell of an actor—or he has no idea what's going on. But that can't be true.

Can it?

I feel a wretched flash of anger. I hate this, not knowing. I can't take his deception a moment longer.

"Stop lying!" I yell, my voice echoing suddenly across the dark quad. "I know everything, Saint. I saw your tattoo!"

"What are you talking about?" He looks at me, still seeming so confused.

"The tattoo! That one on your thigh," I say grimly. "She saw it too."

"Who did?"

"Wren!" I explode. "That night, the one she was taken. It was the only thing she could remember about the man who hurt her. She told me all about it," I add bitterly. "You can't fool me anymore. I know it had to have been you."

Chapter Three
SAINT

S he thinks it was me.

I stare at Tessa in disbelief. This has to be some kind of sick joke. She can't possibly believe . . .

But she does. I can see the brittle suspicion written all over her face. She's already backing away from me, and walking fast through the college towards the gatehouse.

She thinks I'm the monster who hurt her sister.

My God.

"Tessa!" I snap into action, hurrying after her. "Tessa, wait!"

She keeps walking, but I catch up, resisting the urge to pull her into my arms again.

"What happened to your sister . . . You don't really think I could do that?" I ask instead, chilled to the core by her accusation.

"I don't know what to think!" Tessa sobs, tears glittering on her cheeks in the dark. "I thought I knew you, Saint. I thought I was falling—but then I saw that tattoo."

The damn tattoo. I should have guessed something was up when she fled the party so suddenly. "I'm not the only person with this ink," I tell her before she can bolt again.

Tessa stops walking. She turns to me. "W-what?"

I see relief flash in her eyes, and it gives me something to believe in.

She didn't *want* to think it was me.

"I've had this tattoo since I was a student here," I explain quickly. "My mates and I had them done on a dare one night before finals. We designed it ourselves. It was just a drunken prank—"

I stop, realizing just what it means. If the man who hurt Wren had this tattoo . . .

Then one of my friends from that night is the monster who hurt Tessa's sister. Who destroyed her life and drove her to her death.

I exhale. "My God, Tessa, I'm so sorry . . ."

She shakes her head like she's trying to process it. Dark hair falling in her eyes. "It wasn't you?" she asks, her voice lifting in hope.

"No, baby. I swear," I tell her honestly. "The Blackthorn Society party last year? I was at my family's place in the South of France, working on my book. I can get you receipts," I add. "Plane tickets, credit card bills. Whatever you need to believe me. You know me," I insist. "You know I would never hurt someone like that."

Tessa swallows, looking lost in her oversized coat. I try to imagine her feelings of confusion and betrayal, but I know I could never come close. To think that I'd been deceiving her, that I was the one to blame . . .

I could lose her.

Fear grips me, sharp and metallic. This woman has captivated me since the moment we met, and every night we've spent together has only made me want her more. *Need her.*

"I'm so sorry, Tessa," I say again, keeping my voice even despite the furious storm of emotions raging inside. Every instinct is screaming at me to hold her, comfort her. Help her through the shock and conflict that are written all over her face. But I force myself to stay back and give her the space she's asked me for. "I can't imagine what you've been going through, if you saw that tattoo and thought that I—"

My phone sounds loudly in my jacket pocket. I kept the ringer on so I could hear if Tessa called me back. Now I quickly take it out to silence it, not breaking our stare.

"Let's go somewhere and talk about this," I urge her. "Or, if you still want to be alone tonight, I'll understand. But please, don't shut me out forever. I promise, nothing's changed," I vow, shaken by the thought of losing her. "I'm still the same man you've known. I told you, I'm an open book. I'll always be completely honest with you."

Tessa looks like she's wavering, but my phone vibrates again, interrupting what she was about to say.

I stifle a curse, pulling it out to shut the damn thing off this time.

"Who is it?" Tessa asks.

"My mother." I pause, frowning. What's she doing calling me at this hour? "But it doesn't matter," I say quickly. "Nothing matters except you right now."

As soon as I reject my mother's call, another comes through. This time it's from my brother, Robert.

"Answer it," Tessa says, seeing me pause.

"No—" I don't want to lose this chance to get through to her, but Tessa shakes her head, already backing away from me, skittish.

"I can't talk about this right now," she says. "You're right. I need some space to process everything."

"But you believe me, don't you?" Fear shatters in my chest. Fuck, she has to believe me.

Tessa meets my eyes and exhales. Then, reluctantly, she nods.

It's just the slightest gesture, a brief dip of her chin, but it sends relief crashing through me.

Thank God.

"I'll call you when I'm ready to talk," she blurts. "Please, don't contact me until then."

Before I can say another word, she turns on her heel and flees for the lights of the gatehouse.

And fuck, it takes every ounce of self-control for me to let her go.

Robert calls again. I answer with an angry growl. "What, dammit? What the hell is so important?"

There's a pause. Then my brother's voice sounds, tight with tension. "You need to come to London. It's an emergency."

I'm still staring after Tessa, and it takes me a moment to catch up with what he's saying. "Emergency?" I repeat.

"Dad is in the hospital. They're saying it's a massive heart attack. You need to get here, now."

* * *

I DRIVE STRAIGHT down from Oxford. It's past midnight by the time I arrive at the hospital and follow Robert's direction to the VIP section of a new cardiothoracic wing. The place is almost deserted, but a nurse is just exiting my father's room. I pause in the open doorway.

My father is dozing on the hospital bed, my mother fussing over his pillows as Robert talks on his mobile phone in the corner, surrounded by the low hum of machines. There's a tube running into Dad's nostril, and wires disappear underneath the neck of his sagging green hospital gown. He looks pale and weak. Like a shell of the hearty, determined man I've always known.

I stand there for a moment, stunned at the way his salt-and-pepper hair now seems gray with age. The shadows under his eyes are sunken and tired. This man has always seemed like an unstoppable force, the constant thorn in my side. Chiding me with expectations, and always so full of disappointment. But the way he looks now, so fragile, shakes me to my core.

"Saint." My mother notices me standing there and gets up. "Thank God you came."

She crosses to me and pulls me into a brittle hug. The show of physical affection is wildly out of character for the great Lillian St. Clair, and just another sign that this is serious.

I release her, and step fully into the room. "What happened?" I ask, approaching the bed. My father, Alexander, is conscious, I see, and he offers a feeble smile.

"Nothing to worry about," he says. "Lot of fuss over nothing."

"It was a massive heart attack," Robert corrects him. He's pacing, giving off a buzz of anxious energy. The youngest of the family, he works closely with Dad at the family business and is usually an even-tempered optimist. But tonight, he looks almost as haggard as our father.

"When?" I ask.

"A few hours ago. He was working late. Again. The doctors say he could have died if his secretary hadn't found him."

"Could've, would've." My father waves away the concern. "It'll take more than that to see me off. And remind me to give Tricia a raise," he adds, jocular. "I thought she'd need the defibrillators herself, the look on the poor woman's face."

"Darling, you need to take this seriously," my mother chides him.

"I do." My father meets my eyes across the room. "Lillian, why don't you go see if you can find me something to eat?" he asks suddenly. "And Robert, you hunt down that doctor so he can explain everything to your brother."

Robert looks back and forth between us, then nods. "Come on, Mother," he says, steering her to the door. "Let's see if they'll make you a cup of tea to settle your nerves."

"It'll take more than tea to do that," she says, thin-lipped, but she follows him out, leaving my father and me alone.

I move closer to the bed. "How do you feel, really?" I ask quietly, taking note of the slight tremor in his hand when he reaches for the plastic cup of ice water on the table beside him. I pick it up and hand it to him, and he takes a slow sip.

"I've been better," he replies, relaxing back into the pillows with a sigh. "But it's not all bad. I've been thinking about taking a holiday from the office. A little gardening leave, as they call it."

"There are easier ways to get it." I play along with him, even though I'm unnerved by his tone. My father isn't a man to joke, especially not with me. The fact that he's doing it now tells me that this is more serious than he's letting on.

"Perhaps I'll take up bridge. Your mother's always telling me to get a hobby," my father continues. "Or maybe lawn bowls. It's a shame you boys haven't given me grandchildren yet. They would certainly keep me busy."

"What happened to all those lectures about keeping it zipped?" I ask lightly. "I thought you said the world was full of gold diggers just waiting to pounce on the St. Clair family bloodline."

My father laughs softly, but it's swallowed by a hacking cough. He takes another sip of water, settling. "Times change, son," he says, his voice a little shaky. "And moments like this . . . Well, it makes a man think about the future. What's left behind after he's gone."

"You're not going anywhere," I say immediately, more unnerved than ever. "You're barely sixty-five. Plenty of time for you to have a bushel more kids, if you want them."

"I'm not sure how your mother would feel about that," my father says with a faint smile.

"So trade her in for a younger model. All your friends are doing it," I joke—before I remember the hushed conversation I overheard at the Lancaster Media party a few weeks ago. I accidentally stumbled across my father talking with a younger French woman in a heated, intimate-looking exchange. I couldn't hear exactly what they were arguing about, but it didn't take a genius to figure out.

I clear my throat and quickly change the subject. My father's affairs are none of my business. "How long do the doctors say they're keeping you here?"

"Another few days, for observation. My blood pressure's still high, and they say I need to make changes to avoid another incident."

"What kind of changes?" I ask.

"You know, diet, health, lower my daily stress." My father rolls his eyes. "Tricia will make me eat a few salads, and I'm sure everything will be fine."

I'm not so certain, but I don't press him on it. He lets out a yawn, and I get up from beside the bed. "It's late. You should rest," I tell him, still shaken by the change in him. "I'll go talk to your doctors."

He nods, already sleepy. "Thanks for coming, son."

"Of course," I murmur. "Sleep tight."

I leave his room, feeling off-balance. My father and I may not have the best relationship. Things have been strained between us since my older brother, Edward, passed away ten years ago. Suddenly, the future of the family line rested on my rebellious shoulders—and my parents have made no secret about what a disappointment that is for them. I've kept my distance and ignored their lectures about settling down and taking my rightful position as son and heir to the Ashford legacy, the title of duke, the pharmaceutical business, everything.

I've wanted no part of it, and I've been determined to forge my own path in pursuit of pleasure, not responsibility. But seeing my father like this, having to face his mortality . . .

That legacy feels closer than ever, a dread weight pressing down on me.

Reminding me that I'll never live up to Edward's good example.

Reminding me I'll always be second-best.

I'm halfway to the elevators when my mother appears. "Anthony, wait," she says, cornering me. "Are you leaving already?"

"Just to get a few hours' sleep," I tell her, worn out from everything that's happened today. I've been a mess since Tessa disappeared from the party, and I can tell I'm about to hit the wall. "You should try and get some rest, too," I add, seeing her tense expression and the shadows in her eyes. "We can be back here in the morning before he even wakes."

"Just as long as you *do* come back," Lillian says tightly. "We need to talk to his doctors and figure out a plan. This would never have happened if he wasn't so stressed from work, you know. The clinical trials, the new product launch . . . It's too much for one man to handle, and God knows, your brother tries when he can, but he isn't mature enough to take the reins."

I tense. "Are you saying this is my fault?"

"I'm saying you've fooled around with this academic nonsense for long enough." My mother gives me a determined, withering look. "You've had your fun, but it's time to step up and face your responsibilities to this family—before your father works himself into an early grave."

She walks away before I can respond, but her words echo, striking deep into the guilty heart of me.

I've been fighting this part of my life for as long as I can remember. Holding out against all their expectations and pressure, doing everything I can to ignore the fate that's been written in my DNA since the day I was born—and the day that Edward died, leaving me as heir to it all.

But seeing my father in the hospital bed like this, I know deep down that there's no running from my destiny anymore.

Things have got to change.

Chapter Four
TESSA

The early morning Oxford streets are blissfully empty as I pound the pavement, running my regular route through the old part of town, with its historic colleges and ancient architecture. I feel the burn in my limbs, but I don't let up, looping back to Ashford to jog through the quad and down along the riverbanks.

It's quiet here. Fall has arrived in full splendor, and the leaves on the trees are vibrant reds and orange. The air is brisk, dawn mists still hanging low over the meadows. I can see the crew team out on the water for an early practice, but I don't pause to watch. I need to clear my head. Alone.

So much has happened these past few days, I'm still reeling from all the revelations. From trusting Saint, to wondering if he'd betrayed me, and then questioning that all over again . . . I've got emotional whiplash from the changes. I don't know what to think anymore.

But I can't deny how I feel in my heart.

I miss him.

I finally pause to catch my breath, panting hard, my breath fogging in the morning mists. It's been two days since that night outside the library, and I haven't heard a word from Saint. I told him not to contact me—so it makes sense that he wouldn't reach out—but every time I think about calling, I remember the look of betrayal in his eyes when I accused him of attacking Wren.

What can I say to him now?

I was hurting, confused, wishing desperately that it wasn't true—but still, that's no consolation when you've basically accused your boyfriend of being a sadistic monster.

Does he hate me now? I wouldn't hold it against him if he did, even if the evidence did seem incriminating at the time.

The serpent crown tattoo.

Saint said he got the ink on a drunken dare with some friends before finals, and I can't stop the part of me that's fixated on that fact now. Because it means I have a lead again. Maybe the secret society angle wasn't a dead end, after all. Maybe those mysterious notes were pointing me in that direction, because Saint and his friends are members.

The annual party was the hunting ground. Wren was taken—by one of them.

And now I have a new pool of suspects—and it's tantalizingly small. The men with that tattoo . . . I may have fucked everything up with Saint and been completely wrong about him, but it turns out that I'm closer to the truth than ever.

I just have to find out who these other men are.

* * *

I FINISH MY run and slow, stretching. The college is coming to life now, as I stroll back through the quad and stop by the gatehouse to check my mailbox. I'm half hoping for another helpful anonymous note—hell, even a vaguely cryptic one—but today there's nothing waiting for me in my mail cubby except a few random flyers for college events I'll never go to. I cram them in the trash and pause in the old stone gatehouse to say good morning to Bates, the weathered porter on duty.

"Getting chilly out, eh?" He smiles at me, wearing a knit scarf in the Ashford College colors, crimson and black.

"I like the fall," I confide. "All the leaves changing, everything getting cozy."

Bates chuckles. "Just like your sister," he says, and I feel a jolt, remembering he would have chatted with Wren, just like this. "You wouldn't catch her without one of those pumpkin cream coffee drinks in her hand."

I'm hit with a memory of my childhood autumns, playing out in the leaves with Wren. We would spend hours in the backyard, collecting the most vivid colors to make collages and prints.

"It was her favorite season," I agree, before realizing my slip— talking about Wren in the past tense. I haven't told anyone here at college that she's dead, but luckily, he doesn't seem to notice, too busy sorting packages behind the desk. "Anyway, I better get to the library. Essays due."

"You take care." He gives me a friendly smile. "Oh, and send my best to Professor St. Clair. Terrible news," he adds, tutting. "Tell him we're all hoping for the best."

I frown, confused. Is he talking about our breakup? But no, he wouldn't be so tactless. "What do you mean?" I ask.

"His father," Bates replies. "Everyone at the college is praying for his speedy recovery. Course, Alexander St. Clair is made of sterner stuff. I'm sure it'll take more than a heart attack to slow him down."

Heart attack?

"I . . . Of course, I'll pass along your thoughts," I manage to reply, my mind racing. "Bye!"

I leave the lodge, blindly weaving my way through the morning commuter crowds now filling the sidewalks. Saint's father had a heart attack? No wonder I haven't heard from him! For all the thorns of their relationship, the man is still his father, the man who raised him, and if Saint almost lost him . . .

I can't imagine what he's going through.

I break into a run again. Whatever else is happening between us, it doesn't matter right now.

I need to be there for him.

* * *

I QUICKLY CHANGE and catch the express train down to London. On the way, I text Saint's cousin, Imogen, and get the details of the hospital where Saint's father has been admitted. But when I arrive at the crowded reception and ask the clerk for his room number, she stonewalls me.

"I'm sorry," she tells me, staring me down over her bifocals. "We don't give out information about our patients. Are you family?"

"No," I admit, frustrated. "But please, I need to see them. I'm a . . . friend of his son's."

Friend, possible ex-girlfriend, the woman who's been embarking on a wild sexual adventure with him . . .

The woman just glares, unimpressed. "I can't help you," she says firmly. "Please move aside and let the next person through."

I sigh in frustration, stepping away from the desk. What do I do now? I try calling Saint again. I've already left a dozen messages, but he's not picking up.

"Tessa?"

I whirl around. It's Robert, Saint's younger brother, coming through the main doors, balancing a tray of coffees in his hands. "Oh, thank God," I say, rushing over. "I've been trying to get the room details, but the reception lady wouldn't let me through, and Saint's not answering his phone, and—" I stop, realizing I'm babbling. "It doesn't matter. How are you?" I ask. Robert seems worn out, his tow-colored hair rumpled, and his broad frame sagging. "How's your dad? I heard what happened. Is there any update?"

"He's doing better," Robert replies, and I exhale in relief. "The doctors are still running some tests, but he should be able to go home tomorrow—as long as he stays on bed rest, which, knowing Dad, won't be easy for him."

"I'm so glad," I say sincerely. "Is Saint here?"

Robert nods. "Come on, I'll take you up."

He leads me past the desk to the elevators, and up to the fourth floor, which looks to be some kind of VIP wing, a calm oasis compared to the chaos downstairs. But, of course, Saint's father is a duke. His room is down a polished hallway, and Robert goes straight in. I hesitate in the doorway, taking in the scene. Saint is standing by the windows, looking out across the city with his back turned, while his dad—Alexander—sits up in bed. Lillian, Saint's mother, is urging him to drink some noxious-looking green juice.

"It tastes like grass," Alexander is objecting. He looks pale, but seems to be getting his strength back, despite the machines still hooked up, monitoring him. "What's wrong with my usual coffee?"

"The doctors said—"

"Bully the doctors. You like that green mess so much, you drink it. Ah, here we are." Alexander looks up, smiling, as Robert enters with the coffee. "A cappuccino? What about the croissant?"

"Robert," Lillian scolds him, perfectly attired in matching Chanel. "What did we say about his diet?"

"Hush, darling," Alexander says, affectionate. "Let a man enjoy his coffee in peace. Oh, hello," he says, noticing me for the first time. "Tessa, wasn't it?"

At the mention of my name, Saint turns. He looks tired, too, but holds himself with the same confident ease as ever, wearing a crisp button-down and black washed jeans, his dark hair falling rumpled over his eyes, in need of a trim.

So handsome it hurts to look at him.

Our eyes lock across the room, and I offer him a supportive smile, but his expression stays stern. Unreadable.

"Hi, yes. Sorry, I didn't mean to intrude," I add, clocking Lillian's narrowed eyes. "I just heard the news and wanted to see how you all were. Is there anything I can do for you?" I ask.

Saint's mother offers an icy smile. "How sweet. No, thank you, we're all fine."

"OK." I hover there, feeling seriously awkward. Saint isn't saying a word, and I'm beginning to regret showing up here at all. Maybe he doesn't want to talk to me after all the terrible accusations I made.

"Not that we don't appreciate you thinking of us in this difficult time," Lillian continues. "But we'd prefer to keep this a family affair, if you don't mind . . ."

"Of course." I flush. I really don't belong here. "Sorry. I'll leave now. Everyone at Ashford sends their best," I add to Alexander, and turn to leave.

I make it down the hallway and am waiting for the elevator again when Saint emerges, slowly walking over to me.

My heart catches in my throat. "Hi," I say softly, searching his face for some hint of emotion. "How are you holding up?"

He offers a faint ghost of a smile. "I've been better, to tell the truth."

"I can imagine."

There's a long pause, and I try to think of where I can even begin. "Can we talk?" I ask hopefully, gazing up at him. There's a force field between us, a distance I wish I could close.

Saint looks down at me and seems to soften, just a little. He nods. "Not here, though," he says, glancing back toward his father's room. "I need to get some air."

"I saw a café downstairs," I offer, and he nods.

"Let's go."

* * *

WE MAKE OUR way down to the lobby in silence, and out to the café, where Saint buys an overpriced sandwich, and I get a yogurt and granola. We find a table in the little courtyard and sit, but I can't eat anything. I'm too focused on Saint, and the heavy weight playing on his features as he looks at me across the table.

"I'm sorry," I blurt, my heart aching. "Accusing you like that, of hurting Wren. I just didn't know what else to think. That tattoo is the only real detail she remembered about her attacker, and when I saw it on you . . . I panicked. You have to understand, it all seemed to line up," I add, needing him to understand why I could turn against him like that. "But even when I put all the pieces together, a part of me couldn't believe it," I swear. "Wouldn't believe you were capable of doing something like that. I know that's probably no consolation," I add, rueful, but Saint offers me a nod.

"It is, actually."

I blink, surprised. "You mean you don't hate me?"

Saint's brow knits in a frown. "Of course not. Was I shocked and hurt at the time? Yes, of course. The fact you would think I was lying to you, that I could have hurt Wren . . ." Saint shakes his head. "But that's on me, not you. You were just following the evidence. I would have jumped to exactly the same conclusion if I was in your shoes."

I exhale in a massive sigh of relief. He doesn't hate me. He understands. "Then why didn't you call me?" I ask, reaching for his hand. Instinctively I curl my fingers around his, and he does the same. Already I feel better, just being connected to him in this small way. "I know I said I needed space, but with everything going on with your dad . . ."

Saint sighs. He looks down, tracing over my knuckles. "At first, I was just wrapping my head around everything. I didn't want to drag you into it and make you have to deal with my parents—"

"I don't care about that," I insist. "I'm here for you. Whatever you need."

"Thank you." Saint meets my eyes and gives me a soft, heart-melting smile. "But it's not just that . . ." His smile fades. "It's the tattoo. I've been thinking about it nonstop, ever since you told me."

"Oh." I squeeze his hand, wincing. "Right."

"If the man who attacked Wren has the same ink . . ." Saint starts, looking grim. "Then you know what it means, don't you? He was part of the group when we got the tattoos done, ten years ago. The man who took your sister, hurt her like that . . . He's one of my friends."

Silence falls. I've had days to process the uncomfortable truth, but I can see it's so much worse for Saint.

"I'm sorry," I offer uselessly.

"Me too." Saint inhales, then meets my eyes in a determined stare. "Now we just have to figure out which one of them it is."

I blink. "You're going to help?" I ask, surprised by his response. There's no hesitation, no reluctance in his voice, not even for a moment.

"I told you I would." Saint frowns like there's no question. "We're in this together now, no matter what."

"Even if the attacker is one of your closest friends?" I can't help checking. "This isn't just some random secret society member anymore. You know him. You trust him. Hell, if you guys got the tattoos in college, you've known him almost half your life!"

Saint gives me a grim smile. "And if he hurt your sister, then he's no friend of mine." He nods sharply, like that's the end of it, and I can't stop myself. I reach up out of my seat and lean across the table, kissing him square on the mouth.

Saint kisses me back, slow and deep, and I feel the heat burn between us, blotting out the rest of the world.

We're in this together.

"What was that for?" he asks when I finally draw back.

"For being a good man," I reply, trying to ignore the wave of emotion rising in my chest. Trying—and failing. Because every instinct in my body is telling me to throw myself into Saint's arms and never let go. Things have been moving so fast between us, I don't even know what we are to each other anymore. But I know for sure we left "casual sexy fling" way in the rearview mirror.

This is something real.

I clear my throat, feeling self-conscious. "So, what do we do now?" I ask, relishing the feel of the word *we* in my mouth. "Who are these friends of yours with the tattoo, anyway?"

Saint sits back. "There were five of us," he says, and counts them off. "Me, Hugh, Max, you already know them. Plus Sebastian Wolfe and Felix Western."

"Four suspects," I say, feeling a shiver of purpose. I've been looking for a needle in a haystack all this time, but now, suddenly, the stack is more of a small bundle.

But Saint shakes his head. "Felix died that summer, before graduation. Got drunk at a party and decided to take a midnight swim in the lake." He sighs, rueful. "It was a fucking tragedy."

I offer a sympathetic smile. "So that leaves three."

And one of them is already on my radar. Max Lancaster: rich playboy, heir to a global media empire—and a man who's already lied about how well he knew Wren. They were hanging out together during her time in Oxford, maybe even dating.

What else has he been lying about?

Saint's phone buzzes. "The doctors have new test results," he reports, checking the message. "I should get back."

I walk him up to his father's room, and Saint pauses in the hallway. "Thank you for coming down here," he tells me. "I know you've been slammed with studying."

"Of course, that doesn't matter. I can stay as long as you need," I add, but Saint shakes his head.

"Go back to Oxford, hit the books, and keep my bed warm for me," he tells me, his smile turning smoldering. "I'll be back tonight after they discharge him."

"OK." I smile. "I'm just sorry I can't be more of a help."

"You are," Saint reassures me, drawing me into a hug. "Just having you here . . . It's more than enough."

He wraps his arms around me, just holding me for a moment, solid and warm. Then he draws back, tipping my chin up to claim my mouth in a slow, tender kiss. I melt into it, needing him close.

God, I've missed him.

Finally, Saint pulls back, looking reluctant. "Go, before I change my mind and drag you into a cupboard," he says with a wink, as a woman in a white coat walks by, heading for his father's room.

"Dr. Heller?" Saint asks, and she nods, so he follows her into the room. I hear their voices talking, low, about test results and treatment plans.

That's my cue to exit.

I take the stairs down to the lobby, feeling like a weight has been lifted off my chest. Saint's father will be OK, and the two of us are back to being . . . well, whatever it is we are. Except this time, there are no more lies or deceptions between us. I can be totally honest with him about my mission. I can trust him.

Trust him, and *want* him, too.

I shiver, still feeling the burning imprint of his kiss on my lips. I'm lost in thought, eagerly anticipating when we can be alone together again, when I almost bump into someone outside the main hospital doors.

"Sorry," I say, before I see that it's Saint's mother, Lillian. "Oh, hi, Mrs. St. Clair," I add, awkward. "I mean, Lady—or Duchess—"

"I was looking for my son," she says, eyes drifting over me. I grabbed the first clean clothes I could find in my rush to make the train, so I'm wearing jeans and a wrinkled shirt under my jacket, looking a total mess, I'm sure.

"Saint's up with his father. The doctor just arrived to talk," I add.

"Thank you," she says thinly. Then she pauses. "You should know that Saint will be very busy now with all his family responsibilities. He'll be stepping up to help at the company. It's long overdue."

I nod slowly, not sure where this is going.

"I dare say he'll be taking a leave of absence from his teaching at Oxford, too, and moving down here to London full-time," she adds, looking smug. "Of course, he's enjoyed his freedom, having his fun, but that was never going to last. He's the future Duke of Ashford. There'll be no more time for tawdry *distractions*. His family will always come first."

It's clear she sees me as one of those tawdry distractions. In other words, back the fuck off.

I manage to keep my smile pleasant. "Saint's a grown man," I say evenly. "I'm sure he can decide for himself who or what in his life is a distraction. You take care now," I add, breezy. "I'm sure I'll see you again soon."

I hold my head high and walk off before she can respond, but I can practically feel her icy gaze burning into my back as I leave.

I shiver. Something tells me that Lillian St. Clair is not to be underestimated.

Chapter Five
TESSA

Back in Oxford, I make my way to Saint's townhouse, which is located close to Ashford College, on a leafy street filled with expensive historic homes. I let myself in, relishing the peace of the eclectic, historic house—and the absence of any roommates with their passive-aggressive comments.

For now, I have the place to myself.

I grab a bottle of sparkling water from the cozy kitchen and head upstairs. Saint's bedroom is spacious and understated, decorated in shades of cream and navy, with antique rugs underfoot. My things are still packed in bags and boxes where I left them before our fight. Now I'm happy to take the time to unpack properly, moving my clothing into the space he's made for me in the massive walk-in closet, and setting out my toiletries in the gleaming en suite bathroom before I take a long, hot shower.

And all the while, my mind is working overtime.

Hugh Ambrose. Max Lancaster. Sebastian Wolfe.

Three men who share the serpent crown tattoo. Three men who could be guilty of my sister's attack.

And three men who are all wildly rich and well-connected.

I feel a flicker of insecurity even thinking about going up against one of them. I don't have their money or privilege, their army of lawyers, or their powerful friends. All I have is my grief and rage to drive me on, the vow that I swore to discover the truth about Wren.

And now Saint in my corner, too.

I smile, feeling a little better knowing I have him on my side. I'll worry about the battle when I figure out which one of them it is, I decide, putting the last of my things away. For now, I still need to find out everything I can about these men.

I dress in a long comfy jersey skirt and hoodie, go down to the kitchen, pull out my laptop, and settle in with a cup of tea and some snacks, researching my new list of suspects. I start with Sebastian Wolfe, who's a stranger to me. The name is familiar, though, and it doesn't take me long to realize why: he was all over the news last year. Apparently, he's some big-shot finance guy, a billionaire who got accused of killing his own father—and then faked his own death as part of some plot to reveal the real killer.

I skim over the news stories, wide-eyed. Since the scandal broke, Sebastian has been out of the country, photographed occasionally in New York and on some private tropical island with his new wife on his arm. A paparazzi picture shows him leaving a fancy restaurant, glaring at the cameras: tall, cold, and imposing.

Could he have been the one to hurt Wren?

I jot down some notes, then move on. Hugh Ambrose is the next on my list. I pause, reluctant. I know Hugh a little now, and he seems like a decent guy. His father is in the running to become the next prime minister, and Hugh heads a charitable foundation. He offered me an amazing job there, and when I went to check it out, I fell in love with the energy and purpose, and all the great work they do on projects around the world.

But that doesn't mean anything, I remind myself. Plenty of monsters know how to hide in plain sight. He's just as much a suspect as the last man on the list, Max Lancaster.

Playboy. Heir to a media empire. And the only one of the three

I know had a connection to Wren. He's already admitted to meeting her when she first arrived in Oxford. He played it off like a casual friendship—maybe because his fiancée was right there in the room when I asked—but from the things he said, I can tell he knew my sister better than he was letting on.

Were they hooking up? Having some kind of illicit affair behind Annabelle's back? And how does that connection lead to her kidnapping and assault?

I spend the afternoon deep in thought, researching them all, and I'm almost surprised when I hear the sound of a key in the front door.

"Hello?" Saint's voice calls from the hallway.

I close my laptop, smiling. "I'm back here," I call in answer. His footsteps come, and then Saint appears in the doorway, looking tired.

"Hey." I get up and greet him with a kiss. "Did your dad get discharged from the hospital OK?"

Saint nods, dropping his keys and coat, and exhaling in a long sigh. "It took forever, though. My mother kept quizzing the doctors about his medications a hundred times over, and then insisted on having him ride in an ambulance, too. They're settled at the house in Sussex now. He should be able to rest and recover there."

"I'm glad," I say, wrapping my arms around his waist. "Now, what can we do for *your* rest and recovery?"

Saint manages a chuckle. "Honestly, I'm feeling better already, just being back here. With you."

He kisses my forehead, and we stand there a moment, holding each other. God, it feels good to be back in his arms. I rest my head against his chest, breathing in the scent of him, and the steady warmth of his embrace.

"How are you holding up?" Saint asks, looking down at me with a tender smile.

"OK," I say. "I guess I'm still trying to process everything. It's been a crazy few days. The Blackthorn Society party, and then your dad . . ."

"I know." Saint hugs me tightly. "I'm glad you're here, though. It made the last twenty-four hours so much easier, knowing I would be coming home to you."

I smile. "I'm glad I'm here too. You have way better heating than back at the apartment. And much better snacks."

"You found the Choco Leibniz?" He chuckles, noticing the pack of fancy chocolate wafers I've pretty much demolished. "I stocked up, just for you."

"Careful," I tease, smiling. "Keep wooing me with 70 percent cocoa solids, and you'll never get rid of me."

"Well, maybe that's the plan." Saint meets my eyes, and heat sizzles between us.

I look away, suddenly breathless. The bond between us is different now. Stronger, more solid. Not just about the thrill of wild attraction anymore, but something deeper taking hold.

Real emotions.

Real risk.

"Are you hungry?" I ask, stepping back from his arms. A little overwhelmed. "We could grab dinner somewhere nearby," I suggest. "What do you think?"

"That sounds fine," Saint replies, but when I look closer, I can see that he's pretty much exhausted.

"Let's stay in," I decide. "I'll cook."

Saint arches an eyebrow. "Really?"

"Don't sound so surprised." I grin, moving to check out the contents of his fridge and cabinets. "I'm a woman of many talents."

"Oh, I know." Saint's voice turns seductive, and when I glance over, he's giving me a smoldering look. "I remember a few of them. Vividly."

I laugh. "You sit there and keep your hands to yourself," I instruct, pointing to a stool at the farmhouse table island in the middle of the room. "Unless I need them for mixing or chopping. You're on sous chef duties tonight."

"Yes, Chef." Saint salutes, doing as I told him—but not before detouring to put on some jazz music and pour us both a glass of wine. He hands one to me and then steals a kiss, his mouth hot and sweet.

I break away, laughing. "What did I say?"

"To keep my hands off," Saint replies with a smirk. "But you didn't say anything about my mouth."

He kisses me again, longer this time, his tongue sliding against mine in a slow, sensual dance.

I shiver, my blood already heating in anticipation, loving the taste of him. "I thought you were hungry," I whisper as his lips trail to nibble at my earlobe.

"I am."

Damn. The low growl in his voice makes my thighs clench, but I force myself to dance out of reach. "Sit. Stay." I point, and he grins.

"You're feeling bossy tonight? I think I like it."

"You like everything," I reply, flirty, as I start assembling ingredients. I can already tell I don't have the focus to make a real meal, not with Saint lounging there watching me, tempting me, so I figure a simple pasta is best. Luckily, his pantry is stocked with amazing high-end ingredients, and it doesn't take me long to find everything I need for my favorite sauce.

"Here, chop." I pass him the olives, capers, and anchovies as I get started setting a pan of water on the stove to boil. "We're making puttanesca."

"You know why they call it that, don't you?" Saint asks, looking amused as he reaches for a knife.

"No, why?"

"It's from the Italian for whore, *puttana*. It literally translates as 'in the style of prostitutes.'"

"What?" I protest, laughing. "No way."

"It's true." Saint is smiling broadly now, and I'm happy to see him looking more relaxed. "The legend has it, they would tempt their clients with the pungent aroma."

"You're making that up."

"I'm not. I promise. You can look it up."

Saint gets up and brings his chopping board of ingredients to join me by the stove. He sets it down, then stands behind me, brushing my hair to one side so that he can press featherlight kisses along the side of my neck.

"Stop distracting me," I laugh, trying to focus on cooking.

"I thought you were a woman of many talents." Saint's voice hums against my collarbone, and I sigh with pleasure as the sensations ripple across my skin. "Is multitasking not one of them?"

"Not when you're doing *that*," I gasp as his hands come around to my front and gently cup my breasts, molding and teasing them through my sweater.

I sink back against his chest, all thoughts of dinner forgotten as Saint pins me there against the stove, his body hard against me, even as his hands are tantalizingly soft. He slides his hands up under my top and brushes his fingertips over my nipples, caressing them into two stiff peaks as his mouth whispers kisses against my neck.

"Saint . . ." I whimper softly, arching into his hands.

"God, Tessa . . ." Saint's voice is thick with lust as I press back, grinding my ass against the ridge of his hard-on. "I've been going crazy, wanting you."

Suddenly, he spins me around to face him, lifting me by the hips and setting me down on the table. His mouth finds mine, and I kiss him eagerly, wrapping my legs around his waist as our tongues slide together, an inferno rising deep inside. He grinds against me, making me moan with the delicious friction rubbing against my core, until finally he tears his mouth away and fixes me with a look of dark intention.

"I'm hungry . . ." he murmurs, sliding his hands up the insides of my thighs. He rucks up my skirt and pushes me back gently until I'm lying there, spread on the farmhouse table for him.

My pulse kicks as he's tracing hypnotic circles on my skin.

Saint tugs down my underwear, dropping kisses on my skin as his hands keep stroking over my hips and breasts, so soft. It feels incredible, and I prop myself up on my elbows to watch him, the sensations only magnified by seeing his body move with every touch and slow caress.

Saint meets my eyes. "I thought you were the bossy one tonight," he muses, eyes intent with lust. He leans down and lightly nips the inside of my thigh. "And I'm just your willing assistant . . ."

The bite turns to a lick, sliding higher, closer to my core. I gasp in anticipation, tensing, but he pauses, inches from where I need him most.

"So, be the boss of me." Saint's breath is hot against me, and I clench, already aching for him deep inside. "Tell me exactly what I should do, Chef."

He waits there, not moving, ready for instruction.

For me to take control.

I feel a thrill of power. Saint has been the one taking the lead on our sexual adventures, and I've loved every minute of it, but damn, there's a new kind of excitement in seeing him like this, ready to pleasure me any way I choose.

"Taste me," I order him, breathless. I spread my legs wider, inviting him. "I want to feel your mouth on me. Your tongue . . ."

Saint sounds a low growl of approval, and then he bends his head to me, licking against my clit in a slow, delicious stroke.

Oh.

I sink back against the table, loving the feel of his mouth as he laps at me, swirling his tongue softly over my swollen bud in a leisurely rhythm. It's heaven, sinking into the bright rush of pleasure, as Saint explores me with steady, thorough strokes.

"Like this, Chef?" he teases, lapping his tongue slowly, back and forth over my clit.

I moan. "Faster," I gasp, already writhing under his expert strokes. "More."

"As you wish."

Saint returns his mouth to me, lapping faster now, sparking new fire in my bloodstream. I arch against his mouth, feeling the heat rise. "Don't stop," I moan, sliding a hand to the back of his head, my fingers tangling in his hair. "God, don't stop!"

Saint hums a growl of pleasure and throws my legs over his shoulders, yanking me closer, devouring me now. His tongue flicks against my clit in a frenzy of motion, making my hips rise off the table for more.

"Touch me," I gasp, reveling in the control. "I need your fingers. Inside . . ."

Saint obeys me, easing one finger, then two, into my tight cunt. I clench around him, loving the intrusion, the thick stretch of him, filling me up as his tongue lavishes my swollen clit.

Then he starts to pump.

"Saint!" I cry out, lost in pleasure now. Fuck, it's too good. Too full. Too much to resist. I grip his head tighter as I buck against his mouth, chasing the glorious crest of sensation. I hear Saint groan in lust against me, licking in a frenzy as his fingers pulse and beckon, rubbing me just right inside. "God . . . Fuck . . . *Saint!*"

He closes his lips around my clit and sucks, and I shatter into a dizzying spiral of pleasure. I arch up, jerking wildly against his mouth as he licks me right through my orgasm, leaving me gasping and moaning for more.

"More, baby?" Saint echoes, and when I lift my head, I see him looking down at me with a look of pure lust, his fingers still pumping thickly inside, shivers chasing me through my afterglow.

"You," I manage, reaching for his shirt collar and yanking him in for a sweaty, gasping kiss. I taste myself on his lips, a new thrill to the control that's still surging through my body. I pull back, looking him straight in the eye. "Fuck me," I grind out, panting. "Take me, however you want. *Use me.*"

"Oh *fuck.*" Saint groans with a deep, appreciative sound. "Baby . . . You sure about that?"

His grip on me tightens. His gaze roves over me darkly, like he's just planning what kind of filthy, depraved things to do to me.

And fuck, it makes me even wetter.

"I'm calling the shots, remember?" I remind him breathlessly. "I'm telling you—I'm *ordering* you. Fuck me. I'm yours."

The words slip out without me thinking, but damn, they sound good. Because right now, like this, my body flushed from pleasure and my blood still burning up with pure, craven need, I am. *His.*

"On the floor, baby." Saint pulls me from the table and sets me on unsteady legs. He strips my sweater off and tears away my bra, leaving me totally naked now, and lands a stinging slap on my ass, pushing at my shoulders to guide me to the kitchen floor. "Face down, on your hands and knees. It's time to show me what a good girl you're going to be."

I moan. I can't help it. I feel drunk on desire, eagerly sinking to my knees on the cool tile and arranging my body to his orders: palms flat, and my body arched, ass in the air.

"Oh fuck, look at you." Saint growls in appreciation, slapping my ass again. I gasp at the sharp sting, trembling there as Saint tears off his clothing. He sinks to his knees and runs a palm over my back and hips, possessive. "You like to take it as good as you give, don't you?"

"Yes," I gasp, head hanging, my breasts swinging free. I shift my hips, loving the feel of the breeze from the open window, cool against my bare skin. "I love everything you do."

Saint gives a low chuckle, burying one hand in my hair, fisting it tight. "So show me, baby. Show me how much you love to suck this cock."

He yanks, pulling me down by my hair and thrusting his cock at my mouth in one smooth motion. Surprised, I almost choke over the thick intrusion, but Saint holds me in place, sinking deeper down my throat, until I have no choice but to take him all the way.

Fuck.

I gasp for air, overwhelmed—and loving it. His taste, his scent, the stretch of him, owning me the way I crave. I struggle to take him, relaxing my throat and moving my lips over his thick shaft.

Saint answers with a groan. "That's a good girl," he murmurs, his voice as tender as his body is demanding. He thrusts deep again, fucking my mouth, as he gently strokes my cheek and whispers his filthy praise. "All the way, swallow it nice and deep. Christ . . . You look so fucking perfect with my cock in your mouth."

I shudder, moaning in pleasure around him as I suck and lick. "That's right, darling," he praises. "Suck me off. Get me nice and wet for you. Because we're just getting started . . ."

He suddenly leans over and lands a slap on my ass, making me yelp. But just as quickly, he's smoothing over the sting on my ass cheek, touching. Caressing.

Dipping his fingers between my cheeks and stroking against the tight bud of my ass.

I gasp in shock, tensing, even as I shiver from the unexpected pleasure of his illicit touch.

Saint tightens his grip on my hair, pinning me in place. "You said you wanted me to use your body . . . *All* of it."

There's a sharp, filthy spitting sound, and then I feel the wet warmth of his saliva dripping between my ass cheeks. His fingers stroke me there, again, spreading the wetness, and nudging deeper, just inside the ring.

Oh God.

I moan in shock—and pleasure. What is this man doing to me? He's still gripping my hair with one hand, holding my mouth on his cock as the other toys with and circles that forbidden place. And fuck, it's overwhelming, him controlling my body so effortlessly, drawing pleasure from me with every touch.

I can't get enough.

"You like that, darling?" Saint massages, and I whimper, thrusting shamelessly back against his hand. *God, yes.*

He pulls me off his cock, panting. "Down," he growls, and I barely have time to catch the flash of raw, wild lust on his face before the tile floor is cold against my back and Saint is on me, shoving my legs up around my ears and thrusting inside me with a roar.

I scream in pleasure.

His cock drives deep, so deep, I can hardly breathe. *Too much.* I try to pause to adjust to the thick stretch of it, but Saint doesn't slow, not even for a second. He pounds into me, pinning me down on the floor, fucking into me, over and over, a riot of friction and grinding pleasure until I'm mindless, boneless, wailing at the top of my lungs and clawing at him in the frenzy.

"Saint! *Fuck!*"

It's relentless. It's a revelation. My cries mingle with his groans, and the filthy slap of our flesh, dirty and raw, and it's so fucking good I can't even take it. I climax with a howl, digging my nails into his back as my body shatters in ecstasy.

And Saint just fucks me through it. I come again, over and over. Fuck, I lose count, I lose track of everything but the raw grind of his body, and the stretch of his cock, and the delicious grip of his hands on my wrists pinning me, trapping me, so there's nothing I can do but take it.

Take everything he has to give, as I surrender completely to the inferno.

"Tessa!" Saint sounds a hoarse cry, and then he's shuddering into me, roaring his release as our bodies shake, and tremble, until the madness fades; we're left collapsed, almost unconscious on the floor.

Holy shit.

I gasp for air, reeling. Never in my wildest dreams have I ever been fucked like this before. *Owned.* Used, the way I asked him. I let out a stunned laugh of disbelief, pleasure still thick like stardust in my veins.

Saint lifts his head from the tile where he's sprawled beside me, looking just about as spent as I feel. "Alright?" he asks hoarsely, but even in his exhausted state, he still reaches over to brush hair from my sweaty face, his gaze tender and questioning.

I nod. Or at least, I try. I'm still not sure I haven't left my body completely.

"More than alright," I manage, panting. "What the fuck . . . ?"

He laughs, a low, ragged sound. "You're going to kill me, you know that, right?"

"Me?" I drag myself over so I'm nestled against him, recovering. "That was all you, Professor."

"Lies." He idly strokes my hair, his breathing becoming steadier now. "Christ, Tessa . . . You're incredible."

I glow with satisfaction. "Right back at you."

We lie there a moment, just basking in the sense of closeness and satisfaction, until I realize there's a bubbling noise coming from the stove. "The water!" I exclaim, and struggle to my feet. I round the table to find the pan is boiling to the point that it's almost dry. I curse, grabbing a cloth, and Saint gets to his feet, stretching with a lazy yawn. "I'll take it from here," he says, tugging on his boxers. "You just recline over there, looking delicious."

"You sure about that?" I ask with a teasing smirk. "With your record in the kitchen . . ."

"I'm never going to live that down, am I?" Saint laughs and drops a kiss on my lips as he moves me aside, refilling the pan and turning his attention to the sauce ingredients. "Go on, relax. You deserve to be waited on hand and foot after that display."

"You know what? You're right." I beam, feeling like I'm floating on a cloud. If a gorgeous, almost-naked man wants to cook me dinner and tend to my every need, I'm not going to fight him on that. I pull on his shirt and button it, then hop onto a stool and take a sip of the wine that magically wasn't knocked over. "I'll just sit here, enjoying the view."

Saint grins, expertly chopping and sautéing, as I slowly come back down to earth. It's different now, I realize, watching him cook. Our wild chemistry has been there from the start, but before, our sex was consumed by a kind of reckless thrill, the adventure of the unknown. It's still there, driving me to the heights of pleasure, but there's something new between us, too.

Trust.

One that lets me surrender completely, knowing that Saint will take care of me, no matter what. One that lets me be even more bold and shameless than ever before, because I can be certain that when the haze of lust ebbs away, I won't be left with questions anymore.

We're in this together now.

Saint plates our pasta and joins me, sitting at the table. He presents my meal with a flourish, and I hungrily load a fork and take a bite.

"Mmm, this is delicious," I exclaim. "Not bad for a sous chef," I add, teasing.

He chuckles. "I was just following your expert direction." He refills our wineglasses, and we eat in silence for a moment, exhausted and ravenous. Then, when his plate is half-empty, Saint asks, "So, do you want to get started?"

"On what?" I ask, still inhaling my food. It's salty and flavorful, and perfectly filling after the workout I just had.

"The list of suspects. Our investigation."

Oh. That.

I look over and find him watching me with a knowing expression. "You started already, didn't you?" he asks, and I nod.

"Maybe . . . Just some research to fill in their backgrounds," I admit. "I know Max and Hugh a little, but this Sebastian Wolfe guy . . . He's got quite a record."

Saint immediately shakes his head. "It's not Seb. Out of all of them, he is my closest friend." His voice is determined. "He didn't do it. There's just no chance."

I feel a flicker of unease, seeing the instinctive loyalty Saint has for his friends. One way or another, that loyalty will be tested, and soon. "Well, if it's not him, then we'll be able to rule him out immediately," I offer. "That will be helpful all on its own."

Saint slowly nods. "You're right. I'll call Seb and see when we can get together."

"All of us," I remind him. "I have to be there, too."

He pauses. "There's going to be no easy way around this, is there?" Saint asks, and I feel a pang. It's not just my life that I'm upending now in pursuit of justice. It's his, too.

"Regretting it already?" I ask lightly, as I search his face for the truth.

But Saint's gaze is even and honest. No secrets hiding in his eyes. "We'll find the answers," he says, reaching for my hand and squeezing it. "I'm right beside you, whatever you choose."

"Or on top of me," I say, lightening the mood with a flirty smile. "Or behind . . ."

Saint chuckles. "Don't tell me you're ready for another round?"

He suddenly pulls me into his lap, kissing me slowly until I'm breathless. "You're going to need to keep up, old man," I whisper, teasing, as he laughs.

"You'll regret that, darling." Saint nips my bottom lip, and my blood sparks with heat all over again.

"Make me," I whisper, and soon I'm lost in his embrace again. Whatever hard choices lie ahead, we're back together again, and right now, that's all I need.

Chapter Six
TESSA

I take the job at the Ambrose Foundation. I have no idea how I'm going to juggle it with my college work. I'm already falling way behind, but since Hugh Ambrose is on my list of suspects, I can't miss the chance to get closer and find out more.

"That's great news," he says, sounding enthusiastic when I call to let him know. "You'll be a great fit with the team. Our head of fundraising, Priya, is still talking about some of your ideas from the other week."

"I can't wait," I say—and mean it. "Although I'll have to work remotely from here in Oxford while I still have lectures and tutorials."

"Whatever you need," Hugh says immediately. "We can make it work."

"How about I start drafting a real proposal about my plan to use social media influencers to expand our fundraising reach?" I suggest. When I pitched it, everyone was enthused. "I could come into the office at the end of the week to talk it through in person."

"Sounds great," Hugh agrees. "I'll send all the on-boarding information over and get our tech guys to set you up here with all the right accounts. Welcome to the team!"

"Thanks for giving me the opportunity," I reply. "I hope we can make a real difference."

And find out if he's hiding a dark side.

* * *

I SPEND THE rest of the week in Oxford with Saint, catching up on my academic schedule, and preparing the presentation for Hugh and his team. I'm torn. Hugh seems like a great guy, and his foundation is doing genuinely good work, supporting charitable projects all around the world. But I can't trust his genial humor or good deeds—at least not until I figure out if he has an alibi for Wren's attack. He's just as powerful as the rest of them, I remind myself as I click through research online, building my files. His politician father, Lionel, is just weeks away from becoming prime minister, if the polls are to be believed. Hugh has wealth and connections, and that serpent crown tattoo.

And a hell of a lot to lose.

Enough to send some anonymous thug to threaten me? I shiver, remembering my own near-miss attack. I still have the bruises fading on my rib cage from when someone tried to warn me off investigating the Blackthorn Society. This isn't a game. These people will do anything to hide their crimes. But I can't stop now. I'm getting closer to the truth.

Closer to avenging my sister's death. Because whoever hurt her—drugged her, kidnapped her, did God knows what to her in that cell—he's the one to blame for her suicide. He's the one who broke something inside her and sent her spiraling down a dark path. He destroyed the happy, hopeful woman who was going to change the world with her medical research, took away my beloved sister. My protector. My friend.

And whoever he is, I'm going to make him pay.

"Your first day at a new job . . ." Saint's voice breaks through my thoughts. "I feel like I should have got you a briefcase to celebrate."

I look over. We're driving down to London early on Friday morning, with bags packed for the weekend. Saint needs to

check in with his family now that his father is in recovery, and
I've been emailing with Priya and the team all week.

"It's not a real job," I point out as the countryside flies past the
windows. "I'm just using it to get close to Hugh."

"And because you believe in the cause," Saint reminds me with
a knowing look. "Remember, I saw your face after your interview.
You loved the team and the mission. You wouldn't have been
working so hard on your presentation this week if you didn't."

"OK, *maybe* I'm excited about the work," I admit. "The Ambrose Foundation is a great organization."

"So when we clear Hugh, you'll have a great time working
there," Saint says lightly, looking back at the road.

Again, I feel that flicker of unease. Because one day soon,
we're going to uncover the evidence about which of his childhood
friends is really a monster, and when that day comes . . . Well, I'm
not sure Saint is ready to face it yet. He says he's on my side and
will help me find the truth no matter what, but right now, it's all
just suspects and hypotheticals. It's easy to pledge his support
when the guilty party is still a mystery.

But can Saint look the man in the eye and disown him, after
decades of friendship?

"Nervous about your presentation?" Saint asks. "You'll be amazing, don't worry."

"Have you heard from Sebastian Wolfe yet?" I ask, changing
the subject to one of the other suspects on the list. "You said he
might be back in the country this weekend."

"He just texted. He and his wife, Avery, got in last night," Saint
replies. "I suggested dinner later. They're going to see how the
jet lag treats them today and let me know. But we'll meet up this
weekend," he adds.

I nod, glad our plans are finally coming together. I've been
itching with impatience to just barrel ahead and demand the

truth, but I know that this secret is buried deep. It's going to take patience and strategy to uncover what really happened to Wren. "Let me know as soon as you hear anything," I tell him, as the open fields outside give way to the London suburbs. "I'll be at the foundation all day, and then I'll come to your place in Kensington?"

"Yes. That reminds me." Saint rummages in his pocket and produces a key for me. "This is for the house, and I'll text you the security codes, too."

I can't help smirking over how quickly my living situation has upgraded, from grotty student housing to Saint's luxurious properties. "Are you sure there's no more real estate to add to the collection?" I tease, fixing it to my key chain, along with the other shiny new one for his Oxford house. "A pied-à-terre in Paris, perhaps? A bolt-hole in Bermuda?"

Saint smiles. "Well, now that you mention it, we do have some property in Scotland, and a family house in Provence . . ."

"Well, naturally," I joke. I sometimes forget that Saint is Anthony St. Clair, future Duke of Ashford and heir to a pharmaceutical fortune. "Will you be at the office today?" I ask.

He nods, looking reluctant. "Dad's still taking it easy, so I'm going to see what I can do to help out at HQ."

"You're a good son," I say, and he gives a wry laugh.

"Tell that to my mother. She's been hounding me all week to step up and get more involved with the company."

"Well . . . *I'm* proud of you," I add. "Ashford was funding Wren's Alzheimer's research, so whatever the company is working on, I know it's for a good cause. To help people. And clearly, my opinion is the only one that matters, so . . ."

He laughs again, but I can see the apprehension in his eyes. I know he has a rocky dynamic with his family. He's spent years trying to resist the responsibilities that suddenly fell on his shoulders after his older brother died; I know now that his father's recent health scare has made that responsibility weigh heavier than ever.

"You'll do great," I reassure him. "I believe in you."

"I thought that was my line?"

I wink. "I'll be sure to credit you in the footnotes."

* * *

SAINT DROPS ME off at the Ambrose Foundation offices, located in a cool area of East London in a buzzy converted warehouse full of open office space and vibrant art. Hugh is out at meetings all morning, I learn, so I'm able to focus on completing all the HR on-boarding paperwork and prepping my notes for my big presentation.

"Ready to go?" Priya asks, stopping by my desk to collect me. She's in her forties, a brisk, no-nonsense kind of woman who I know I need to impress. Especially since Hugh hired me out of nowhere on a whim, because I happen to be dating Saint.

"Yup!" I bolt to my feet and clutch my folder of notes. "I'm all set."

At least, I hope I am.

"We're just up in the conference room," she says, leading me upstairs. "It's all really low-key here," she adds, probably catching the terror in my eyes. "You don't have to give a flashy presentation or anything. Just chat to us. Tell us what you're thinking and how we can activate the plan."

I nod, relaxing a little. Priya introduces me to the rest of the fundraising team, another four people who all seem friendly enough. Then they look at me expectantly. I take a deep breath and begin. "So, I've been putting together an action plan focused on your next campaign, for the clean water initiative . . ."

I keep talking, getting a little more confident as I see the interested expressions on their faces. Hugh told me the foundation has been pretty old-school in its approach to fundraising, relying on fancy galas and high-society charity auctions to bring in the big bucks—even though those kinds of events often cost a huge portion of the proceeds to host. Now he's looking to take a new approach. I suggested that we look to more modern, youthful avenues for raising awareness and money, using social media influencers and partnering with them on campaigns to reach their audience.

"I've drawn up lists of the influencers we should be targeting," I explain, handing out the materials I prepared. "The top ten names I listed alone have a combined reach of over twenty million followers."

"Twenty million?" Priya echoes, looking amazed. "That's more eyeballs than we'd get for a full national ad campaign."

"And for a fraction of the price," I agree. "I've already reached out to them to ask about sponsorship rates, and honestly, I think we can get most of them to partner for free. It looks great for them," I add. "Social awareness, a charitable mission. Everyone wins."

"Sounds great to me."

I look over and see that Hugh is in the doorway, smiling. "Seems like you've hit the ground running," he says, and the others make noises of agreement.

"You should run with this." Priya nods. "And keep me posted. Let me know what you need to make it happen."

The meeting wraps up, and I feel a glow of pride—and relief that I haven't made an ass of myself on my first day in the office. "I knew you'd be an asset to the team," Hugh comments, walking out with me. "What changed your mind about taking the position?"

"Oh, well, it's such a great cause," I reply vaguely. I'm not about to tell him that he's a prime suspect in my investigation now, so I just flash a smile. "You talked me into it."

"I can be persuasive like that." Hugh smiles. He's got rumpled dark blond hair and a slightly nerdy vibe, with gold-rimmed glasses and a button-down shirt. I've always thought he was the nicest of Saint's rich friends, understated and sincere, but now I'm looking at him with new eyes, searching for some sign of a duplicitous double life.

"So, how have you been?" I ask, friendly, as we arrive back at my desk. I give Hugh an encouraging smile. The whole reason I'm here is to strike up a friendship with him and to learn as much as possible. "I haven't seen you since . . . It was the Black-thorn party, right?"

"Right." Hugh nods. "That was a fun night."

"It was," I agree. "Although . . . I guess I was expecting more, you know, from the great Blackthorn Society."

He gives a chuckle. "Turns out secret societies can be rather run-of-the-mill," he agrees, dropping his voice confidentially. "We just let everyone believe we're up to wild adventures so they think we're much cooler than we really are."

I smile. "That was a regular meeting, wasn't it?" I ask, keeping my voice casual. "Do you attend a lot of those things?"

"I should." Hugh makes a face. "My father is always telling me they're important for legacy and tradition, but to tell you the truth, I find them kind of stuffy. Still, they're great for business," he adds, nodding around us. "Most of our big-money donors are members of the society, so really, those events are just a network-ing tool. At least, that's what I tell myself when I'm stuck making small talk about the cricket scores with Humphrey Hewton-Littlegate, class of '74," he adds with a grin.

I laugh along with him.

"That's why it's great that you're here," Hugh says, giving me a friendly smile. "You're going to shake things up for the founda-tion. I can tell. Plus, I shouldn't say it, but I've never seen Saint happier," he adds. "I mean, for him to show up at one of those meetings is a rarity, but to do it with a smile on his face? Unheard of. Whatever's going on with you two, I hope it works out."

"Thanks. Me too," I agree. I realize my phone is buzzing on the desk and check the number. "Speak of the devil. Or should I say, the Saint . . ."

Hugh grins. "Tell him he owes me a squash game," he says, and leaves me to answer in peace.

I pick up.

"How did it go?" Saint asks right away. "I bet you knocked their socks off."

I smile. "The team here is too cool for socks," I report back, glancing around. "But it went OK . . . Better than OK."

"That's my girl."

Saint's casual praise sends warmth right through me. "What about you? How are things at Ashford?" I ask.

He sighs. "The usual. Reports, financials, endless passive-aggressive disappointment."

"Well, as long as you're having fun," I joke, and he laughs.

"I heard from Seb. They can meet for dinner tonight."

"Really?" I feel a shock of anticipation. "That's great."

Saint doesn't sound so enthusiastic, but he continues: "So I'll meet you at the house after work, and we'll drive over to the restaurant together to meet them there."

"It's a plan," I agree, my mind already racing over just how I can approach the topic.

"And I sent you a little something," Saint adds cryptically. "Enjoy."

He hangs up before I can ask more. *Mysterious.* I look around, wondering if he's having more flowers delivered, but there's no sign of anything. With a shrug, I get back to work, and spend the next hour drawing up next steps on the plans I presented. But when I pause for an afternoon coffee, I'm surprised to see a familiar face crossing the office floor.

"Tessa." Saint's cousin, Imogen, greets me with smooth air-kisses on both my cheeks.

I blink. "Hey," I say, surprised. "What are you doing here? Planning a fundraising party with Hugh?"

Imogen is in her late twenties, polished and sophisticated, and runs a successful event-planning business. "No," she replies bluntly, running a hand through her glossy blond hair. "I thought it was high time we got to know each other a little better. Plus, Saint told me you were in town and could probably use my expert shopping knowledge," Imogen adds, already steering me to the exit. "He even gave me his credit card, so the sky's the limit."

"You're joking." I stop in my tracks, a little offended. Saint thinks I need to change the way I dress?

Imogen smiles. "Darling, I never joke about fashion."

I shake my head, still weirded out. "I'm sorry, but . . . I can't spend his money. That would be way too *Pretty Woman* for me."

Imogen arches a perfectly sculpted eyebrow. "So, you have a cocktail dress for dinner tonight, and a tennis outfit, in case Max and Annabelle decide to put on a mixed-doubles this weekend, and another two, three formal ball gowns, because Lord knows the St. Clairs have a packed social calendar, and then of course, there are the fundraising luncheons . . . ?"

"OK, OK," I interrupt her, getting the point. Maybe my dressed-down college student wardrobe isn't going to cut it in Saint's aristocratic world. And if I'm trying to blend in and stay under the radar for my investigation . . . "When you say sky's the limit, just what are we talking about?" I ask, curious.

Imogen smirks. "Now, that's more like it!"

* * *

IMOGEN CALLS A car and takes us to the chic, exclusive boutiques on Bond Street. I can tell from just glancing at the windows that they're way out of my price range, with gleaming floors, luxurious furnishings, and snooty assistants. But of course, Imogen is right at home. She just breezes into the first store, eyes the displays, and beckons over a stylist to pull some looks—who, obviously, she already knows by name.

"Samantha, hi," she coos, flipping through the racks. "Can we see some of the new collection for my friend here? Maybe those gorgeous silk separates. I'm thinking the navy will be great on her skin tone."

"With pops of jewel tones, perhaps?" the girl eagerly adds.

"Yes, exactly!" Imogen beams. "Tessa, what are your sizes?"

"Um, a US eight, but I'm not sure what that translates to," I reply, a little dazed by the speed of their back-and-forth.

"Oh, don't worry. Sam will figure it out. She's a genius." Imogen moves on, and soon I'm cloistered in a lavish dressing room, trying on half a dozen outfits. I pause to take a peek at the price tags and feel faint. Just one of the blouses alone costs more than my entire stipend for the semester!

"How are you set for outerwear?" Imogen calls through the thick velvet curtains.

"Um, what do you mean?" I call back, taking a deep breath. Saint was the one who offered to pay for this wardrobe overhaul, I remind myself. Hell, he pretty much insisted on it.

"Coats, jackets, capes . . ." Imogen yanks the curtains open without ceremony and eyes me in the pair of tailored pants I'm trying.

"Capes?" I repeat, amused.

"You know, for the opera and formal events. Yes and yes," she adds, moving to fix the buttons on the back of my silk top. "Love it. Try the red next."

"Whoa." I hold up a hand, stopping her. "Can we take a breath? Or, you know, just move at a human pace, instead of this super-speed you have going on?"

Imogen pauses and gives me a rueful smile. "Sorry. I can be a little . . . efficient sometimes. Habit of the trade. When you have sixteen rose arbors to construct, and a panicked bride in melt-down over her fiancé's wayward dick, you tend to try and solve problems fast."

I smile back. "Well, how about you sit down and take advan-tage of the champagne and cookies?" I say, eyeing the spread some assistant has brought in. "And also, tell me about this way-ward dick. I have half the store in here. It's going to take a while," I add.

Imogen laughs and goes to relax on the plush couch. "Well, it started at the rehearsal dinner," she begins, and proceeds to tell me the story of her newest clients, who had a meltdown— and a threesome with the maid of honor—just days before the big event.

"They didn't go through with it, did they?" I ask, wide-eyed, pulling back the curtain and emerging in another outfit. This one is a long silk column dress in an inky shade of blue. It shimmers like petrol under the lights, and I have to admit, I love it.

"Oh, they did," Imogen replies, getting up to help me adjust the tiny straps. "The amount of money that family spent on the weekend? They couldn't call it off. Rumor has it the special friend joined them on the honeymoon, too."

She stands back and gives an approving nod. "We'll say yes to this one, too."

I swallow. We've been saying yes to an awful lot of expensive things, and even though I'm supposed to just wave Saint's credit card around, I can't help adding up the total and coming up with a jaw-dropping figure.

Imogen must see the panic in my eyes, because she smiles. "Don't worry. He can afford it."

"Can he?" I venture. We've already picked out three gowns, two cocktail dresses, and a ton of chic pants and sweaters, not to men-tion the pile of boots and accessories Imogen has assembled . . .

There must be over fifty thousand pounds of merchandise here, draped casually around the room!

"You really don't know?"

When I turn back, Imogen is looking at me, curious. "Know what?" I reply.

"The St. Clairs are loaded," she says, as matter-of-fact as ever.

"Yes, but Saint is just a professor," I argue. "He's an academic—"

"With an eight-figure trust fund he inherited the day he turned twenty-five." Imogen finishes for me. "And that's just for starters. He likes to run around acting like one of those libertine poets he teaches, living off passion and pleasure alone, but the man is heir to one of the oldest, richest estates in the country. And then you have Ashford Pharma too . . ." She shrugs. "Look, us Brits like to be terribly tight-lipped about money, but you should understand the situation. Especially if things are getting serious between you."

I take a seat, processing her words. I always knew Saint was wealthy, but in a vague, distant way. I had no idea just what that really meant.

"What else should I know?" I ask finally. "About Saint, I mean. You know him better than anyone, and God knows you don't sugarcoat the truth," I add. Imogen is every inch the perfect debutante, but she has a direct intelligence and wit that I like. I can trust her for more than just the usual polite small talk.

Imogen takes a sip of champagne, thoughtfully assessing me. "Well, you're aware of his taste for wide-eyed students, I'm sure?"

I nod. "I've heard the stories. He has a reputation at Ashford."

"And it's earned. He likes variety. Fresh adventures, new conquests," Imogen continues, rolling her eyes. "Don't get me wrong, I love the man like a brother, but he's never met a committed relationship he didn't turn and run from in the opposite direction. Until you," she adds, sounding curious. "He seems different now. Clearly, you know how to keep him on a short leash."

I get a flash of memory from that sex club he took me to, the woman leading her partner around by a leash. I cough, spluttering over my champagne. "Sorry," I blurt, recovering.

Imogen seems so polished and self-contained, I'm not about to shock her with any news about Saint's wilder side.

"Things are rocky with his family," I add, scoping for more information. "After what happened with Edward . . ."

Imogen nods, looking sadder. "Saint worshipped him. We all did. Edward was one of the good ones, and when he was killed in Afghanistan . . . Nobody knew how to deal with it. Out of nowhere, everything was different—for Saint especially. He'd never been expecting to inherit the title, and even now, I think he's still in denial about what that means."

"His younger brother, Robert, seems more suited to the role," I say. "Saint says he's already working at Ashford Pharma and helping out with family stuff. Why can't he take on the official duties?"

Imogen gives me a rueful smile. "It doesn't work that way. Unfortunately, the Ashford estate is entailed through the male line. Saint is now the oldest son, so he's the one who'll get it all. Whether he wants it or not."

"That doesn't seem fair, on either of them." I frown.

"Welcome to the wonderful world of the British aristocracy." Imogen smirks. "Fairness and equality are *not* on the menu, I'm afraid."

I nod, processing. Saint isn't just from a foreign country to me. He's from a foreign world. One where birthrights and legacy seem to have these people locked into a destiny the moment they were born.

"His mom . . ." I start, hesitant. Imogen looks over. "She doesn't seem to like me that much."

"Aunt Lillian doesn't like anything except Chanel, show jumping, and her pack of poodle schnauzers," Imogen jokes. "Don't worry about it."

"She sort of warned me off from dating Saint," I add, remembering the scene at the hospital, and all her icy determination.

"Of course she did." Imogen sees my expression and softens. "Look, in this world, marriage is still seen as something of . . . a merger," she declares. "Sure, nobody's forcing us down the aisle anymore, or writing marriage contracts when we're still in the cradle, but there's still an awful lot of pressure to make the right choice. The right person, from the right family, with the right pedigree, who'll bring advantage for everyone. There's a reason Max Lancaster is marrying an aristocrat like Annabelle, who's thirty-eighth in line for the English throne—and an even bigger billion-pound reason why she's marrying him. And it's not just young love. You're an outsider, with no money or bloodline," Imogen continues. "You're the last person they're going to want for him."

"Well . . . That's just great," I say dryly, and she laughs.

"Look, Saint doesn't buy into any of that nonsense. So if things are working for the two of you, don't concern yourself with Lillian's opinion."

I nod. "What about you?" I ask curiously. Imogen hasn't mentioned any partner or romantic life. "Is a *merger* in the cards for you?"

She smirks. "I prefer to build my own empire."

"The party-planning business."

"Right. Immersive event staging," she explains, and a flash of intrigue crosses her face. Then, just as fast, it's gone. "You know, tea parties and galas, terribly dull," she adds quickly. "Nothing new there."

Something tells me a woman as smart as Imogen wouldn't be spending her time on anything that boring, but she's already steered the conversation onwards. "I think we have time for a couple more outfits," she says brightly, shoving a fancy blouse into my arms. "Then I better get you back to Saint in time for dinner."

"Right. That." I follow her orders back into the dressing room, but I'm already thinking ahead to meeting Sebastian Wolfe tonight. I feel a shiver of nerves, wondering just what this man is like. Everything I've read says that he's a force to be reckoned with. Powerful. Cold.

Heartless.

But Saint swears he's his closest friend, and can't believe he's the one behind the attack.

Who is this man? And is he the one who hurt Wren?

Chapter Seven
TESSA

I f I'd known you were going to look like that, I would have insisted we stay home," Saint murmurs, sliding a hand to the small of my back as we arrive at the restaurant that evening.

I flush, unable to deny the rush of heat that comes simply from the feel of his palm caressing my bare skin. "You're a fan of my shopping expedition, then?" I ask, flirty.

He chuckles. "A very big fan."

"And you haven't even seen the lingerie I picked out," I whisper, making him exhale fast.

"Now you tell me . . ." Saint's eyes rove over me, as if he's trying to see through the blue silk dress I wound up choosing for dinner, paired with some strappy sandals. My hair is down in loose waves, and the whole effect is casually elegant. At least, I hope it is. Saint definitely seems to appreciate the outfit as he leans in to whisper in my ear. "Didn't anyone tell you it's cruel to tease?"

"Think of it as an exercise in patience," I reply, smiling.

He holds open the door, and we step inside. It's a buzzy, high-fashion Japanese place, with low neon lighting and sleek counters. The other guests are all young and impossibly glamorous, and I send silent thanks to Imogen for making sure I was styled right for the evening.

The hostess materializes and greets him by name. "Mr. St. Clair. Please, this way. You're the first of your party to arrive."

I exhale. Good. My nerves about this dinner have been bubbling under all afternoon, but now that we're here, they're wound tighter than ever.

How the hell am I going to do this? I wonder as I follow them to the table, which is set back in a private corner, the VIP seats. I wanted to look the man in the eye, but what am I supposed to say?

By the way, you didn't kidnap and assault my sister last year, did you?

I don't think that would go down too well.

Saint holds my chair out for me, then places his hand comfortingly on my shoulder as I sit. "Relax," he murmurs. "It's just dinner."

Except it's not. Not to me. The stakes keep rising higher, and the more I discover, the more I wonder who could have been capable of such a cruel, premeditated attack.

The person I'm looking for is a monster. And he's hiding in plain sight.

"Here he is." A voice comes from behind us, and then Sebastian Wolfe arrives, tall and impeccably dressed in a bespoke suit. "The sinner himself." He draws Saint into a back-slapping hug, and the men laugh, clearly old friends. Then he turns to me. "And this must be the famous Tessa." His eyes sweep over me, ice-blue and cool. He has similar coloring to Saint—all dark hair and aristocratic chiseled features—but everything about Sebastian seems sharper. Sterner. Carved from stone. "It's a pleasure to meet you," he says. "Saint has told me very little about you, but the fact we're meeting at all means a great deal."

"It's good to meet you, too," I say, shaking his hand as Sebastian introduces me to his wife, Avery. She's a few years younger than me, but seriously intimidating, in black jeans and chunky boots, with smudgy dark eyeliner and a tough-girl vibe. But it's clear the pair of them are head over heels, from the way Sebastian keeps one hand touching her—resting on her shoulder, taking her hand—even as they sit.

"Fair warning, I'm not sure how long we'll last," Seb says. "We came from Miami last night."

"He's fine," Avery adds with a knowing smirk. "I'm the one who's not used to all the jet-setting, time zones."

"You're American?" I ask, pleased to recognize a familiar accent. "Where are you from?"

"New York," she replies, smiling—but her gaze is sharp and assessing. I can tell nothing gets past her.

"So how did you two meet?" I ask, making an effort to seem friendly and casual. After all, this is supposed to be a fun dinner between old friends, not the Spanish Inquisition.

Avery and Sebastian exchange a look. "Oh, we were . . . introduced by a mutual friend," he replies, smiling. "And then Avery found herself in England, and . . . we grew closer."

"He means he won me in a poker game after I swore to destroy his life," Avery says sweetly, taking a sip of her water. "Which I did. We just wound up falling in love, too."

I blink. "I . . . OK. Wow."

I look to Saint, but he's just smiling, amused. He seems fine with all this drama.

"What about the two of you?" Avery asks, looking curious.

"We met at Oxford," I answer quickly, not about to be quite so honest about what brought the two of us together. "I'm studying there."

"I'm her professor," Saint says with a smirk. "She walked into my seminar and shamelessly flirted with me. I was helpless to resist."

"I did not!" I protest. "He was actually being a real asshole, lording it over me," I tell them, as Saint chuckles. "So I told him exactly what I thought of his bullshit smoldering routine."

"I smolder?" Saint asks, grinning.

I grin back at him. "You know you do."

He laughs, and I can't help but smile along too. When I finally look back at Sebastian and Avery, they're watching us curiously. "Well . . ." Sebastian finally says, smirking at Saint. "Isn't this interesting . . ."

"Watch it," Saint replies. "I expect you to be on your best behavior, so you don't scare Tessa away. You too," he adds to Avery, who offers an innocent smile.

"Who, me? I'm always a good girl."

Saint coughs and takes a drink of water. "Should we order now?" he says, changing the subject suddenly. The waiter approaches and recommends an array of sushi dishes while I sit back, trying to figure out the vibes here. Clearly, they're all good friends.

But just how good?

"So, how are things at Ashford?" Sebastian asks. "The master of the college still fighting off retirement?"

"He'll hang on until he keels over in the main quad," Saint replies, and the two of them catch up, reminiscing about old friends and teachers as the food starts to arrive. I carefully follow the conversation, smiling along, and waiting for my chance to delve a little deeper.

". . . I'll have to see if he's around," Saint is saying. "Get the guys together again."

Sebastian nods. "It's been a while since we were all in one place."

"Do you ever get back to Oxford at all?" I ask Sebastian brightly.

"Sometimes," he replies. "I'm not exactly an active alumnus, but I do have some business interests in the area, so I'm there from time to time."

Vague.

"It's a beautiful city," I continue. "I've heard it's changing though, lots of new development. Have you been up recently?"

"Not in a while, no."

Still vague.

I'm trying to think of a way to pin down his movements when I catch a curious glance from Avery. *Whoops.* I fall silent, waiting until the conversation moves on to their recent travels, before trying again.

"Barbados?" I remark, after Avery describes the beach house there where they spent a few months, escaping the press frenzy after a scandal last year. "I was talking to someone about there at the party a couple of weeks ago," I add. "You know, the Blackthorn Society get-together."

Saint looks amused. "What part of *secret society* don't you understand?" he asks, and I give a bashful laugh.

"Oh, sorry. I just assumed, you know, that Sebastian was part of the group."

"Not me." Sebastian takes a gulp of sake. "My blood isn't blue enough for the likes of them," he adds with a friendly smile.

"And back at Oxford, he was only filthy rich, instead of offensively, stinkingly loaded," Saint adds with a laugh.

Sebastian just gives a modest grin. "What can I say? Business is booming."

I smile too, but I'm disappointed I'm striking out again. How am I going to tactfully get the answers I need? "Excuse me," I say, rising. "I'll be right back."

I cross the restaurant to the bathrooms and take a moment to regroup. They're just as modern as the rest of the place, with low concrete sinks and moody dark lighting. I shut myself in a cubicle and try to think of a strategy. Saint is being no help; aside from the introduction, he's acting like this is any old reunion between old friends.

Except he did agree to let you take the lead.

I sigh, hoping the night isn't already a bust. But when I flush and emerge back into the main bathroom, I'm surprised to find Avery is waiting for me.

"Hi," I blurt, surprised. She's leaning against the wall, arms folded, watching as I wash my hands. "It's great seeing Saint catch up with old friends," I add, pleasant. "Hearing all the old stories . . . Although, I get the feeling they're not telling us half of the trouble they got up to," I add with a grin.

Avery doesn't smile back. In fact, the way she's looking at me right now is intimidating, like a woman that knows how to kick some ass and would be perfectly willing to do it.

"What are you playing at?" she asks, narrowing her eyes.

I blink. Adrenaline spikes in my bloodstream, but I force myself to act calm.

She can't know anything.

"I'm sorry," I say, keeping the friendly smile fixed to my face. *When in doubt, play dumb.* "I don't know what you mean."

I dry my hands and carefully check my reflection, painfully aware of Avery's sharp stare still burning into me.

"You want something," Avery says slowly. "And you're asking a lot of questions to find it out. I don't know what it is yet, but I'm not buying this friendly curiosity routine."

I force a nervous laugh. "Really, I don't know what you're talking about. I'm just trying to learn more about Saint's friends, that's all." I turn back to face her and give a bright smile. "Hopefully we'll all be hanging out more in the future."

Avery narrows her eyes at me, but she doesn't say anything more as I exit the bathroom. She trails after me, following me back to the table, and I take my seat again as Saint flashes me a smile.

"We were just deciding about dessert."

"What's there to decide?" I ask. "Yes, always."

"I thought so." Saint reaches over and squeezes my hand. He leans in, whispering in my ear. "That doesn't mean we won't have any later . . ."

I shiver at the brush of his lips. "Like I said," I murmur back, flirty. "Yes, always."

Saint chuckles, sitting back. He lifts my hand to his lips, kissing my knuckles as he gives me one of those smoldering looks. Just as I'm just relaxing again, Avery announces bluntly, "I think it's time you two dropped the act and tell us what's going on."

I freeze, and even Sebastian looks surprised. "What do you mean?" he says to her, frowning.

"Ask them." Avery nods to Saint and me. "They're up to something. And I thought we knew each other well enough to be honest instead of playing games. At least, the three of us do," she adds, giving me another long, suspicious glare.

"It's not a big deal," Saint says, immediately trying to smooth things over. "Tessa just has something she's trying to find out, and there's a possibility that—"

"You have the tattoo?" I ask Sebastian bluntly. There's no point being subtle about this anymore. "The serpent and crown symbol."

He frowns, surprised. "No."

What?

"But Saint said—" I start, and Sebastian holds up a hand for me to let him continue.

"I got it removed. No offense," he adds to Saint with a wry grin. "But it's not exactly my style."

"None taken," Saint agrees.

"When?" I demand, trying to stay on track. "When did you have it removed?"

Avery speaks up again. "Tell us why you want to know." She fixes me with a glare. "I don't like liars, and you've been lying since the moment we sat down."

I hold her stare. "Because my sister was kidnapped and tortured and God knows what else by a man who had that tattoo," I reply, just as fierce. "And I'm trying to figure out who it was from the group."

There's silence.

Sebastian and Avery look shocked, and Saint clears his throat, awkward. "More sake, anyone?" he asks, like he's trying to make a joke.

They ignore him.

"You think it was Sebastian?" Avery asks, sitting forward.

"I think he's on the list of suspects, and I have to rule him out," I reply, direct. I'm expecting anger at the suggestion, or even for them to get up and walk out, but instead, Avery just gives a cool nod.

"When? When was your sister attacked?"

"Uh, last year, in the fall." I tell them the weekend it happened, and Avery looks to Sebastian.

"That was before we met," she says, and he pulls out his phone to check his calendar.

"I had the tattoo removed over five years ago, and that weekend I was in New York on business," Sebastian reports, glancing up.

"Can you prove it?" I shoot back.

"Tessa . . ." Saint gives me a furious look, but I don't care if I'm being impolite. I have to be certain, one way or another.

"Seb?" Avery prompts him, seemingly in my corner. Or maybe she's just in a hurry to get this over with, but either way, I'll take it.

"Hold on . . ." Seb scrolls on his phone, then shows me the screen. It's a photograph of him on a red carpet, looking dapper. The caption reads, "New York society turns out for a gala performance at New York City Ballet." There's more description, of the guest list, and the date. "I'm sure I can pull other photos and evidence from the night if you need. My flight records, and testimony from the staff there, too."

I sit back, exhaling. The dates match. It wasn't him.

"Satisfied?" Avery asks coolly.

"Yes." I nod, feeling a wave of relief. Saint clearly cares about this man and their friendship. I'm glad he was right about Sebastian in the end. "Thank you," I add, glad he's no longer a suspect. But when I look to Saint, it's clear he's not pleased.

He looks furious, his jaw set with barely contained tension. "I think it's time we were leaving." He rises, tossing down his napkin. "Tessa."

It's not a question but an order.

Shit.

"It was nice meeting you both," I blurt, getting to my feet. I flash an awkward smile at Sebastian and Avery. "I mean, aside from the whole interrogation part. Maybe we'll see you again soon!"

Saint takes my hand and practically drags me away. I have to hurry to keep up with him, but he doesn't say a word, not until we emerge onto the dark sidewalk outside the restaurant.

"Christ, Tessa!" Saint whirls on me, exploding in anger. "What the fuck were you playing at?"

"I was getting answers," I reply, yanking free. "The way I said I would."

"These are my friends!" Saint yells, his voice ringing out in frustration. "And fuck knows, Seb's had enough false accusations thrown in his direction. Would it have killed you to use a little tact and subtlety?" he demands, dragging a hand through his hair.

"I tried tact!" I protest. "It wasn't getting us anywhere! So I figured I'd be direct."

"And insult them right to their faces." Saint paces, agitated.

"It worked, didn't it?" I shoot back. "We can cross him off the list."

"But only because he's innocent!" Saint exclaims, his eyes flashing in the dark. "You think the real attacker will just put his hands up and come clean? 'Gee, sorry, you've got me there,'" he mimics. "You've got to be smarter than this. For Christ's sake, I had a plan!"

"How was I to know that?" I demand hotly.

"Because this is my world," Saint yells back. "My friends, *my life* you're bulldozing to the ground. The least you could let me do is figure out what kind of dynamite is best to use before you go and blow it all to hell!"

Saint's voice echoes in the night, and we stand there in silence for a moment, breathing hard.

His world . . .

I realize with a pang just how much I'm asking of him. To turn on people he trusted, lie and interrogate them, to help me find the truth.

And he hasn't hesitated, not for a moment.

"I'm sorry," I whisper, closing the distance between us. "I know this is hard for you. Having to pick sides, and to choose who you'll be loyal to . . ."

"But it's not!" Saint yells, flexing his fists at his sides, his body still racked with tension. "That's the really fucked up part. Because it's not hard to choose. Not even for a minute. It's always you."

I inhale in a rush, staring at him there on the sidewalk.

It's always you.

Emotion swells, a rush of passion too strong to resist. I reach for him, all but hurling myself into his arms and pulling him down to meet me in a hot, wild kiss.

Saint groans against me, and in an instant, all our frustration and anger are channeled into white-hot desire, blazing there in the dark. He kisses me back, hard, yanking me closer, his strong arms pinning me in place as he takes control. I melt against him, eagerly parting my lips for him to taste and plunder as I hold on for dear life.

More.

I swear, the way the lust takes us over, I could have torn his clothes off right there in the street. Somehow, Saint pulls away long enough to hail a cab, and we make it back to his place, careening through the door in a messy tangle of mouths and hands.

He puts me back against the wall, kissing me furiously, his eyes still hot with frustration there in the dim hallway.

"You should have trusted me," Saint growls, kissing his way down my neck. "Fuck, tell me that you trust me, Tessa."

"I do," I moan, as his tongue finds the sensitive hollow of my neck. "I'm sorry. I do trust you."

He lifts me, and then we're stumbling up the stairs to the bedroom, shedding clothes as fast as we can. "Damn," he groans, seeing me bared in my new black lingerie. "I'm going to need a full show of what you got."

"Later," I manage, yanking him back to me by his collar. "Now, just take it off."

"With pleasure." Saint shoves me onto the bed with a bounce, covering me with his body, devouring me inch by inch. His mouth is on my breasts, his hands already parting my thighs, petting at my damp core as I gasp and writhe against him.

"Saint!" My voice rings out, echoing with need as he pulls down the lacy cups of my bra and feasts on me, teasing and toying with my nipples until they're stiff and aching for him. I arch against his hand, needing the pressure, wanting *more*.

He lifts his head, dark eyes and breathing hard. "Show me," he orders, spreading my legs wider, throwing my ankles up around his shoulders. "Show me you trust me. That you can follow a damn order. Don't you dare come until I say."

He buries his head between my legs and laps against my clit, sending me reeling.

Oh fuck.

I reach up blindly, hanging on to the bars of the headboard for leverage as Saint sets about licking me into a frenzy. "Yes!" I cry as he thrusts two fingers inside me, pumping in time with his wicked mouth. "Oh God, right there. *Yes!*"

Saint is relentless, licking and swirling over my clit with devastating precision. I whimper helplessly, writhing beneath him, lost to the incredible friction and thick stretch of his fingers, curling deep inside. Pleasure surges, cresting, and it doesn't take long before I'm trembling and close to the edge. He's just too talented, his fingers and tongue driving me wild. "Please," I beg, my voice rising with need. "Oh my God, Saint, *please . . .*"

I'm gripping the headboard so tightly, doing my best to hold the pleasure at bay, but it's too good, too strong. I'm not going to last. "Saint!" I scream as he pumps his fingers deeper, thicker—

He lifts his head, stilling his motions as I gasp and writhe. "You'll follow my plan next time?" Saint demands, watching me.

I make a noise of frustration. "Not fair," I exclaim through my haze. "I thought we agreed . . . no using sex as a—*ohhh!*" My complaint is lost in a moan as he flexes his fingers inside me, making my body arch. "Weapon," I finish, breathless.

"But it's more fun than a fight," Saint counters, smirking, and I have to laugh, even though I hate him a little right now. "Do we have an agreement?" he presses, flexing his fingers again. Beckoning, rubbing my inner walls just right.

I moan, so close to release. So fucking close. "Yes," I surrender, clenching helplessly around his fingers. "Fuck, yes, whatever you want, just let me come. *Please . . .*"

He sounds a low chuckle. "So soon? But you look so pretty like this, begging for me."

"Saint . . ." My voice is hoarse and desperate now.

His gaze is steady. Stubborn. Proving a point. "Oh, baby, I could do this all night."

But I won't.

In a breathless shift, I sit up, grabbing Saint and pulling him down to the mattress, rolling us in one swift movement until I'm straddling him, pinning him to the bed now. He laughs in surprise, and I muffle him with a kiss, greedily tasting his mouth as

I unsnap his belt and yank his pants and briefs down. "You had your fun, teasing me . . ." I scold him playfully as I free his cock. I wrap my hand around the thick length, fisting it slowly. Making him groan. "Now it's time for me to take what *I* want."

"Go right ahead." Saint sinks back into the pillows. He stares up at me, voice thick with lust. Cock straining in my hands. "Fuck, Tessa, take it all."

So I do.

Straddling his lap, I rise, positioning his thick head against my aching core. Then I sink down on him, taking him deep, *fuck*, taking him all the way to the hilt.

Oh God.

My head falls back with the pleasure of it, every inch of him stretching me open, rubbing with a delicious friction. I moan from deep in my chest, and Saint answers with a fevered curse.

"Fuck, Tessa. *Fuck.*"

His hands come to my hips, gripping so tightly I know they'll leave marks, but I don't care. Nothing matters right now except the heat glittering in my bloodstream, and the pleasure clenching hard as I rise up and grind down on him again, fuck, feeling that thickness, chasing the rush.

"That's right, ride me." Saint growls, splayed there beneath me. He moves my hips, finding my pace. "Ride my cock, baby. Let me feel that pussy clench."

I moan, moving faster now, panting as I start to bounce. Everything I need, fuck, it's right here, each stoke of his cock, every perfect grind of his hips. I'm unleashed, using his body shamelessly as I chase the ultimate high. "Saint . . ." It's closer now, fuck, my climax rising like a tidal wave. I throw my head back, gasping, so fucking close . . .

"Touch yourself," Saint demands, thrusting his hips up to meet my pace. His eyes are lust-filled, his jaw clenched with desperate self-control. "Show me how you like it, darling. Rub that clit while you ride my cock."

Oh God. I slip a hand to where our bodies join, finding my swollen bud and rubbing it as I grind. Pleasure sparks through me, inside and out, the sweetness curling low at the base of my spine. "Yes," I cry, feeling my whole body start to shudder. "Oh, God, *yes*!"

Saint sounds a desperate roar, rearing up, his mouth finding my breasts to nip and lick, the added sensation driving me wild. He closes his mouth around my nipple and sucks so hard I let out a scream, clenching my core as the sensation shatters through me.

I come apart with a howl, my whole body convulsing there as he pins me to his cock, thrusting up into me over and over as I climax in his arms. "Fuck, yes, choke my cock," he groans, his eyes rolling back. "I can feel you, baby. Don't stop. Milk me out!"

A fresh wave of pleasure shatters through me, and I scream, but Saint doesn't stop. He bounces me harder on his cock, the friction driving me crazy until I'm sobbing, out of my mind. *"Fuck—"* I hear Saint's desperate roar as he flips us over and fucks me deep into the mattress, embedding himself deep inside and bearing down, coming in a hot rush that makes me moan. He shudders into me, ragged, face buried in the pillows, until finally his body goes limp and he collapses in my arms.

I lie there, mindless, until slowly I begin to think in complete sentences again. "You know you didn't have to bargain like that," I murmur, gently stroking Saint's sweaty back.

He lifts his head, face slack with pleasure. "What?"

"I trust you. I'll be better about working together next time."

He smiles, catching his breath. "But still, it was fun, making you beg."

I laugh. "Maybe. Just a little," I admit, curling closer.

"And you were such a good, obedient girl for me . . ." Saint's voice drops, husky. "I think you earned a reward."

I yelp in surprise as he pulls me up, taking hold of my hips and settling me directly over his face. "Saint, wait, I only just came—"

But his tongue finds me, soft and wet, lavishing my clit in a delicious sweep. I moan, tilting forwards and grabbing hold of the headboard again.

I should beg him more often.

Chapter Eight
SAINT

To say I'm not a morning person is an understatement. I usually sleep until noon, tired out from the debauchery of the night before—or take an early stroll home to avoid whatever misbehaviors I got into last night. But waking early Monday morning with Tessa sprawled in bed beside me, naked in the sheets with a peaceful smile on her sleeping face, I begin to see the appeal.

I watch her for a moment, relishing the chance to see her so unguarded, almost innocent. She lets out a breathy sigh, wriggling under the covers, and I feel an unfamiliar tightness in my chest.

Mine.

I reach over and brush a stray lock of hair from her cheek, careful not to wake her. After the drama of dinner on Friday night, we've spent a relaxing weekend together, just strolling the city, showing her the sights. Evenings we've spent here at the house, watching old movies and getting wrapped up in each other's arms. It's been quiet. Understated. Domestic, even.

How the mighty have fallen . . .

I stifle a wry chuckle. Christ, I've never been possessive over my women; my sexual adventures are the very definition of temporary. A partner is there to be enjoyed, educated, explored—even *shared*, as my past exploits would attest. But no matter what kind of sensual, wild fun I had, the ending was always the same: we'd go our separate ways. No promises, no commitment, nothing but a brief interlude of mutual satisfaction—and then on to the next one.

But lying here, with Tessa in my arms . . . ?

I understand now what makes Sebastian willing to kill for his bride. And why watching Tessa slide my house key onto her key chain sparked some deep protective instinct.

This is only the beginning.

Tessa stirs, slowly blinking a couple of times as she wakes. "Good morning," she murmurs, stretching with a sleepy yawn. Her body shifts under the sheet, baring her breasts, and I can't resist leaning over to kiss each nipple in turn.

"It is a very good morning . . ." I lick her softly, and Tessa gives a satisfied moan of a laugh.

"Now, this is much better than my alarm." She smiles, pulling me up to meet my mouth with a slow, sultry kiss. Goddamn, she feels perfect in my arms, warm and naked, wrapping herself around me like she never wants to let go.

Which would be just fine with me.

Finally, she pauses for air, her cheeks flushed and rosy. "What would you do for me right now?" she asks, a playful sparkle in her eyes.

I rock my hips into the cradle of her thighs, letting her feel my straining erection. "Any fucking thing you want." I kiss her neck, finding that sensitive spot that makes her tremble.

"Breakfast," Tessa says, pulling back. She grins at me. "Make me breakfast, darling. I'm so hungry, I could gnaw down on this pillowcase right now."

I chuckle. *Darling* . . . I like the sound of that. "You didn't enjoy dinner?"

Tessa gives me a look. "Eating wasn't exactly the first thing on my agenda for the evening."

"Good point." I release her and climb out of bed. "Eggs? Toast? Bacon?" I ask as I pull on some boxers and a robe.

"All of the above." She beams, getting up.

"Wait." I stop her halfway to the bathroom.

"What?" She pauses, looking at me expectantly.

I drink in the sight of her naked body there in the morning sunlight. Fuck, the curve of her hips . . . the swell of her breasts . . . it could drive a man to poetry. And when I remember how she looked bouncing on my cock last night, shamelessly taking her pleasure and screaming out for more . . .

"Nothing," I finally reply. "Just I'm understanding now what made the great writers devote their lives to their craft. How can you find the words to describe something like you?"

Tessa blinks in surprise, then rolls her eyes. "Quit it," she says playfully, like she doesn't believe me. "You already got me into bed. You don't need to bring out the fancy lines." With a grin, she sashays into the bathroom and slams the door.

I head downstairs to get started on breakfast, enjoying the morning peace. I can't deny feeling a lot of relief, too, that we've officially crossed Sebastian Wolfe off her list of suspects. He's one of my closest friends, and I didn't believe for a moment it could be him. But still, now that Tessa believes it too, it's a weight off my mind.

Until I think about the fact that we just have two people left: Max and Hugh. Also my longtime friends. Also unthinkable that they could be to blame.

Soon enough, Tessa joins me, dressed down in jeans and a familiar college sweatshirt. She's heading back to Oxford for the week to attend her classes, while I stay here in London to check in with things at Ashford Pharma. "What happened to all your new clothes?" I ask, sliding food onto a plate for her and setting it down beside the coffee I've just brewed. "The credit card company called to check I hadn't been robbed by a woman with exquisite taste."

She laughs. "They're lovely, but . . . I don't want to show up for class in couture," Tessa says, diving into the food. She shoves a piece of toast in her mouth and talks around it. "You know everyone else dresses down. I don't want to stand out."

"Tough," I tell her, adding orange juice to her spread. "You always do, just by walking into the room."

Tessa rolls her eyes again. "Do you think I can make it back for my nine a.m. lecture?" she asks, changing the subject. Clearly, she's not comfortable with compliments, which is crazy to me. I've been singing her praises since the moment I walked in on her impromptu break-in during the Ashford welcome tea.

I knew she was trouble then; I just didn't realize how sweet that trouble would be.

I check my watch. "I already called the car, but it'll be close," I note. "Why not skip it and spend the morning here with me instead? I'll have you back to Oxford by noon . . . after at least three orgasms," I add with a smirk.

She grins back. "Only three? You must be getting bored of me."

Bored? Fuck, she has no idea how obsessed I'm getting. Nobody else could drive me so crazy, practically yelling right there in the street after dinner—or send me out of my mind with her wanton moans. But I know, as much as she says she trusts me now, she's still skittish. She's spent so long alone with her grief and anger, her defenses are a mile high. If I'm going to show her just how good we could be together, I need to take it slow.

So I give her a smoldering grin and play it cool. "Well, you are rather predictable," I tease, using her own favorite insult against me. "Tessa Peterson, just your ordinary, average kind of girl. Run-of-the-mill, even," I add, flashing to the first night at the Midnight party where she spread her thighs for me in the darkness and moaned like a goddess, working herself into a frenzy for a room of strangers.

For me.

"What you see is what you get," she agrees, a flirty smile play-ing on her lips. "I mean, I would *never* be the kind of woman who wears French silk panties under her jeans. The kind that you could just slip aside when you bend me over . . ."

Fuck.

Lust surges, and I reach for her, but Tessa ducks away with a giggle. "Not now," she scolds me with a wink. "I have a lecture to get to. And you have a busy week ahead, too, thinking about exactly what you're going to do to me this weekend." She leans up on her tiptoes and whispers hotly in my ear. "And yes, in case you were wondering, the bra matches, too."

And then she dances away, grabs her toast and her bag, and leaves.

And I go take one hell of a cold shower.

* * *

WITHOUT TESSA HERE to distract me, there's no avoiding my commitments, so I finally head into central London, to the glass and chrome monstrosity that is the Ashford Pharma HQ. Sub-tlety is not my father's style, at least not when it comes to busi-ness, and so the new construction rears up above the historic streets, with sweeping views of the river, and gray skies beyond.

I pass security with a nod in the lobby and take the elevator up to the executive floor. Then I pause, looking around. My fa-ther isn't here—he's recuperating at the family estate down in Sussex—and I can't say I'm familiar with any of the other staff. I've made it a point to steer well clear of the family business.

Of any family business, full stop.

But with my father out of commission after his heart attack, I know there's no more avoiding my official duties as eldest son and heir.

I find Robert in his office, frowning at a stack of files. "Nice view," I comment, strolling in.

He looks at me in surprise. "Saint. What . . . What are you doing here?"

"I'm sorry, I must have gotten confused. I was looking for the bar," I joke, looking around.

"It's nine in the morning," Robert sighs.

"All the more reason to crack open a bottle of something strong."

Christ, this office is more like a prison cell. It's all bland and corporate, his desk positioned facing away from the windows so nothing will distract him from his computer screen. But then again, Robert always was the hardworking one. He even has family photos lined up on a credenza, smiling happily with our parents.

And a picture of Edward, too, hiking some mountain terrain.

I pause over the frame, feeling the echo of a decade-old grief. *You should be here, big brother. Not me.*

Never me.

But things don't turn out the way we plan, so I set down the photo frame and turn back to Robert. "I'm here to help," I explain. "Dad is going to be in recovery a while longer, and even after the doctors give him the all-clear, he'll have to scale way back."

"I know all that," Robert replies, looking annoyed. "I was in the meeting, too. I just didn't expect you to actually follow through."

"Look, I'm not here to make your life harder," I say, putting my hands up. "If you don't want me around, I'll just go and leave you to it . . ."

"You think you're getting off the hook that easily?" Robert finally grins and shoves a thick stack of folders over to me. "Nice try, but we could use all the help we can get."

"Even me?"

"Even you. Come on," he adds, leading me out and down the hall. "You can work out of Dad's office while he's gone. It's safer

that way. Tricia's probably the only secretary here who's immune
to your charms," he says, giving me a knowing look.

"You underestimate me." I smirk. And I'm a one-woman man
these days. "But no need to worry. I'll keep my hands to myself,
and my eyes on the . . . *Annual Adjusted Forecasting Matrix*," I
say, reading the folder on the top of the pile. I whistle. "Not exactly a blockbuster title, is it?"

"The title doesn't matter, just the top line," Robert says, grabbing yet more files from a desk as we pass. "The quarterly newsletter is going out to investors, and I need you to pull some highlights.
Good news we can use to keep them happy, tide them over until
the big trial results announcement next month."

"The Alzheimer's drug?" I ask, and Robert looks surprised.

"You're keeping up to date with our trials?"

I roll my eyes. "I'm not completely oblivious to what goes on
here," I tell him, even though if it wasn't for Tessa's connection
to the project, I probably wouldn't know anything about it. But
since her sister worked on the early trials phase, I know that the
project matters to Tessa—a way of Wren's legacy living on. "How
are the trials going?"

"They finished a few months back," Robert replies. "Now they
just crunch the numbers and fast-track through peer review before we can announce."

"That's good." I glance at the folders Robert's given me, but
there's nothing about our new drugs or interesting research, just
thick, dull-looking files about cost-cutting.

"Isn't this newsletter a job for the PR department?" I ask, sighing.

Robert makes a face. "Dad insisted on doing it himself. The
personal touch. So . . ."

". . . now you're fucked without him." I nod. The downside of
a control freak CEO. "Got it. Anything in particular you need?"

"Anything with a positive spin. Overhead savings, new grants,
helpful side effects for the diabetes drugs. Everything you need

will be in the internal update reports." He pauses. "You have been reading the internals, haven't you?"

"I may be a few weeks behind," I reply. More like years. "But I can handle it," I assure him. "Good news, massive profits, rah-rah Ashford."

"Alright . . ." Robert looks reluctant, but one of the other staff members scurries over and pulls him away for a meeting, so I let myself into my father's office and get started, grabbing the first folder at random.

Leveraged Cost Analysis—Southern Europe Division.

Oh boy.

* * *

FIVE HOURS, TWO espressos, and some gourmet donuts from the snack room later, I've got financial projections and medical terminology coming out of my eyeballs. There are a dozen reasons why I've stayed away from Ashford all these years, and the dry, corporate nature of the work is moving fast to the top of the list.

Adjusted Laboratory Expenditures—United Kingdom.

I yawn, scanning the next folder. I've already pulled a number of positive stories from the files and almost have enough to keep any investor happy with Ashford's world-beating prowess, but as I scan the financial breakdowns of our Oxford location, I pause.

That can't be right.

I frown at the dense print, but the numbers don't change.

Incidentals, the spreadsheet calls them, but they total over £50,000 a month above usual spending levels, and when I check the footnotes at the very back of the report, I find they've been paid out personally to Dr. DeJonge.

I quickly search for her name in our internal staff database and discover she's the lead scientist in charge of the Alzheimer's drug project. There's a photo of her, too: chic, dark-haired, with a severe bob and cool blue eyes.

Valerie DeJonge.

She's the French woman my father was arguing with at the Lancaster party. And he's been paying her a massive amount of money off the books for almost a year now.

Dammit.

I grab the file and stick my head out of the office to where my father's trusty secretary, Tricia, is working at the desk in front. "I don't suppose you'd know who could give me some more information about these numbers, do you?" I ask.

"Accounting should be able to help," she replies. "Try Harold. He knows everything."

I pause, and Tricia looks amused. "Fourth floor," she explains.

"Much obliged."

I take the elevator down and go in search of the all-knowing Harold. I find him in a windowless cubicle, a middle-aged man with balding hair hunched over a limp supermarket sandwich.

"Harold?" I ask. He looks up, and chokes on his egg salad at the sight of me.

"I . . . Um . . . Mr. St. Clair," he blurts, trying to blot mustard from his shirt. "Shoot. I mean, wow. Hello. Um, are you lost?" he asks, puzzled.

I smile. "Call me Saint," I tell him. "I was hoping you could help me with something . . ."

I look around. Christ, this place is depressing, just cubicles as far as the eye can see. Clearly, they spent the interior decorating budget upstairs.

And the catering budget, too.

"What do you need?" Harold asks, setting his lunch aside and putting his reading spectacles on.

"It's these budget line items," I explain, pulling up a chair and showing him the spreadsheet. "I must be reading them wrong. The new incidentals seem awfully high to me."

"Hmm . . ." Harold flips through, quickly assessing the figures.

"No, see, it says here they started breaking out the laboratory equipment budget in more detail starting at the beginning of the year," he explains, looking up again. "The incidentals used to be lumped in with the main budget. That's why they suddenly seem to have increased."

"But wouldn't those payments go to vendors?" I ask, still stuck on my instinct that something's not right.

"Yes, they would. See here, the supplementary breakdown." Harold shows me another row of figures—matching the £50,000 every month, all legit and aboveboard. "Your father signed off on it personally, so you shouldn't worry," he reassures me. "It all adds up."

Except it doesn't.

But instead of pointing out those footnotes with the direct payments to Dr. Valerie DeJonge's personal account, I close the folder. "Thanks, Harold," I say, getting to my feet. "You've been very helpful."

He coughs. "Well, thank you, Mr.—I mean, Saint. I'm always around if you need answers."

I nod and say goodbye, but as I head back up to the office, it's clear there's only one person who can give me the answers I need. The man who knows exactly why Dr. DeJonge is getting such a large personal bonus straight from the company accounts.

My father.

* * *

WHEN I CHECK his calendar with Tricia, I find he's scheduled for a follow-up appointment at St. Guy's hospital this afternoon. I'm glad. I'd rather keep this conversation as far away from my mother as possible. But when I head over to the hospital and up to his suite in the VIP wing, I'm surprised to find he's not alone.

A now-familiar French voice is audible inside with him. The door is ajar, so I pause outside, listening to the discussion going on.

"I can't keep going like this," Valerie is insisting. She sounds emotional, and I can tell from my father's harsh, frustrated tone that he isn't happy, either.

"You knew what you were getting into. Nobody forced you."

"Is that so? I'm your employee, after all. Perhaps people will see it differently if I tell."

"Is that a threat?" My father's voice rises, shaken.

"Take it how you like. You can't hide this, Alexander," she adds. "And I can't hide it for you much longer."

"Don't you dare—"

I hear the anger in his voice, and smoothly push the door open. "Hello, Father," I say loudly.

They freeze, caught together across the room. My father's face is set with anger, and he's gripping Valerie's arm tightly. Up close, I realize I've seen her at various parties and Ashford events. Except then, she always had an expression of brisk impatience, as if she had better places to be.

Now she looks shaken.

"I'm not interrupting, I hope," I say pointedly.

"Of course not," my father blurts loudly, releasing her. The moment she's free, Valerie backs away from him. She recovers and offers me a polite smile. "I was just leaving, Alexander." She nods at my father. "This conversation isn't over. We'll talk soon."

She stalks out, her high heels tapping on the floor.

My father exhales and sinks onto the bed. "Everything alright?" I ask carefully.

"Oh yes," my father says immediately. "Just a few hiccups at the lab. Deadlines and so forth. You know how scientists can get. Brilliant, but highly strung."

He takes a handkerchief and mops his brow. His hand trembles. *Dammit.*

I wanted to stay out of his personal affairs, but clearly, this is spiraling out of control.

"You don't have to pretend with me," I say slowly. "I know what's going on."

My father looks up, and panic flashes across his face. "Son—"

"This affair with Valerie." I cut him off before he can deny it. "I've seen the two of you sneaking around. Here, the Lancaster party . . . It's only a matter of time before somebody else catches you in your little tête-à-têtes."

There's a pause. "You're right." My father hangs his head, and I would swear he even looks relieved. "I'm sorry."

"You don't owe me an apology," I say coolly. "It's none of my business who you fuck around with. But the payments? Fifty thousand pounds a month, straight out of the company funds? That's just sloppy, Dad. No matter what kind of creative accounting you did to try and hide it," I add. "Hell, if I can find it right there in the books, anyone can."

My father looks up, brightening. "You were in the office?"

"I said I'd help. And you're lucky I did," I continue. "Do you really want your mistress payoffs coming out in an official audit? Wouldn't look too good in the investor newsletter, that's for certain."

He nods, looking chastened. "You're right. I don't know what I was thinking. You don't have to worry," he adds. "It's over. I'll end it, I promise."

"Good," I reply, relieved. For once, I'm the one lecturing my father about his life choices, but the role reversal is no consolation for having to consider my father's peccadilloes, even for a moment. "How was your checkup?" I ask, glad to change the subject. "Everything looking alright?"

He nods. "The usual lectures about taking it easy and eating more leafy veg. Your mother is having smoothies delivered twice daily," he adds with a wince. "What I wouldn't give for a nice rare steak."

"Well, as long as you're on the mend." I get up, more than ready to leave. "And the sooner everything is wrapped up with Dr. De-Jonge, the less stress you'll be under."

"I guess I couldn't resist temptation. Like son, like father, eh?" He offers me a weak smile, and I grit my teeth at the idea.

"Not anymore."

My father looks surprised. "That American girl still keeping you occupied?"

"Her name is Tessa, and yes." I head for the door. "Oh, and I'm giving Harold in Accounting a promotion. And a raise."

I walk out.

God knows someone should come out ahead in this mess. Since Valerie's been banking a small fortune from my father, and he's certainly benefited from the affair himself, it looks like it's going to be Harold and his egg salad sandwiches getting the last laugh. Good. The less I have to think about my father's sex life, the better. But as I exit the hospital, his words linger.

Like son, like father.

It's true, I've never turned down the pursuit of pleasure, but I like to think my moral code stops short of cheating and deceit. Especially now, with Tessa, there's no room for another woman in my mind, when I'm so consumed with thoughts of her.

Her playful, teasing smile.

Her rare, brilliant laugh.

Her tight pussy clenching me to oblivion and back.

I pull out my phone and start to type a message. *Missing you.*

But I stop and delete it just in time. It's too much, too soon. I want to take my time with her and do this right.

Because something tells me she's the one. And we've got forever to make this work.

Chapter Nine
TESSA

My focus might be a million miles away from Oxford—going over my list of suspects, and caught up in memories of my lazy weekend with Saint—but my academic schedule for the week is clear: I need to get my act together, before I lose my scholarship and visa and get sent packing back to America.

I have to hit the books, and hard.

Luckily, Saint's townhouse is perfect to hole up in and study, and without him around as a tempting distraction, I manage to blitz through my reading list and make good progress for the week. The luxury espresso machine and cupboards full of snacks sure don't hurt, either. By Tuesday, I've just about finished an assigned essay due today, and I'm feeling like I might be able to scrape through this semester, when I hear the doorbell sound.

I bounce downstairs from where I've adopted Saint's library as my study den. "Jia," I say, surprised, when I find my old roommate standing on the steps outside. She's got a box in her arms and a judgmental stare on her face as she pointedly looks up at Saint's home.

"Nice digs," she says, peering past me into the hallway. "Guess I know why you're not slumming it with us back at the flat anymore."

"Hi," I say carefully, used to her passive-aggressive comments now. "Nice to see you, too."

"You left some stuff behind," she says, unceremoniously shoving the box at me. I grasp it, off-balance, and notice some of my books and papers crumpled carelessly inside.

"Thanks for bringing it by," I say brightly.

"Well, we thought about holding on to it for you," Jia adds, giving me a smirk. "For the next time you and the professor break up. Kris bet five pounds you'll be back by the end of the week, but I think you could last all the way until November."

"Gee, thanks," I reply flatly. "Your confidence is touching."

"Well, what do you expect?" she asks. "You're together, you break up, you're back here fawning over him again . . . It's not a good look. People are talking around college," she adds. "About you, and Saint, and your dirty little affair."

"And I'm sure you're telling them all to mind their own business." My cheerful act is straining now. It's clear she isn't here because she's genuinely concerned about me. She just wants to stick the knife in. "Anyway, thanks for the box. I better get to college. I don't want to be late for my tutorial."

"Why, is Saint teaching?" Jia smirks, backing away. "I would have thought you'd already got your grade all sewn up."

She walks off, and I slam the door on her, scowling. At first I enjoyed hanging out with Jia and Kris, and thought we could be real friends, but soon enough it was clear that lurking beneath their fun adventures and gossip was a real nasty streak.

Now she's just proved it.

But I don't have time to dwell on her bitchy comments; I grab my books and jacket and hurry over to the Ashford College campus, where my next tutorial is set to start. The professor's office is in the East Wing, up a creaky staircase, and when I enter the room, I'm surprised to find that the class is already underway.

"I'm so sorry," I blurt, looking around the room at the other four students, who are all sitting with their notebooks out and studious expressions on their faces. Oxford prides itself on its small, demanding study groups, but damn if it doesn't make it hard to sneak in unnoticed. "I thought we were meeting at four thirty?" I ask, scrambling to check my printed schedule.

"I emailed this morning, moving the time to four o'clock," the tutor, Professor Abernathy, explains. She's a tall, hearty woman in her forties, renowned around college for her love of Romantic poetry—and the two poodles who are lying at her feet.

"Oh, I'm so sorry," I say again, finding a seat. "I've been so busy; I didn't think to check. Here." I thrust my printed assignment at her, now crumpled from my rushing again.

My classmates exchange looks, and I brace myself for a dressing-down. Abernathy is harsh but fair, and she hates lateness, but today, she gives me a surprisingly understanding smile.

"Of course, you must have a lot on your plate right now. How is he?" she asks.

I blink. "How is who?"

"Alexander St. Clair," the professor continues. "Saint says you've been in London with him, supporting the family. It's perfectly alright if you'd like to take some more time with your essay this week," she adds, sympathetic. "I understand this must be a difficult time."

"Oh." I swallow, surprised. *Saint called her?* "Thanks. That's . . . That would be great. And he's doing better, Mr. St. Clair. Saint says he's expected to make a full recovery."

"Excellent news." Abernathy smiles. "Please send our best, and tell Saint I'll have a bottle of his favorite scotch waiting on his return."

"I will."

I sink a little lower in my seat, catching more glances from the other students. Abernathy restarts the discussion. I'm able to keep a low profile for the rest of the tutorial and only offer an occasional half-baked comment, but the moment the session ends and we all head downstairs to the quad, I'm suddenly the center of attention again.

"Must be nice," one of my classmates comments sarcastically. She's perky and polished and has *straight-A student* written all over her. "Having a duke on-call to excuse your absence."

"Some of us don't have friends in high places to ring and get us off the hook," another pipes up with a sneer. He's an athlete type who always likes to have the last word. "I should try that, asking for special favors the next time I'm late with an essay."

"Sorry, Professor, I couldn't do the assigned reading, but look, I brought a note from my boyfriend!"

They laugh meanly, and coming after Jia's little bitch-fest, something in me snaps. "I'm sorry, are we back in high school?" I demand, looking at them in turn. "Because I got confused with all this juvenile gossiping. Why don't you grow up and focus on your own lives, and I'll get on with mine?"

There are raised eyebrows and surprised looks, but nobody seems ruffled by my outburst.

"It's your round at the bar, Tarquin," the girl says without skipping a beat. "Jules says they're screening *Blackadder* tonight in the JCR, and we have the bop tomorrow, too . . ."

The group moves off, chatting about upcoming social plans and laughing over in-jokes like they've known each other for years.

I feel a wistful pang, watching them go. Sure, they're acting like brats, but that's because they can be. I remember my college experience the first time around. The parties, and late nights, and blissful freedom of it all. Oxford may be a pressure cooker, but it's still carefree for these kids compared to adult life. They don't have the same burden as I do pressing down on their shoulders.

They couldn't imagine that I'm on this dark mission that I've sworn to pursue no matter the cost.

Wren.

With Sebastian Wolfe crossed off my list of suspects, I'm getting closer to the real culprit, and I know it won't be long until I have the answers my sister deserves. Let my classmates and Jia score cheap points bitching about my special treatment. I have more important things on my mind.

* * *

I HEAD BACK to Saint's place, stopping to pick up some groceries from the shop on the corner before letting myself into the house. It's quiet here without him, and I'm surprised to find myself missing him more with each passing day, despite our frequent calls and texts.

How's your new bestie, Harold? I message as I unpack the milk and eggs.

Saint replies with an emoji. *We're bonding over profit/loss statements. Was class OK?*

Fine, I lie.

I feel worn out by all the drama, even though I've done nothing but sit at a desk for days, so I decide to pour myself a glass of wine and go upstairs to take a relaxing bath. I set the lights on low and pour half a bottle of some expensive lavender oils into the massive claw-foot tub. Soon the bathroom is filled with fragrant steam.

I strip off my clothes and sink into the hot water with a sigh. *Ahhh.*

It feels amazing against my bare skin, and I luxuriate in the bubbles, letting my mind wander.

And my hands . . .

I stroke over my wet skin, remembering the last time I was in this tub—with Saint. He climbed in with me fully clothed, not caring that he was getting totally drenched. I sigh in pleasure, recalling the feel of his mouth on my neck . . . His hands sliding over my breasts . . .

I'm just dipping my fingers between my thighs when my cell phone vibrates on the little stool beside the tub. It's the man himself.

"Can you sense when I'm naked and thinking about you?" I answer huskily, setting the phone to speaker and placing it down again.

Saint's chuckle is low and throaty. "What would you do if I was on speakerphone right now?"

"I'd say hello to Harold," I reply, smiling.

He laughs. "No Harold. We finally called it a night at the office. Now I'm home. Alone. Wishing I was there with you."

"I wish you were here, too. I'm taking a bubble bath . . ." I tell him, flirty.

He sounds a low groan. "Now you're just tormenting me."

"I'm all wet, and naked, and did I mention wet . . . ?" I tease, lifting one leg out of the suds and stretching, watching the bubbles slide down my skin.

"Tell me," he demands. "Tell me where your hands are."

"You decide," I breathe, feeling a shiver of anticipation. "Where do you want them to be?"

"On your breasts," Saint growls, and the lust in his voice makes my stomach curl. "Touch yourself. Play with your nipples."

I do as he says, sinking back into the water, stroking and teasing the sensitive swell of my breasts. I circle my nipples, imagining it's his hands pleasuring me, his fingers pinching the stiff peaks . . .

I moan aloud, and Saint hisses a breath down the line. "Fuck, Tessa . . ."

I smile, loving that I can have this effect on him, even when I'm not in the same room. "I want you," I moan again. "Inside me . . ."

"Damn, I want that too. But you'll just have to take care of yourself without me, won't you, baby?" Saint's voice is low and seductive, urging me on. "Play with your pussy for me. Stroke your clit nice and slow."

I trail my hand lower, over my stomach, down between my legs. I find my clit and start to stroke slowly, just like he's telling me. Pleasure ripples through my body, radiating out from my gentle touch as I—

A noise comes from outside in the backyard. A clattering sound, close to the house.

I sit up with a splash.

"Did you hear that?" I ask, my heart suddenly racing.

"You moaning for me?" Saint replies, still smoky, but seduction is the last thing on my mind right now.

"No, there was a noise," I tell him, climbing out of the bath. I grab a robe and wrap it around me, moving to the window to look.

It's dark outside, but the security lights are all shining brightly. "The lights only come on if there's something out there, right?" I ask, trying not to panic.

"It's probably just a fox. They're always trying to get into the rubbish bins," Saint says, trying to calm me.

"I swear I heard someone," I repeat, peering around. The yard is shadowed, and I can't see from here, but still, it's like I can feel someone out there. Watching. "Saint, I'm not kidding around."

"It's alright." Saint is immediately reassuring. "I'm logging into the security app now. Everything looks fine," he reports a moment later. "All the doors and windows are alarmed. There's nothing on the cameras. You're safe, baby. I promise."

I exhale. "OK . . ."

I step back from the window and tug the curtains closed. The bath is still steaming hot, but the mood is ruined. "I think I'm just going to bed now," I tell Saint. "It's been a long day."

"You're not going to worry about this, are you?" Saint asks, sounding concerned. "I can drive up tonight, if you want—"

"No, I'm fine," I insist, feeling a little foolish now. "It's like you said, probably just a fox, or a horny raccoon."

"Those randy bastards," Saint agrees. "Alright, sleep tight. Call me if you need anything. Anything," he repeats.

"I will. Good night."

I hang up, looking around the empty room. I've been relishing the peace and quiet of being in the house alone, but now, I can't shake the feeling of unease.

If someone is out there . . .

I've already been hurt on this mission: stalked through the city and attacked by some creepy mystery man who warned me to stop digging into the Blackthorn Society. Now I wonder just how dangerous this is going to get.

The man I'm hunting has everything to lose if I expose him.

How far would he be willing to go to keep his crimes a secret?

Chapter Ten
TESSA

I don't sleep. I try to tell myself that the sound I heard was nothing, but I can't shake the feeling of unease, that prickle of awareness that stays on high alert as the hours tick past, and I toss and turn alone in Saint's bed.

Is someone watching me?

Maybe I'm overreacting, but I can't help wondering if it's self-preservation, instead: my fight-or-flight instincts telling me that something's wrong. Either way, I startle at every sound all night, and by the time dawn breaks outside the windows, I'm exhausted and ready to bolt. There's no way I'm staying here alone for the rest of the week, scared of shadows, alone in an empty house, so I pack up my books and catch an early train down to London instead, leaving the eerie old streets behind for the noisy bustle of the city.

My tension eases with every mile, but still, I'm feeling a little foolish by the time I make my way to Kensington and show up on Saint's doorstep. Is he going to think I'm needy and para-noid? But the moment he answers the door with a coffee mug in his hand and messy bed head, I know I've made the right choice.

I feel better just burying myself in his arms for a hug.

"Well, this is a lovely surprise," Saint says, drawing back to land a welcoming kiss on my mouth. "What are you doing here?"

"I missed you," I say, which is the truth. I decide to gloss over the whole getting-scared-of-my-own-shadow part.

"Well, I missed you, too." Saint smiles wider, and draws me in for a longer, slow kiss. I sigh, sinking against him, finally feeling safe in the warmth of his embrace. "Come on in," he says, taking my bag and leading me inside. "There's fresh coffee and cinnamon buns."

"You *baked*?" I gape.

He grins. "No, I stole them from the office yesterday."

"You own the office," I point out, smiling. "Technically, you could walk out with all the furniture, and it wouldn't be stealing."

"Good point." Saint leads me to the kitchen and pours a fresh cup of coffee for me, placing it in my hands as he breaks off a piece of pastry and pops it between my lips.

Sugar and caffeine and a good morning kiss? It makes me wonder why I've been sleeping alone up in Oxford all week.

I settle in at the table, sipping my coffee and watching as Saint gets ready to leave for work. It already feels like I left the foreboding unease miles away, back in Oxford, and now there's nothing but light banter and affectionate kisses, making me feel more like myself again.

It feels right.

"What?" Saint notices me looking.

I shake my head, smiling. "Nothing," I reply. My feelings for him are growing deeper by the day, but I'm not ready to think about what that means just yet. "It's great your dad is doing better," I say instead. "Any new updates?"

Saint pauses. "I saw him at his checkup appointment yesterday," he says, but he doesn't seem happy about it.

"Family stuff?" I ask softly.

He nods, looking relieved that he doesn't have to explain. "Family stuff."

"Well, I think you're great for helping out," I say warmly.

"You mean when I could be tying you naked to my bed all day instead?" Saint shoots me a smoldering look, and I match it.

"It's not either/or, you know . . . Your bed will still be here tonight. And so will I."

"Then count on it." Saint leans over and kisses me, hard and hot, leaving me in no doubt that he'll follow through on every one of his filthy promises.

Finally, he pulls away. "I wish I could stay, but I have a bunch of meetings this morning that I really can't miss."

"I don't need entertaining," I promise him, straightening up his button-down shirt. "I still need to hit the books. I have a ton of reading, and an essay due, too. You go be a productive member of the Ashford Pharma team."

Saint winces. "Don't say it like that," he protests, collecting his jacket and keys. "Next thing, I'll be wearing a gray suit and playing bridge with Harold."

I laugh. "I think you're a ways off becoming a boring corporate drone," I reassure him. "Unless Harold also has a taste for wild sex parties on the weekend . . ."

Saint laughs, too. "You never know. I saw a photo of his husband, Clive. A real silver fox."

I know I should let him leave, but I can't resist asking, "Have you thought about how we can approach Max or Hugh next?"

Saint's smile slips, just a little. "Max is still in Europe," he replies. "Doing God knows what, but it probably involves a yacht, bottle service, and half the women's ski team. I was supposed to play squash with Hugh, but he pushed it to next week. I think he's tied up with work, too."

"OK." I stifle my impatience. A day's delay, a week . . . It makes no difference, in the end. If I bide my time and play this smart, I'll find the answers I need.

"You're not going to rush into anything, are you?" Saint asks, searching my face.

I shake my head. "I promised you, didn't I?" I ask, going to kiss him goodbye. "I'm fine waiting for you to call the play."

Saint smiles again, pulling me into his arms. "Is that some American sports phrase?" he asks, teasing.

I grin. "Why? Do you have a thing for tailgates and cheerleaders?"

"I only know what one of those is, and yes, now that you mention it . . ."

He nuzzles my neck, and I playfully bat him away. "Tonight," I promise, already anticipating his wicked touch. "We'll see if you can give me something worth cheering for."

"You can count on it."

* * *

SAINT HEADS TO the office, and I settle in to plough through my reading list—without flinching at every bird chirping outside the windows this time. Still, although I'm finally able to relax now without panic distracting me from my schedule, I can't stop my mind from wandering to the next suspect on my list.

Max Lancaster.

Handsome, charming, a media mogul in the making . . . His CEO father is pretty much all-powerful, and I already know that Max was closer to Wren than he's letting on. But beyond that, their relationship is still a mystery, and I have no idea how it might be connected to her attack.

But maybe someone else does.

Getting a flash of inspiration, I pull out my phone and text Max's fiancée, Annabelle. She's my age and has been the most friendly to me out of any of Saint's friends. Her bubbly good humor has already confirmed details about the Blackthorn Society for me.

What other information might she have?

I'm in London . . . want to get lunch? I message her, and a moment later, a reply flashes up.

Omg yes! Spa day? Come join me.

She texts an address and time, and even though I know I should be focused on my studies, I reply with a thumbs-up. *It's research*, I tell myself, closing my books. And no matter what else is going on in my life, finding Wren's attacker has to come first.

Besides, after a tense night, I have to admit that the idea of a spa day is pretty tempting. And when I arrive at the address Annabelle sent and find a chic modern spa, all marble and luxurious fresh roses, I know I made the right call.

"Tessa! Babe!"

Annabelle greets me in the lobby, wearing white leather knee-high boots with fur trim and a matching white parka that looks like she's about to hit the slopes, not stroll Bond Street. "It's so great you're in town," she exclaims happily, flashing me a perky smile. "I was just thinking we should get together, have some girl time. I want to hear *all* about you and Saint."

Annabelle breezes us through check-in, and soon we're both stripped down to our swimwear, steaming in a dimly lit plunge pool and sipping on cucumber waters.

"Ahh." Annabelle sinks into the water with a sigh. "I needed this. I swear, I've aged ten years just trying to keep this wedding from turning into a total shitshow. You know Max's stepmom is trying to stick her nose into the planning? It's like, babe, you're wife number four, and even I know Cyrus is sniffing around for your replacement already. Ease up with the big opinions about my bridal bouquet!"

I smile. The plunge room is tiled like a Moroccan spa, with candles flickering, and just a couple of other people braving one of the ice baths in the far corner. "What does Max say about it all?" I ask, steering the conversation to my main topic of curiosity.

"Oh, he couldn't care less about the planning." Annabelle splashes a wave. "He's still pushing for some wild elopement, but I mean, come on, my parents would kill me, and even the Lancasters want the full court press. Cyrus even suggested I do a full wedding shoot for *Hello!* magazine," she adds, beaming.

"Will you?"

She shakes her head. "Oh, Lord no. It's so sweet of him to offer, but that's a little too try-hard. *Vogue* is one thing, but the tabloids? But that's typical for Cyrus," she adds, confidential. "He thinks bigger is always better. It's weird—you'd think running the biggest media company on the planet would make a man relax, but nope, I suppose he'll always have something to prove."

"Is Max like that, too?" I ask, sipping my water casually.

"With work? No." Annabelle looks thoughtful. "But I suppose he has the same instincts as his father, that sort of animal drive to be the alpha dog: crush his enemies, seduce every beautiful woman around . . . the thrill of conquest, and all that jazz."

I pause, filing that information away. Did his urge for conquest drive Max to kidnap Wren, in some kind of twisted show of dominance and power?

"Saint said he's traveling right now," I reply. "You must miss him."

Annabelle trills a laugh. "Miss the drinking and debauchery, and his stinky hungover morning breath? No thank you. He has his fun, and I have mine."

"And you're OK with that?" I ask, thinking of that woman I saw Max with in Oxford. The glamorous brunette who most definitely wasn't his fiancée.

"More than OK, darling," Annabelle replies, lifting her leg

from the water and admiring the bright purple pedicure. "It's the only way to make a relationship work long-term. You both need to have your freedom. Otherwise things just get stale and stifling. Let Max frolic in the South of France all he wants. I know he'll always come back home to me. With some gorgeous Van Cleef diamonds to make it up to me, I'm sure."

Annabelle flashes another bright smile, but I swear I see some tension in her eyes. Maybe she's not so relaxed about Max fucking around, and this is just her way of keeping her pride. Or perhaps I'm projecting my own feelings onto her, because I know I could never be that relaxed about Saint seeing other women. Even the idea of it makes me feel a sharp slice of jealousy. Wild, sexy games are one thing, but cheating?

No way.

Annabelle gives me a knowing smile. "So, things really are heating up with Saint then, if he's tempting you down to London all the time."

I nod, feeling a little bashful. "I'm still trying to figure out how I fit in his life, how he would fit in mine . . ."

Especially since my mission could wind up tearing apart one of his oldest friendships.

Annabelle gives another vague wave. "Don't worry about that sort of thing. There are only three questions that matter in a relationship. Does he worship the ground you walk on? And is the sex good enough?"

I laugh. "Yes . . . and yes," I admit, blushing.

Good enough? Try mind-blowingly, panty-meltingly out of this world.

Annabelle claps her hands together in delight. "Well, he ought to, given the man's reputation," she says with a smirk.

"Wait, what's the third thing?" I ask. "You said there were three questions that matter."

"Oh, yes." Annabelle pauses, and that flash of tension returns on her face. "Do you get what you need from him?" she asks simply. "If you do, well . . . that has to be enough, doesn't it?"

The question hangs between us, and I wonder again what, exactly, Annabelle needs that Max Lancaster is giving her in their relationship. It can't just be about his money, can it? Imogen said that Annabelle was from a very old, well-connected family.

I guess connections don't pay for luxurious spa days and Van Cleef diamonds.

But the question wasn't about her. It was about me, and Saint. Now I consider it. In the beginning, I was clear about what I wanted from him: wild sexual adventure, and access to his rich social circle for my investigation. But quickly, all that changed. Our bond is deeper now, and the one thing I value more than anything else is how he's stepped up to join me in my mission. Backing me up, making me feel safe and supported, no matter what.

Not just a lover, or a wild fling, but a partner now. *Mine*.

"Yes," I answer finally, feeling that unfamiliar swell of emotion in my chest again. "He gives me what I need."

"Then that's the only thing that matters right now," Annabelle declares. "Of course, being a hot future duke set to inherit the entire Ashford estate doesn't hurt either," she adds with a laugh, and then launches into a discussion about honeymoon destinations, and whether Max should buy them a little vacation island in the Caribbean for parties, since it's just *so* much nicer to have the whole beach to yourself.

* * *

WE GRAB SOME lunch and finish up at the spa. Annabelle has to get to a dress fitting. "For your wedding gown?" I ask, and she laughs.

"No, my third reception dress. But this was so much fun! We

must all hang out soon. Double date, you and me and Saint and Max. We'll have a fabulous time!"

"Sounds great to me," I agree, hoping that Max isn't the evil bastard I'm looking for—for Annabelle's sake, if nothing else.

But if it's not Max, then that just leaves Hugh Ambrose as the only other man with the serpent crown tattoo. And I hate to imagine it's him, especially with all the good work he's doing at the charitable foundation. Still, I can't rule him out yet either, so I decide to swing by the Ambrose Foundation office before I head back to Saint's place.

"Tessa, love the links you sent over." The head of fundraising, Priya, meets me on her way out. "Can't talk now, but let's hop on a Zoom or call soon and talk. I think we could schedule the campaign kickoff as soon as the new year."

"That fast?" I blink, surprised.

"We move quickly here." She smiles. "Put together a preliminary schedule, and we'll make it happen!"

She whisks away in a swirl of silk and red lipstick, and I continue inside, pleased. I shouldn't be sneaking time to work on my project for the foundation, but it means a lot to me to carve out a small part of my days here that are about me and my passions, and not just avenging Wren.

Plus, it gives me the perfect excuse to get to know Hugh better, and figure out what he has going on beneath the nerdy, ruffled surface. But when I get to his office, I don't see him around. "Is Hugh coming in this afternoon?" I ask the nearest intern, who's stationed at a desk right beside his door.

"Let me check . . ." the guy replies, helpful. Peter, I think his name is. He clicks on his desktop computer, and I can see from the angle that he's looking at Hugh's schedule. "No," he reports. "Sorry, it looks like he's out in meetings for the rest of the day. Did you need anything?"

I pause, thinking fast. If I can just get a closer look at that calendar . . .

"Actually, yes," I reply. "Hugh said he was pulling some information for me, the donation data and distribution information for the last three months . . . ?"

"Sorry." He gives an apologetic shrug. "He didn't mention it."

"Oh, that's a shame," I reply, looking concerned. "I need them ASAP, and I really can't move ahead without them." I give him a hopeful look. "I don't suppose you could track them down for me?"

"Of course." The intern efficiently clicks into a few different documents. "I can email them right over."

"I meant printed!" I blurt, remembering from my tour that the print room is way in the back of the office, out of sight line from Hugh's corner. I flash him another smile. "And bound, if that's OK. In triplicate."

"That might take me a little while," he says, getting to his feet.

"No problem!" I beam. "I can wait."

Peter heads off to the copy room, and I look quickly around. The main floor is open-plan and buzzing, but luckily, everyone seems occupied.

I slip into Peter's chair and tap through to Hugh's calendar, which is still up on-screen. It's a daily schedule, blocked out with meetings, trips, calls . . .

I quickly click back to last year and focus in on the date of Wren's attack. Whoever took her kept her in that cell for more than twenty-four hours, and I'm hoping I can find enough in Hugh's schedule for that time period to count him out—or at least give me an alibi to verify.

November, October . . . *There.* I find the weekend in question and check his commitments for the dates.

The whole weekend is blocked out.

I gulp. There's a notation to show he's not available—but

there's no meeting or event listed which might explain him being tied up for that period of time.

Dammit.

My hopes fall. I wanted to rule him out easily, but instead, this looks more suspicious than ever. The Blackthorn party wouldn't take up the whole weekend; Hugh told me himself he only attends them as a family obligation and networking opportunity. I click around some more, thinking maybe there's a side note or something to justifying the blackout, so I can—

"Tessa, hello!"

My head snaps up. Hugh is crossing the office towards me with a genial smile on his face.

Shit!

I quickly click out of his calendar and manage to bring up the documents Peter found, so by the time Hugh reaches me, the screen is covered with perfectly innocent spreadsheets. "Hi!" I blurt, bouncing out of the chair. "I thought you were in meetings all day."

"I am," Hugh says, looking rueful. He's dressed smartly in a suit and tie but carries a battered leather messenger bag slung across his chest. "I left the shiny new pitch folders behind, and God forbid we try and woo donors without some glossy pictures of all our good deeds."

"God forbid!" I echo, too loud. My heart is racing from the near miss, but I try to act casual. "I just stopped by to pick up some numbers, help pitch the influencers with data about our other campaigns," I add.

"Priya shared some of your emails to keep me up to date with the project," Hugh says. "It's all shaping up wonderfully."

"Well, I wouldn't go that far," I reply, bashful. "They're just ideas for now."

"Everything starts as just an idea," Hugh corrects me. "And believe me, I've seen some terrible ones."

"You mean it's a low bar around here?" I joke, and he chuckles.

"Learn to take a compliment. Or is Saint not showering you with enough of them to make you used to high praise?"

Praise . . .

I get a flash of Saint groaning *good girl* as I take his cock all the way, and blush deeply. "Well, thanks!" I blurt brightly. "I'm having a great time with the project—when I can steal the time away from my studies."

"Ah yes, I remember the Oxford pressure cooker." Hugh gives me a sympathetic smile. "The best advice I can offer is to carve out time to protect the things you really care about. Otherwise you can wind up working yourself into a minor breakdown."

"Oh, minor breakdowns are no trouble to me," I joke. "That's amateur hour."

Hugh chuckles as Peter returns with an armful of paperwork. "Printed, bound, and triplicate," he says proudly. "Just the way you wanted."

"Uh, thanks." I heave the folders from his arms. "I really appreciate it." I turn to Hugh. "You know, Saint said we should all get together for a drink sometime . . ."

"I'd love to!" Hugh agrees. "Let's check our calendars and set something up."

I say goodbye and leave—already regretting the heavy packet of documents I have to tote around town now—but my mind stays on Hugh's calendar and that mysterious blocked-off weekend.

Where was he? And was it with Wren?

* * *

BACK AT SAINT's mews house in Kensington, I find he's already home: drinking a glass of wine in the living room with his shirt already unbuttoned, bare feet up on the coffee table.

He looks deliciously undone, giving me that sleepy, happy-to-see-me smile.

"I'm brain-dead," he tells me with a yawn as I lean over and kiss him hello. "They got me with three solid hours of depreciation projections. Do you know the breakage rate for glassware in a laboratory setting? Because I do. Quiz me."

He gulps the wine, and I laugh in sympathy. "Poor baby," I coo, climbing into his lap. "What can we do to wake you up?"

I slide my hands over his bare chest, and kiss him, slow and deep. Saint makes a noise of appreciation, setting his wineglass down and wrapping his arms around me without even breaking the kiss.

"Well, that certainly helped," he murmurs, eyes bright again when we come up for air. He shifts me on his lap, pulling me closer against him, and trailing soft kisses down my neck. "How was your day studying?"

I bite my lip. "I kind of played hooky," I admit. "I hung out with Annabelle instead, and stopped by the office to see Hugh. I checked his calendar," I add. "He doesn't have an alibi for Wren's attack. At least, not one I know about yet." I sigh. "I understand a little of how you feel now," I add, nestling my head against his shoulder. "I hate having to suspect him of doing something like this."

"It's awful," Saint agrees. "I can't shake it now, wondering about the truth. All day, it's lurking in the back of my mind. I wish we could just forget all about it for a little while."

"You mean, take a time-out from the investigation?" I ask wistfully.

"The investigation, my work at the company, all of it." Saint brushes hair from my face. He looks worn out, and stressed, and I know exactly how he feels.

"Why don't we?" I ask, feeling a reckless urge. He arches an eyebrow. "Take a time-out," I explain. "Do something wild and crazy and fun tonight; just let go, and have a good time. I'm sure you can think of a few ideas," I add, flirty. "Wild and crazy is kind of your expertise."

Saint slowly smiles at me. "Just how wild are we talking?" he asks, sliding his hands around my waist and squeezing with a new purpose.

I shiver with anticipation. "Try me," I whisper, and watch the lust flare in his eyes.

"Done."

Saint gets to his feet, lifting me and setting me down in one smooth motion. "Upstairs," he orders, landing a light slap on my ass.

The anticipation flares into hot desire.

"Yes, *sir*," I murmur, and practically skip up to the bedroom. Saint strides after me, but when we reach his room, he doesn't just throw me down and ravish me—he crosses to the closet instead.

"Wear . . . *this*," he says, browsing my new clothes and plucking down a hanger. "And these, too . . ." He picks out lingerie for me, gorgeous, sensual pieces in inky silk and lace.

"I'm liking this plan already," I reply, stripping off my clothes and tossing them to the floor. Saint sits on the bed, watching me, so I make sure to put on a show for him: wriggling into the panties and lace bra, and bending way down to slide the stockings and suspenders into place.

His expression is smoldering, his eyes devouring every move I make, but he doesn't reach for me or touch me at all, just leans back, watching me as I tug the dress he selected over my head. It's a black silk number that pours over my body like water, hugging my curves and flaring out from the waist in a swirling knee-length skirt. I add a pair of wicked black stilettos with sexy leather straps and let my hair down in a tousled mane.

"Do you like it?" I present myself to him with a little pose, enjoying the subtle shift in power dynamic, how I'm obeying his instructions and seeking his approval now.

Saint slowly nods. "Beautiful," he replies, his voice a little husky. "Wear red lipstick, too. I'm going to want to see everything you do with that sweet mouth tonight."

My stomach gives a delicious flip. *Oh wow*. I asked for wild and crazy, didn't I?

Something in Saint's eyes tells me I'm going to get everything I wanted . . .

And more.

We catch a cab over to the private members club that Saint belongs to, my anticipation growing by the mile. He doesn't touch me in the car, just rests a casual arm over my shoulders, idly drawing soft circles with his fingertips on my bare skin, until I'm burning up by the time we reach our destination.

"Welcome, Mr. St. Clair," the handsome host greets us politely on sight, and ushers us through the luxurious, dimly lit lobby area. His touch lingers on my arm as he gives me an appreciative smile. "Please, enjoy your evening. And let me know if you need anything, anything at all . . ."

I flush at the suggestion in his tone, and the way his eyes drift over my black silk dress, but Saint doesn't skip a beat. "Thank you. We'll let you know."

Saint leads me through the ornate doorway and into the hallway beyond. "Well, you certainly have an admirer," he comments, amusement in his voice.

"Jealous, are we?" I tease, and Saint laughs.

"Not at all," he replies. "In fact, if you'd like him to join us tonight for a drink, just say the word. A drink . . . or more," he adds, giving me a wicked smile.

I flush, a little shocked at the suggestion. "Really? You'd be OK with that?"

"With watching another man lick your pussy until you're begging me to fuck you?" Saint smirks matter-of-factly. "Oh yes, darling. I'd be more than alright with that."

Oh wow.

My head is still spinning over the outrageous proposition when Saint suddenly backs me into a dim alcove. My pulse kicks, trapped against the wall with his body hard against mine and his hands gripping my waist. "Would you like that, baby?" he asks softly, his eyes glittering with dark, seductive promise. "Sucking his cock like a good girl, while I fuck you from behind. Being shared between us, *consumed . . .*"

I feel a thrill, trying to imagine it. Then I remember something in a flash: the intimate vibe at the table with Sebastian Wolfe and his wife the other night.

"You've done it before, haven't you?" I realize, looking up at him. "Sharing a woman. You, and Seb, and Avery."

Saint slowly strokes my cheek. "We've enjoyed each other's company, yes."

"Oh." I swallow hard. His smile softens.

"It was all just for fun," he reassures me. "And it was, very fun. Especially for Avery," he adds, breath hot in my ear again. "After all, if you enjoy being worshipped by one man . . . why not be worshipped by two? Two pairs of hands on your body," he muses, tracing down over the swell of my breast until I'm gasping. "Two mouths, exploring you . . . Two fat cocks, filling you all the way up."

My cheeks burn. I'm suddenly breathless picturing the illicit scene.

I couldn't . . . could I?

"He's not my type," I quip lightly, ducking under Saint's arm, and sashaying a few paces ahead of him down the hall. I hear him chuckle as I catch my breath, and then he reaches me, slinging his arm around my shoulders as we step into the main bar area.

"Interesting . . . So, what is your type?" he asks, looking around the lavish, exclusive club. "Young and eager, perhaps?" He nods to where a blond man is waiting by the bar, fresh-faced and clean-cut, wearing jeans and a plain white T-shirt. He looks wholesome and corn-fed, and Saint leans in closer to murmur to me, "I bet he'd love to get on his back for you, so you could ride his face while you suck my cock."

I swallow hard. I thought I was prepared to play it cool in this place, not gawk like a wide-eyed newcomer, but already, the suggestions Saint is crooning are making me burn up inside with a strange new thrill.

"Not him," I manage, feeling tongue-tied. Oh my God, I can't believe this is really happening.

Is he seriously proposing this?

"Then maybe you'd like to be the one following orders . . ." Saint doesn't skip a beat, still musing casually, like we're picking a restaurant for takeout, not proposing a wild, thrilling night. He points out a stern-looking man in an expensive suit, sipping whiskey at a table in the corner. "What do you think? Would you like an older man?"

Saint moves behind me, his arms encircling my body, whispering in my ear as he caresses me through my dress. "You could try and be a brat, of course, but together, we'd put you in your place . . ." He pinches my nipples, making me moan. "Yes, he'd make sure you're a *very* good girl for us . . ."

As we watch, the man beckons a woman over and points to the floor, ordering her to her knees in one swift motion. She goes eagerly, already reaching to unsnap his belt and free his cock for her willing mouth.

"Would you like to taste him, too?" Saint whispers as I watch the couple. Saint is still caressing me lazily, his touch like fire on my burning skin. I sink into his embrace and his casually wandering hands. Getting hotter. *Getting wet.* "I could watch you suck him off . . . give you plenty of instructions, so you'd swallow his cock just right."

I watch, entranced, as the woman sucks him deeply; arching her back, sliding a hand between her thighs to play with herself. The dim lights reflect off her curves spilling out of a tight dress; the man's hand knotting in her dark curls to control her movements.

Beautiful.

"Ah, I see . . ." Saint's voice turns smug. "Maybe we've been looking in the wrong direction . . ."

Saint turns me towards the bar. There's a woman relaxing there, sipping her cocktail, and surveying the room curiously, just like us. She's about my age, with expressive blue eyes and blond hair pulled up in a messy bun, but unlike the other women here tonight, she's dressed casually, in a tank top and long silk skirt that flows around her legs when she rises, crossing to a booth in the corner with the effortless grace of a dancer.

"She's pretty," Saint murmurs approvingly. "What do you say, baby, want to ask her to come play?"

My stomach tightens. *Oh God.*

"I've never . . ." I whisper, blushing furiously.

But I can't deny that I've thought about it. Wondering. *Imagining . . .*

As if sensing my thoughts, the woman looks in our direction. Her eyes sweep over the two of us, openly curious, then meet my gaze. She smiles at me, friendly, and I find myself smiling back.

I can't believe I'm really considering this, but . . .

I want to.

Saint turns me to face him, and my secret curiosity must be written all over my face, because he chuckles knowingly. "Tell me. Use your words, baby."

I swallow again, dry-mouthed. My heart pounding in my chest. "Yes," I manage, jerking an eager nod. "Yes please."

"Oh *fuck*," he murmurs lustily, and my thrill intensifies. "We won't do anything you don't want to do," he adds. "This is about you, so if you change your mind, or feel like you want to hit the brakes, just say the word."

I nod, but I already know I won't be changing my mind tonight.

I want it all.

"So, what happens now?" I ask breathlessly.

Saint produces a small gold key from his pocket. "Why don't you freshen up and meet me in room six?" he says, handing me the key. "I'll go get us some drinks and see if our new friend would like to join us."

I nod. It feels like I need to dunk my whole head under cold water right now, so I gladly slip away to the luxurious, pink-tiled bathroom, done up with vintage Tiffany lamps and fringed chaises, with old Hollywood glam mirrors at every station.

Deep breaths, I tell myself, rinsing my hands under the cold water. I grab a paper towel and dab some water on my chest too, but I can tell that there's no cooling down, not with my blood already racing like wildfire, sensual anticipation in my veins.

How does Saint know all my secret desires? I marvel, giddy with excitement and nerves. From the moment we met, he's tapped into my most forbidden dreams, taking my hand and leading me into a new world of pleasure and discovery.

And now that I trust him completely, I know that the pleasure is only going to be sweeter.

The door to the club swings open behind me, and the blond woman strolls in. Our eyes meet in the mirror, and I freeze, but she doesn't seem at all ruffled as she strolls to the mirror beside me and checks her lipstick. "Hello," she says, giving me another friendly, curious smile.

"Hi," I blurt, feeling wildly self-conscious. Did Saint talk to her yet? Does she know?

I realize I'm staring, so I quickly say, "I, um, really like your necklace."

It's true. She's wearing a thin gold chain with a tiny flower pendant swinging low between her small, shapely breasts.

The woman smiles. "Thank you," she replies in a soft English accent. "I was just going to tell you, I love your dress. I'm Rose," she adds.

"Tessa," I reply, relaxing a little. I'm not sure if she's giving me her real name, but now that I'm up close, I can see that Rose has a quiet, warm vibe about her that immediately puts me at ease.

"Is this your first time at the club?" she asks, pulling out an eyeliner pencil and touching up her makeup.

"Almost," I confess. "I came here once before, so I thought I was over being shocked and naïve, but then I look around the room, and, well . . ."

She laughs. "I know how you feel. The first time a date brought me here, I felt like one of those cartoon characters, you know, with their eyes *that* big. You're here with someone, aren't you?" she adds, turning to me.

I nod. "Yes. Did he, um . . . ?" I trail off, not sure how to ask.

Rose smiles. "He did. And I'm definitely interested," she adds, her gaze trailing over me in a way that feels both new and familiar all at once. "But I wanted to talk to you first," she adds. "Some guys . . . well, they have this fantasy, and then strong-arm their partner to go along with it. I don't have any interest in that kind of rubbish," she adds, so self-assured and clear, I can't help but be impressed.

"It's not like that," I say quickly. "It was my idea. I mean, I want to . . ." I trail off again, blushing furiously. "Sorry," I mutter, looking down. "I don't know how this works."

"It works the same way as anything." Rose strolls towards me and places a fingertip under my chin, tilting my face up to meet her playful gaze. "You just follow your instincts," she whispers, eyes sparkling. Like a partner in crime. "Surrender your inhibitions and do whatever feels right. What happens in the club stays at the club," she adds with a wink. "We're all just having fun."

Fun . . .

And just like that, my curiosity drowns out the last shivers of nerves. I smile back at her and take her hand. "Follow me," I find myself saying, and then lead her out of the room and down a long, dim hallway. We pass other people, and I feel a fresh thrill, knowing that their eyes are on us. Knowing where we're going.

Knowing what I'm about to do.

I find the room Saint mentioned and go to unlock the door, but it's already open. Inside, Saint is waiting, his jacket thrown over the back of a wingback chair, as he pours three glasses of champagne. There's a low bed, and luxurious lighting, bathing the room in a soft glow. It looks like an expensive hotel suite—if expensive hotels came with metal bars hanging parallel to the ceiling, and an entire wall of smoked-out glass.

"You found her," he tells Rose with a smile as I close the door behind us. He saunters over, handing us both a glass.

"I did. And I see what you mean," she says, taking a sip.

"What did he say about me?" I ask, looking between them.

Rose smiles. "That you were delicious," she says, flirty. "Although I'll just have to test that part for myself."

And then she puts the glass down, leans in and kisses me.

Her mouth is cool, and unfamiliar, sweet with the champagne bubbles, and soft where Saint's is demanding and rough. It's intoxicating, new and unfamiliar. My pulse races as I lean in, stroking her soft cheek, marveling at the silky texture of her hair. Her tongue nudges, wet between my lips, and I open to her, sliding my tongue against hers in a sensual, foreign dance.

"Damn . . ."

I hear Saint let out a low groan of appreciation, and then he's moving behind me, sandwiching me between them, his hands on my waist as hers cradle my cheeks; his body hard and unyielding as hers presses softly against my curves.

My head spins. It's incredible. Already I feel like I'm having an out-of-body experience, floating there between them. Rose breaks the kiss, dancing kisses along my jawline and neck, as Saint tugs my dress straps over my arms, peeling my bodice to my waist.

"How does she feel, baby?" Saint asks, teasing. "Do you want some more?"

I moan in answer, sinking my head back against his chest and closing my eyes, reveling in the wave of sensation.

"No," he scolds me lightly. "Open your eyes. Watch her touch you . . ."

I do as he orders, my knees weak as I watch Rose bend her head, hair spilling around her face as she licks across the swell of my chest. Saint helps her, cupping each lace-clad breast in his hands, offering them to her to lick and suck in turn.

Oh God . . .

I shudder, overwhelmed with the incredible feel of her mouth, and her soft, eager tongue teasing me through my bra until I'm aching, arching against her, whimpering with need.

Saint chuckles. "I think she likes it," he muses to Rose, who lifts her head, her cheeks flushed, and her gaze playful as it locks on mine.

"Touch me," she whispers, taking one of my hands and placing it over her own breast. "Don't be shy. You know what will feel good for me."

I bite back another moan, squeezing at her command. She's not wearing a bra, and I can feel the stiff peaks of her nipples through the thin silk as I stroke and toy with them, acting on pure instinct, doing all the things I know make me ache.

Rose sighs in pleasure, pressing into my hands. "Don't stop," she whispers, kissing me again, her mouth consuming mine as

Saint's hands rove hungrily over my body and his erection presses hard against my ass. He drags Rose from my mouth and kisses her too as I wriggle back against him, grinding, lost in the rush of pure sensation, giving in to the heady thrill.

What the hell is happening? I don't even have words for it anymore. All I know is I want *more*. Hands and mouths and searching, eager tongues as we kiss and caress, stroking each other into a frenzy.

Saint pulls back. "Strip her," he orders Rose.

"Yes, *sir*," she says, and obediently peels my dress the rest of the way off, unfastening my bra and tugging my panties down, too, stroking over my body with every touch until I'm naked and trembling. Standing bare there between them while they're still fully clothed, sends a fresh surge of electricity through me.

"Your turn," he tells me. "Take it off her."

I do as he says, sliding the silk skirt over her body until Rose has stripped down to her panties, a hot-pink shock of silk running between her thighs. I drink in the sight of her body, curious, before reaching for Saint.

"Not so fast." He moves back to sit on the edge of the bed. Then he slowly unsnaps his belt and tugs his pants down far enough to free his thick, straining cock. "Now, be a good girl," Saint instructs me, his eyes dark. "Show our new friend how to suck my cock."

Oh fuck.

I sink to my knees, moving between his thighs. I lean in, taking the head of Saint's cock in my mouth and sucking him deep.

He sounds a ragged groan of approval. "That's right, darling. Every inch."

I moan around him, angling my head to suck him deeper, just the way he likes. That's when I feel Rose settle to her knees behind me, and the brush of unfamiliar kisses trailing down my spine.

Oh . . .

Rose's lips are soft on my skin, her hands stroking over my body, roving around to cup and toy with my breasts, as Saint starts to thrust down my throat.

"Hold her," I hear Saint say. "Keep her steady. Make her take it all."

I don't know what he means until Rose's hands knot in my hair, and I feel the pressure of her pushing me down on Saint's cock, controlling my movements.

Fuck.

The domination is intoxicating. I shudder, trapped between them, blissfully overwhelmed. Rose moves my head faster, forcing me to take him deeper as Saint thrusts wildly, fucking my mouth. I moan, dizzy, lost to the rush of it all, clenching my thighs, so turned on I'm dripping, drenched from the wicked thrill.

Suddenly, Saint pulls me off him and hauls me onto the bed, settling beside me. I gasp for air, lying there beneath him, my whole body trembling with need.

"You're doing so good, darling," Saint praises me, leaning over to drop a soft kiss on my forehead. "I think you deserve a reward."

He moves down my body, but Rose places a hand on his shoulder. "Me first," she murmurs, kneeling above us, looking down at me with a wicked smile on her face. "You did say she was delicious, after all."

"You're right," Saint says. "Ladies first. I'll just have to keep her mouth occupied a little longer . . ."

He kisses me again, deeper this time, plunging his tongue in my mouth like he's claiming it as his territory. I rise up to meet him, wrapping my arms around his neck, savoring the taste of him.

And then Rose settles between my thighs and licks up against me.

Oh my God!

I moan against Saint's kiss in surprise—and pleasure. He doesn't stop, stroking my mouth with his thick, insistent tongue as her soft one laps against my clit. It's overwhelming, and I struggle against the two of them, out of my mind with the unfamiliar pleasure.

"You like the feel of her tongue in your cunt?" Saint growls beside me, pinning me down so I have no choice but to submit to Rose's soft, insistent lapping. "I know you do. Christ, you're shaking like a leaf. Look at her, baby, eating you up."

I lift my head, gasping, dizzy at the sight of Rose between my thighs, her blond hair spilling over my skin and her tight grip digging into my hips. "Oh my God, *oh!*"

"Use your fingers," Saint instructs Rose, his voice thick. "She loves it when you fill her up."

Rose does as he says, slipping two, then three fingers inside me as she sucks on my clit. I scream, clenching around her, but her fingers are too slender. It's not enough. *Fuck, not nearly enough.* She lifts her head. "Come join the party," she tells Saint with a grin. "She's wet enough for the both of us."

Saint barks a laugh and releases me long enough to slide a hand between my legs from behind and thrust his fingers inside.

"Fuck." I shudder at the thick invasion and bear down hard, loving the stretch. "Don't stop!"

"You heard her," Saint says with a smirk, pulling me tight against him so my back is flush with his chest, and he's using a knee to prop my leg wider, spreading me to Rose. "You need to feel her when she comes. It's like a fucking earthquake."

"I'd say we're not far now," Rose teases me, bending her head and nipping at my tender inner thighs as Saint begins to thrust his fingers deeper. I shake in his arms, whimpering, not caring how loud or desperate I seem. My whole body is a live wire, crackling, coiled and tense, begging for release.

"Please," I gasp, trying to buck against her mouth, clenching around Saint's rhythmic fingers. "Oh God, *please . . .*"

"Louder, baby," Saint chuckles in my ear. "Don't you want them to hear you outside?"

He turns my head, and I see that the wall of glass running the length of the room is no longer smoky and opaque. I can see into a lounge area filled with people.

Oh fuck.

"It's one-way glass," Saint continues as I just about lose my mind. "But I could make it two-way with just the click of a button . . . Would you like that?" he whispers hotly as Rose licks my clit again, devouring me. "Would you like everyone to watch you coming with her tongue in your cunt?"

I shatter with a cry, coming so hard I swear I see stars. Pleasure crashes through me, over and over, until I'm left blissed out in Saint's arms. In one smooth motion, he flips me onto my back, yanking me to the very edge of the bed and replacing Rose between my thighs. He gives my pussy a possessive stroke, then sinks his cock into me slowly, all the way to the hilt.

Fuck.

I moan aloud again, still shaking from my first climax as Saint thrusts his way inside. He lets out a hiss of satisfaction. "Christ, baby, I can still feel you clench."

I gasp for air, my body strung out and trembling on this incredible high. But I want more. "Your turn," I manage, pulling Rose to lie beside me, struggling to keep my wits even as Saint's cock drives me wild. "What do you like?"

She kisses me, slow and sensuous, her curves pressed against mine. "Why don't you find out?"

Rose takes my hand and guides it down her body, in between her legs. I feel another unfamiliar thrill, sinking my fingers into her core, finding her wet and eager for me. I stroke the swollen bud of her clit curiously, and she sounds a breathy moan. "Yes . . ." she gasps, arching closer. "Just like that."

I stroke again, learning from every moan and gasp she makes, finding the right pace until she's mewling softly, face buried in the curve of my neck. I hold her close, locking eyes with Saint over her head.

"How does it feel?" he groans as he sinks into me again, stretching me open with every slow, relentless thrust. His expression is blissful, even as his voice sounds low and ragged, his whole body taut with self-control. "Driving the both of us crazy like this? Holding our pleasure in your hands?"

I don't have words to describe it, the thrill of power and lust that pounds through me. I stroke Rose faster, sinking my fingers inside her as I clench around Saint's cock; hearing them both groan in pleasure, gasping, grunting, begging me for more.

I give it to them. I give it to *him*. Eyes still locked with Saint's as I rise to meet his thrusts, until I feel Rose break beside me, orgasming around my fingers with a high-pitched cry. And then only Saint matters, and everything else melts away. He bears down on me, pinning my legs high, grinding deep, so fucking deep, it makes my body ignite. My eyes roll back, and a desperate plea falls from my lips.

"Don't stop . . . *Please*, oh God, *right there*! Don't stop!"

And he doesn't. Saint doesn't let up, not even for a moment. He pounds into me, hitting that sweet spot inside me just right, so I'm already cresting when Rose's own nimble fingers slide between us, applying the perfect pressure to my clit as Saint fucks me senseless into the sheets.

Oh my God!

I climax again with a scream, the friction inside me so perfect, so pure, I can't even breathe for the sheer bliss of it. My orgasm blots out the goddamn world, until I'm left sobbing, collapsed between them on the bed in a tangle of spent limbs.

Holy shit. I'm reeling, dazed. Drunk on pleasure like I've never known before.

And in the midst of the rush, deep down, I feel a wave of unexpected sadness. Because for all the adrenaline racing through my body, and wild, reckless joy of release, I know that I can't surrender to it completely; I can't let go, or truly live in the moment with Saint.

Not until my mission is complete.

Not until I deliver justice, in the name of Wren's memory, and can finally move on for good.

Because I want to. Lying there safely in Saint's arms, feeling his ragged breath, my body humming with the new pleasure he's introduced me to, I wish with everything I have that I could simply let myself fall in love with this man.

I think a part of me already has.

But the rest of me . . . The rest of me can't be truly happy until I bring Wren's attacker to justice. I need to find him, more than ever. And something tells me I'm running out of time.

I can't be free until I know who he is.

And make him suffer for his crimes.

Chapter Twelve
TESSA

*H*ow does she feel, baby? Do you want some more?

    Memories of Saint's low, commanding growl make my blood spark, and when I recall the way Rose's soft tongue whispered over my body and nudged against my core . . .

My cheeks flush, heated in the cool autumn air. It's a good thing I chose a sidewalk table outside the coffee shop this morning, because I'm just about burning up remembering the wild, sexy adventures we had last night.

Saint certainly delivered on his promise. Wild and sexy fun? Try a mind-blowing sensual adventure that still makes my pulse race just thinking about it.

I take a gulp of coffee and try to focus on my essay assignment half-finished on my laptop screen, but I can't help slipping into daydreams, replaying every moment of our wild night at the club. The shocking rush when I first felt Rose's unfamiliar hands stroking over my naked body . . . The intensity of the pleasure they both drew from me, my senses overwhelmed to the point of ecstasy . . . And *oh*, the thrill of reckless abandon that took me over, consuming me, making me bold.

Making me beg for more.

God, I've never felt anything like it. And not just because of Rose, either. Somehow, Saint knows all the secret desires I've dreamed about exploring; all the filthy, illicit fantasies I've never even whispered out loud. He sees the hunger that's burning deep inside me—and goes right ahead and stokes the fire.

There's no shame, no judgment with him, just a total acceptance. I've never felt this safe with a man—even as he pins me to the bed and fucks me senseless.

It's an intoxicating combination.

My phone buzzes, and I check the message, smiling when I see it's a text from Saint. He only dropped me at the café an hour ago before heading to the Ashford Pharma offices nearby. But clearly, he's still thinking about last night, too.

> *They're trying to tell me about Q2*
> *projections, and all I can think about*
> *is the way your pussy clenched*
> *when she sucked your nipples.*

My blush deepens, and I feel a rush of desire.
Are you hard? I text back, surprised by my boldness.

I am now.

> *Good. Because I'm wet for you.*

Fuck, baby . . . Don't torment me.

This is nothing, I text back with a smirk. *I'm about to go lock myself in the ladies' restroom and get myself off thinking about your cock in my mouth . . .*

The text bubble appears, and then disappears, and then appears again.

I grin wider, just picturing Saint stuck in a boring meeting, trying to conceal his lust. Finally, his answer appears.

You'll pay for that later.

I feel another delicious shiver. I can't wait.

I tuck my phone—and thoughts of Saint's punishment—away and try to focus on my essay, but the themes of antiestablishment rebellion in the eighteenth century can't compare to the question still haunting me.

Max or Hugh? Which of them is the man Wren remembers?

I'm still no closer to discovering if Max has an alibi, and the block of time x-ed out in Hugh's schedule that weekend is still concerning me. My patience is already wearing thin. I need to know what he was up to. I've been running internet searches on both men for more information, but there's nothing I can really use to judge their guilt one way or another. They both have a ton of information and public appearances posted online, mainly VIP parties and playboy antics for Max and more serious philanthropic events for Hugh, but that's just PR: the version of themselves they show the world.

I need to know who they are when the cameras and crowds aren't around.

I scroll idly through some photos from a polo tournament over the summer when both Max and Hugh were in attendance. Then I spot another familiar face in the frame with them: Imogen.

I perk up, wondering if she could know more about them. From what I've seen, Saint's cousin knows everybody and everything, and since she's a professional event planner, maybe she has an idea about what kept Hugh out of commission that whole weekend.

I pull out my phone again and shoot her a quick text, inviting her to lunch.

Sorry, she replies right away. *Setting up for the big Ashford event Friday.*

I pause. Saint hasn't mentioned anything about an event, and now that he's working there full-time, I'm curious to learn more about the company.

How about I bring something by for a quick break? I message, and a moment later, I get a thumbs-up.

Perfect.

I stop by a deli nearby and grab some salads, then walk over to the impressive modern building that houses Ashford Pharma's European headquarters. It's a towering chrome and glass building with a cavernous main lobby area buzzing with activity—and security. I'm hoping to surprise Saint as well, but when I tell the receptionist to call up to his office, I'm told he's out to lunch with the accounting team.

"Do you have an appointment?" the man asks me, pleasantly icy.

"No, I'm supposed to meet someone. Imogen Alcott?" I offer, but he just stares back, unmoved.

"If she didn't sign you in, I'm afraid I can't help you. What extension number is she?"

"She doesn't work here," I'm trying to explain when I catch sight of a familiar face. It's Phillip McAlister, Wren's nerdy coworker from the lab, just entering the building with a thermos in one hand and a security pass in the other. He's dressed down in battered corduroy pants and a rumpled sweater, and I call over loudly, "Phillip? Hey!"

He stops, looking surprised to see me. "Tessa, what are you doing here?"

"I'm supposed to be meeting my friend, but she didn't sign me in . . ."

"It's OK," he tells the receptionist, flashing his badge. "She's with me."

"Thank you," I tell him as I'm waved to the security barrier. I wait while a guard searches the food bags, too. "Are they hiding the crown jewels in here?" I joke when I'm finally ushered through to meet Phillip on the other side.

"As good as," he replies with a chuckle. "They house the VIP laboratory in the basement, so they keep things rather tight. All their precious trade secrets and so forth."

"Hence the full-body pat down and armed guards," I reply as Phillip steers us to an elevator—and then has to swipe his badge and enter a few numbers just to get the damn doors to close. "What floor?" he asks.

"Um, executive level?" I guess.

"Fancy." He grins as the doors slide shut.

I laugh. "I wasn't expecting to see you here," I say. "I thought you lived up in Oxford?"

"I do, but we've been summoned here to HQ for some big event," Phillip explains, running a hand through his mop of curly brown hair. "We're supposed to circulate and talk up the research. Using plain English," he adds with a wry smile. "They keep stressing that part. No big science words."

I smile back. "Well, good luck. Is everything still going well?" I add. Phillip is under some serious nondisclosure agreements, but he's hinted that their Alzheimer's research is proving a big success, and the clinical trials for a new drug are going to revolutionize the field. My sister worked on the early phases of the research, and it's nice to think she's contributed to something that could change the world like this. "And by 'everything,' I mean the top secret project you're working on that I know absolutely nothing about," I add with a grin.

Phillip gives a confidential grin. "Hypothetically, if I was working on a top secret project, that project would be going great," he says.

"I'm glad."

We reach the twentieth floor, and the doors slide open. It's modern and luxurious up here, with stunning views of the city, and serious-looking executives having serious-looking meetings. Phillip lets out a whistle. "So this is how the other half lives," he says, looking around. "Pretty sweet. But what brings you here? Are you not at Ashford College anymore?"

"I am, technically," I reply, taking it in. "I'm just splitting my time. My boyfriend lives in London," I add, feeling a little self-conscious describing Saint like that for the first time. I barely blush when he gets me off in front of a crowded room, but sure, calling him my boyfriend gives me butterflies. "Hey, you probably know him," I add, realizing I hadn't put the pieces together when I saw Phillip last. "Saint—I mean, Anthony St. Clair."

Phillip's eyes bug out. "Your boyfriend is the rebel heir?"

I snort with laughter. "That's what you call him?"

"Shit, don't tell him," Phillip says quickly, looking embarrassed. "It's just a stupid nickname around the lab. You know, because he refuses to get involved in the company."

"Not anymore," I report. "Since his father's heart attack, he's been working at the office. He's here now, actually, helping out."

"Wow, well . . . I hope you're happy with him," Phillip says slowly. It's clear he knows the rest of Saint's wayward reputation, but he doesn't comment on that.

"I am." I nod. "Very happy."

And very turned on.

Phillip checks his watch. "I better get back to it," he says. "Down in the basement with the other science nerds. It was good running into you, though. Hey, did you ever find out more about that secret society you were looking for?" he adds as he steps back onto the elevator.

I shake my head. "Turned out to be a dead end," I reply, thinking of the Blackthorn Society party. I'd gone in with such high hopes, but it had turned out just to be a bunch of rich, privileged people drinking and chanting Latin mottos together.

"Maybe that's for the best." Phillip gives me a rueful smile. "I know you wanted to find out more about Wren's time at Oxford, but I don't know . . . Sometimes it's better to just move on. Keep the happy memories alive and let the rest of it go."

"Maybe," I echo, even though I don't believe it for a second.

Let go of what happened to Wren? I wouldn't even know how.

The doors slide shut, and I turn my attention back to the office. I'm just wondering who to ask about locating Imogen when the woman herself breezes down the hallway, dressed impeccably in navy silk pants and a little cashmere cardigan, her blond hair in a neat French braid. "So sorry," she exclaims, greeting me with a kiss on the cheek. "I got tied up over the music before I realized I'd stranded you downstairs with the gestapo."

"It's fine." I smile and hold up the lunch bags. "I come bearing carbs."

"Angel. So what brings you over?" Imogen asks as she leads us down a hallway. "Not that I'm not happy to see you, of course. I've been drowning in centerpieces all morning. I could use the break."

"And Gino's finest antipasti," I joke. "I was just in the neighborhood, and, well, to tell the truth, I've been curious about this place," I say, looking around as we go. "Saint's been tied up with meetings all week."

"Everybody's slammed." Imogen nods. "Lionel Ambrose decided to hold a last-minute campaign event here. Of course, nobody's calling it a campaign event," she adds, rolling her eyes. "That would be unseemly. Officially, it's a celebration of British business, with Ashford Pharma as the shining example of innovation. Somehow, I got roped in to plan the thing," she adds, throwing open the doors of a massive conference room. "And you can see how well that's going."

I blink. The room looks like a hurricane just touched down, crammed full of lavish centerpieces, event furniture, and boxes of linens and glassware. "Wow," I manage. "And the event is tomorrow, you said?"

Imogen grins. "Don't worry, I have a team of well-trained minions assisting me, and there's a method to my madness," she reassures me, cleaning off a table and pulling up two chairs for us. "By Friday night, this whole floor will be a tasteful testament to Ashford's world-beating results. Or whatever the latest investment prospectus says."

I set out the food, and we dig in. "Saint doesn't talk much about the business," I confide, looking around. "But they mainly develop new drugs, don't they?"

Imogen nods, picking at her salad. "Technically, Ashford has feelers in everything," she explains. "Plastics, beauty products, baby food, even a random chocolate factory in Belgium."

"Really?"

She grins. "Saint's grandfather fell in love with a buxom chocolatier in the fifties, I think it was. Set her up with her own little empire out there when the affair ended. Now the family sends out the best Christmas samplers every year. But yes," she adds, "pharmaceuticals are the core business. It's a billion-pound industry, and everyone's racing for the next big wonder drug."

"Like Alzheimer's," I reply without thinking.

Imogen blinks, surprised. "You know about that?"

I remember too late that Phillip said the clinical trials were top secret. "My sister was working on the research," I explain quickly. "Why? How do you know?"

Imogen glances around. "It's kind of an open secret around here," she says, but she still drops her voice so the people passing outside the open door can't hear. "My parents liquidated the rest of their stock portfolio to buy more Ashford shares," she confides. "And all their friends have done the same. See, the minute Ashford announces the trial results for the Alzheimer's drug, the company value is going to skyrocket."

"Isn't that . . . I don't know, insider trading?" I ask, frowning.

Imogen laughs. "Maybe, but everyone does it. We scratch your back, you scratch ours . . . That's why they're doing this event here," she adds. "Ashford rolls out the red carpet for Lionel Ambrose's campaign and helps him win the leadership election. Then, once he's prime minister, he can push for the new drugs to be available on the NHS. The National Health Service," she adds, translating her Britishism to me. "It would mean massive government orders, which will send the Ashford shares even higher. It's all connected."

It's all corrupt, sounds like to me, but I don't say anything. Billion-pound industry, national political campaigns . . . It's way over my head, and a million miles from my life.

"It seems like the families are close," I say instead, thinking of Hugh.

Imogen nods. "Saint's father and Lionel go way back. Cyrus Lancaster, too. He's one of Lionel's biggest donors, and I think he's invested in Ashford, too. They've all risen to the top together."

And all the families have a lot to lose.

I swallow, again reminded of the stakes at play here. Whether it's Max or Hugh who is behind Wren's attack—or both of them—they're both just as powerful and untouchable.

There's a knock on the door, and a harried assistant sticks her head in. "Miss Alcott—I mean, Imogen? There's a truck in the delivery bay with a thousand black balloons."

"Black?" Imogen is on her feet immediately. "No, no, I said red, silver, and white."

"I'm sorry." The girl looks helpless. Imogen turns to me with a sigh.

"I really have to—"

"Of course! Don't worry about it." I get up, realizing I haven't even begun to quiz her about Hugh and Max. Still, I've learned some interesting intel about Ashford and the families, so my trip hasn't been a complete waste. "You go fix the balloons. I'll see you soon, I'm sure."

"Are you coming with Saint to the event?" she asks.

"He hasn't said anything about it yet."

Imogen sighs and shakes her head. "Ah yes, the usual, 'if I ignore something long enough, my attendance will be optional' move. Somehow, it never seems to work for me!"

"Probably because you're necessary to the whole thing," I point out, and she smiles.

"Clearly I need to work on that!"

Imogen whisks away to conjure the correct balloons, so I take my time packing up and wandering towards the elevators again, looking curiously around. It's clearly a hive of activity up here, but I can already see why Saint has stayed away: everyone looks so corporate and serious, dressed in sensible suits, dashing around like they have a million urgent fires to put out. I try to picture Saint's devil-may-care attitude and dark-wash jeans blending in for a team meeting and have to smile.

The rebel heir . . .

I just know that I'm going to tease him like crazy over that nickname. I'm about to send him a text when I hear my name being called.

"Tessa?"

I turn to find Saint's younger brother, Robert, striding down the hallway. I guess this place really is the epicenter for the St. Clair family right now. "Hi," I greet him, smiling. If Saint is the rebel, all chiseled jawline and wicked, tempting smile, then Robert is the opposite: broad-shouldered, with blond hair and more rounded, friendly features. He looks perfectly comfortable in a button-down shirt and tie, clutching a bottle of mineral water, and checking his phone in his other hand. "Sorry." He tucks it away. "Things are hectic right now. It's good to see you. Stopping by to see Saint? I'll walk you out."

"Actually, I was here to see Imogen," I reply as we step onto the elevator. "But she's racing around setting up for the big campaign event."

"Right, I almost forgot about that." Robert gives a chuckle. "There are always a million things on the calendar. I'd say things will calm down soon, but Ashford seems to only have one speed right now, and that's flat-out."

"Well, it seems like an exciting time. I know Saint's been working hard."

"And we have you to thank for that."

I frown. "What do you mean?"

Robert gives me a conspiratorial smile. "Come on . . . I know my brother, and he'd never willingly step foot in this building even once, let alone put in a full workday. Not unless he had an angel on his shoulder pushing him in the right direction. Whatever you're doing, keep it up," he adds, his voice turning urgent. "It's high time he came home to what matters in this family. The stakes have never been higher for us."

I blink, a little unsettled by his intensity. Maybe the stress of filling in for his father is getting to him. "I can promise you, I'm not an angel, and I definitely haven't been pushing Saint anywhere," I reply firmly. "This is all him. He wants to help out," I add. "Your father's heart attack was a big deal; he's been different ever since. Well, at least when it comes to Ashford and his family responsibilities," I say, thinking of the reckless, sensual streak that's still just as dominant as ever.

"Really?" Robert looks surprised. "Still, he's a changed man, ever since you two started seeing each other."

"Different good, I hope?" I say lightly as we step out into the bustling lobby on the ground floor. I'm still weirded out by the idea they have that I'm some kind of role model, dragging Saint back onto the straight and narrow.

In fact, with all my investigations, I'm the one leading him astray.

"Different excellent," Robert assures me. "I hope we'll see you both tomorrow at the Ambrose event," he says, still a little urgent. "It's important that he be there, so we can show a united front."

"I hope so too," I reply evenly. Then I try to change the subject: "I'd love to find out more about the work you're doing here. You know, my sister was actually working on an Ashford Pharma research project before she died," I add as Robert takes a sip from his bottle of water. "At the lab up in Oxford. Wren Peterson. Maybe you met her?"

Robert chokes on his drink. "Sorry," he splutters, hitting his chest. "Went down wrong." He takes a moment to recover, red-faced, then gulps the rest of the bottle. "Wren, you say? I don't recall crossing paths," he answers finally. "My dad runs all the cutting-edge research operations, you see. At least, he did. It's a big company."

I nod. It figures.

"I better get going," Robert says, already backing away from me. "Meetings, calls, you know."

"I'll try and drag Saint here for the event tomorrow," I reassure him, but Robert barely offers a smile.

"Don't trouble yourself. Saint is, well, Saint. Take care!"

Then he turns and bolts, leaving me alone again.

* * *

I HEAD BACK to Saint's place, thinking about Robert and his weirdly urgent vibes. I guess that he's under a lot of pressure, too. He's been the one holding things down at Ashford Pharma without Saint until now, and with their father out of commission, it must be even more stress for him, prepping for the big launch.

I wonder how it must feel, being the second son in a family like this. As much as Saint doesn't want the responsibilities of being heir to the Ashford fortune, I wonder if Robert ever resents him for it, or wishes it was him that was next in line to be duke. After all, he's the one putting in the hours at the company, while Saint has been following a different path in life.

It doesn't exactly make for a sibling bonding experience, that's for sure.

I turn onto Saint's street, a pretty, leafy road lined with luxurious mews houses. After our wild adventure last night, I'm ready to spend a lazy evening curled up, taking it easy. Maybe we could order some food in, put on a movie, and—

As I unlock the door and step inside, I find a skinny brown envelope sitting on the mat, with my name printed in black marker on the front.

I stop dead, a shiver of unease trickling down my spine.

I pick it up slowly. There's no address or postage mark, which means somebody pushed it through the letter box by hand.

I glance to the empty street outside, then slam the door firmly, my unease growing.

Who knows I'm staying here?

I remember what happened in Oxford, hearing that strange noise in the night, and the chilling feeling that I was being watched. Not to mention the man who attacked me to warn me off investigating the Blackthorn Society.

No, it's probably nothing, I tell myself. Something from Imogen, or Hugh at the foundation.

Hand-delivered?

I walk slowly through to the kitchen, bracing myself. A part of me wants to just toss it away without reading it, but my curiosity is too strong for that. I take a deep breath and tear the envelope open. There's a single page of cheap white paper inside, with a line of typed text:

You don't know what you're dealing with. Stop asking questions before it's too late.

I read it, then read it again.

Too late for what?

Suddenly, there's the sound of a key in the door. I startle, whirling around with my heart in my throat, before I see it's Saint just arriving back from work.

"Well, aren't you a sight for sore eyes?" he greets me from down the hallway with an affectionate smile. "It felt like this day would never end. How about you? How was your day?"

He pauses by the door to strip off his jacket and take out his wallet. In a split second, I decide:

I can't tell him about the note.

He'd only worry, and maybe even want me to drop the investigation completely. But I've come too far to back down now; not when we're finally closing in on the right suspects.

"Fine!" I blurt, quickly tearing it up and crumpling the pieces into the recycling can. I shove the envelope on top, pressing them both down and out of sight beneath some junk mail. "Good. I saw Imogen, and your brother, too."

"A regular family reunion." Saint strolls into the room and pulls me into a warm hug. "While I was stuck entertaining a room of accountants all day. If you want a joke about standard deviation, just let me know," he adds with a smirk. "I'm an expert in maths puns now."

I force a smile, even though my heart is still pounding. "There's nothing standard about your deviant behavior," I joke, and he laughs.

"See? You're a natural. You'd fit right in." Saint drops a casual kiss on my lips, then steps back. "Thai food? Ramen? What do you think? You're going to need your energy," he says, giving me a wicked smile. "Don't think I've forgotten you deserve a spanking, I was hard as a fucking rock all morning after your texts."

I exhale, trying to forget about the crumpled paper just a few feet away from us. *It makes no difference,* I tell myself firmly. I've known the risks in hunting Wren's attacker.

There's nothing they can throw at me that could make me stop now.

And if they're getting worried enough to send this threatening note and warn me off my quest?

That just means I'm getting close.

Chapter Thirteen
SAINT

D ammit!"

I reach uselessly with my racquet as another killer squash shot flies past me, careening off the polished wall with a loud *thwack*.

Hugh laughs, gleeful beside me. "You're getting sloppy," he gloats, barely breaking a sweat in his workout gear. "Too many late nights will do that to you, old friend."

"Au contraire," I pant, trying to recover. "Just hitting my stride."

"Of course you are. You're up." Hugh tosses me the hard rubber ball, and I slam it against the wall in a serve. I've been putting off this squash game for a while now—ever since I learned he could be behind Wren's attack—but I made an early appointment with him today at Tessa's urging. She's still pushing to figure out if he has an alibi for that weekend.

I can't believe for a second it could be him, but I know the possibility will drive both Tessa and me crazy, so here I am, serving another shot, and wondering what questions I could possibly ask to rule him out. This time I manage to keep up a decent rally before Hugh sends it flying at an angle I just can't reach.

"About that stride of yours . . ." he teases, and I scowl good-naturedly.

"Remind me again why I ever agree to play you, when you crush me every time?"

"Because it's good for that enormous ego of yours," Hugh replies, pausing to gulp from a bottle of water. I grab mine and take a drink, too. "We've all known it for years. The Great Anthony St. Clair needs to be humbled, and often. Otherwise you're just unbearable."

I can't help but laugh. Hugh and I go way back. We all do. "You don't need to worry about that," I remark wryly. "Tessa keeps me humbled every damn day."

Hugh arches an eyebrow. "Still going strong, then?"

I nod, mopping sweat from my brow. Strong. Deep. Wildly, recklessly out of control . . . Whichever way you look at it, I'm mad about her. "What about you?" I ask, not in any hurry to describe the hold Tessa has on me.

Or the way it felt, watching her orgasm with another woman's head buried between her legs.

"Weren't you seeing that Belgian chick?" I continue. "The one with the vineyard."

Hugh shakes his head. "Didn't last. And these days . . . well, it's a circus, with the leadership contest. Journalists sniffing around anything remotely connected to our family. Not many women ready to sign up for that level of scrutiny."

"And the ones who are, are the wrong ones," I agree. I've never been in the public eye the way Hugh and Max are, but we've all had our share of fortune-hunting party girls chasing after us, eager to have their photo in *Town & Country* magazine. "Remember that Tara girl you were seeing last year?" I comment, finding a way to steer the conversation to his whereabouts the weekend of Wren's kidnapping. "Didn't Max say she tried to crash the Blackthorn party?"

"Christ, I forgot about her." Hugh chuckles. "Yes, she showed up with a coterie of school friends, already drunk on cheap Lambrusco. We had to tactfully steer them out the back door before Cyrus threw a fit."

"Wild . . ." I reply, casual. "I heard the after-party was crazy that year. Sorry I missed it."

"I didn't stick around long." Hugh gives a shrug. "You know it's not my scene. Just another networking event for my father, to mingle with all his donors."

I'm about to ask what he was doing instead when Hugh leans back against the wall of the squash court with a sigh. "Christ, I'm telling you, this campaign can't be over too soon. I'm counting the days. I feel like I'm under a microscope," he adds, mopping his brow. "And the memos . . . All these damn consultants, vetting every move. Should we go out for a family meal at the curry house, and show Dad's commitment to a multicultural United Kingdom? Or get a full roast at the pub, to signal his traditional English values?" Hugh rolls his eyes. "I made the mistake of showing up late to a strategy meeting the other day and got a full-on lecture about family responsibility and obedience."

"Ah yes, I know it well." I raise my own water bottle in a rueful toast. I can't help but feel for the guy. We've commiserated about our fathers and all their expectations many times before over the years. "Legacy. Commitment. Protecting family name."

"It's true, though." Hugh looks serious for a moment. "At the end of the day, that's the most important thing, isn't it? Making sure we don't fail them. Securing the legacy that they've built . . . however high the price. We owe it to them. We owe everything to them."

"Someone's been listening to too many Blackthorn Society speeches," I tease him, surprised. Hugh's never gone in for much of the whole tradition routine. He's not a black sheep like me, but I thought he wanted to go his own way. "Next thing, you'll be quoting Latin. What is it Cyrus likes to say? 'The past points our way to the future.' The past chains us to it, more like."

"Right." Hugh shakes his head, giving a faint smile again. "Prime minister. Christ, as if my father wasn't holier-than-thou already. He's going to be unbearable once he's the leader of the entire nation."

"Think of it this way. There won't be a VIP ticket in town out of reach. Never mind the club. You'll be jet-setting to Davos with the best of them," I point out. "And those parliamentary fangirls, desperate for a taste of power . . . they'll be all over you, mate." I whistle, teasing, and he chuckles.

"I'd say you don't need those kinds of perks to make them come flocking around, but you're a bloody duke-in-waiting, after all."

I groan. "And you know I'd give it up in a heartbeat, to be free from all the family bullshit that comes along with it." I think of my father and his affair with Valerie. He swore he'd end it right away, and I've checked into the finances: the payments have stopped at the very least.

But does that mean it's over, or just that he's figured a different way to cover his tracks?

Hugh and I head back to the locker room and hit the showers, but the question stays with me. I just hope that my father finds a way to get out of it before anything blows up in our faces. Hugh's right about one thing. We're all under a ton of scrutiny right now: his family with their political campaign, and mine with the Ashford Pharma business and our upcoming drug announcement. And of course, those two fates are tied now. Our families are connected, and scandals are the last thing we need.

A scandal like Hugh being revealed as a violent predator . . .

I study him combing his hair and fastening his watch. We go back so far. I know that the battered leather strap on his wrist is the original, bequeathed by his grandfather, and that after a disastrous close crop with a fancy stylist, he'll only visit one ancient barber in Bethnal Green to get his hair trimmed. I can't imagine him doing the awful things Tessa described, not Hugh, nor Max, or any of these men I've known for years.

But someone did it. Someone's been lying and hiding their dark side from everyone—me included.

Not for the first time, I wonder if this tattoo clue is as reliable as Tessa thinks it is. I haven't mentioned it, but a part of me wonders if Wren might have been mistaken somehow. Tessa said herself that her sister's memories were a jumble, splintered fragments from whatever drugs had spiked her drink. What if it was a different design, and we're looking in the wrong direction? Allowing the real perpetrator to get away with the crime . . .

Then we'll cross that bridge together, when we confirm Max's and Hugh's alibis beyond a shadow of doubt, I decide. I meant it when I told Tessa I was her partner in this now. No matter what friendships it costs me, we're going to find out the truth eventually. I just have to hope it's before the constant suspicion and mistrust drive me mad.

* * *

I SPEND THE day at the office, working on some budget issues with my new best mate in accounting, Harold. It's dull enough work, but I can tell that everyone's distracted by the big Lionel Ambrose event setting up for tonight. I see Imogen flying around the offices, her minions trailing after her, and by the time six o'clock rolls around and I make my way back up to the executive level, I can see she's been hard at work. Hundreds of people have already arrived: the toast of British media, government, and society. Balloons, canapés, and tasteful floral arrangements are everywhere, all of them in Ashford colors of red and silver, despite the fact the event is technically in honor of all British industry—not just our company.

"You've outdone yourself," I tell Imogen, raising a glass of champagne when she appears through the crowd, looking surprisingly serene in a tasteful cream dress.

"I have, haven't I?" she says, looking around at the buzzing party with a satisfied smile. "Despite every best effort from the Ambrose team. You know his PR girls wanted Union Jack flags hanging from every surface? They have zero sense of taste or subtlety."

"I don't think subtlety and politics mix," I remark. "At least, not if you want to win."

Imogen rolls her eyes. "We all know he's got the race sewn up," she points out, rearranging a table set with glossy brochures about Ashford's world-beating innovation. Brochures I've been overseeing. "The Lancaster papers have been pushing him hard all week. 'The only sensible choice,' they say. Did you see those photos of Hugh and the family?" she adds with a smirk. "'The British Kennedys,' they called them."

I snort. "Hugh will sock Max for that."

"Or shake his hand for propelling them into Number 10 Downing Street." Imogen looks around the room and sighs. "Does it ever make you feel . . . I don't know, icky?"

"Icky?" I echo, amused.

"Uncomfortable. Wrong. That this is the way the world works." Imogen frowns for a moment. "Lionel Ambrose and Cyrus Lancaster shake hands in a back room somewhere and decide who ends up running the country. Your father pitches in, and suddenly, Ashford's drugs get a nice government stamp of approval, and they all get a massive payout. And here we are, blowing up balloons and waving flags along the way."

"Well, shit, when you put it like that . . ." I drain my champagne. "But this is the way it's always worked, isn't it? Before Lionel and Cyrus and my father, it was their fathers, and their fathers before them."

"But what happens next?" Imogen asks, arching an eyebrow. "Are you going to follow obediently in their footsteps, making backroom deals with Hugh and Max twenty years from now?"

"Absolutely not," I vow.

"What about Robert?" she asks pointedly.

I look across the room to where my brother is shaking hands and smiling for the cameras, posing with my father and Lionel in front of one of those unsubtle Union Jack flags.

"What's got you so contemplative?" I ask, studying Imogen.

She gives a little shrug. "I am capable of deep thoughts from time to time," she says lightly, plucking a loose thread off her dress. "It's not all tea parties and *Tatler*, you know."

"Anyone who underestimates you is a fool," I tell her affectionately, and she smiles back at me.

"I'd say the same, but we both know your whole devil-may-care intellectual image is just an act." She smirks. "It's a good thing you're so pretty, to make up for that lousy brain of yours."

I laugh out loud—and then stop, catching sight of Tessa as she makes her way tentatively through the crowd. We arranged to meet here for the event, so this is my first glimpse of her wearing a figure-hugging navy dress: conservatively cut, high at the neckline and low to her knees, but clinging in all the right places. She has her hair pulled back off her face in loose curls, and looks fresh-faced and impossibly beautiful.

I feel Imogen hit me on the arm.

"What?" I ask, dragging my attention away.

"Oh, I've been saying your name for the past minute." She smirks again, glancing over to Tessa. "You've got it *bad*."

I don't bother denying it. She's right, I'm crazy about Tessa—and I don't care who knows it. "If you see my mother, steer her in the opposite direction, OK?" I ask, grabbing another champagne glass for Tessa. "The less time she spends around Tessa, the less likely it is she'll send her fleeing back to America to escape the icy chill."

Imogen laughs. "You'll owe me, cuz!"

I cross the room, single-mindedly brushing off greetings and attempts at conversation. There's only one person I want to see.

"Oh, thank God," Tessa exclaims when I reach her. Clearly, the feeling is mutual. She holds my hand tightly, looking around. "Someone asked me if I was with the Department for Trade and Industry, and what I thought about the tech policy being negotiated at the upcoming G8 conference. I was worried I was going to start an international trade war!"

I smile, tugging her closer for a kiss. "You should have told them you favored protectionist policies and were pushing for tariffs. You could have sent the stock markets reeling tomorrow morning," I joke, feeling better already with her in my arms.

Somehow, she makes everything better.

Tessa takes a breath, stepping back so there's a polite distance between us. "Lionel Ambrose looks comfortable," she says, nodding to where the man himself is holding court with my father and a crowd of journalists, imposing and charismatic. "Is Hugh here yet? How was the squash match?" she demands. "Did you find anything useful?"

I shake my head regretfully. "He was at the party last year, but we knew that already," I reply, knowing she'll be disappointed. "He says he left early, but there wasn't really a way for me to quiz him on what else he was doing."

Tessa looks downcast. "What about Max? Is this the kind of event he shows up for?"

"Not if he can help it."

"So there's no new information at all." Tessa presses her lips together, annoyed. "We're running out of time."

"How do you figure that?" I ask, frowning. I've noticed a change in Tessa's mood the last couple of days, a new focus and determination in her hunt for Wren's assailant. She's stayed up late, running internet searches, looking for clues; blowing off her college work to obsess over Hugh and Max's possible alibis, and trying to brainstorm ways to trap them in a lie.

I know this search matters to her, but I can't help feeling uneasy, seeing how much it consumes her thoughts. Even talking on a night like this, I can tell that a part of her brain is on alert for anything that might link back to Wren.

"Well, the longer I'm asking questions and digging around, the more chance there is that her attacker will find out I'm looking for him and cover his tracks," Tessa explains, looking away, almost guilty. "The Blackthorn Society found out I was looking into their business and sent that guy after me," she adds. "If this man feels threatened . . . who knows what he might do?"

"I won't let anyone hurt you," I vow, drawing her closer. That attack in Oxford still haunts me, knowing I should have been there, protecting her. "You don't have to worry. You're not going after the society anymore."

"No, but that doesn't mean my target isn't just as dangerous," she points out, her face still shadowed.

I lean down and kiss her softly, trying to banish the shadows from her eyes. "We'll find him," I promise her, even though I still have no idea how.

And once we find the right man, what happens then? I haven't talked about it with Tessa, but she has to know that we can't just go to the police or expect the legal system to offer any kind of justice at all. Wren is long dead, there are no witnesses—only secondhand fragments of information—and no one would press charges, let alone convict a man on evidence like that. Not to mention the fact that the Ambrose or Lancaster family would never stand for so much as an official investigation. Their lawyers would send even the most determined prosecutor running.

So what is Tessa's endgame here?

Do I even want to know?

I grab another glass of champagne. This just got too dark, too fast—and I see my parents across the room, too. It's only a matter of time before they decide to come say hello, so I grab

Tessa's hand and pull her down the hall, away from the main party. "How about a tour?" I ask, wanting to lighten the mood.

"I've already visited," she protests, but she's smiling again as I tug her into an alcove behind the main reception area.

"Yes, but you haven't had a special, personal, private tour . . ." I murmur, dropping kisses on her neck and collarbone. She catches her breath in a rush, shivering as I find the sensitive spot I know she loves.

"Don't you need to circulate?" she asks, but her cheeks are flushed, and her eyes are already sparkling with temptation. "Play the dutiful son?"

"I'd rather hear that moan you make right before you come."

"Saint!" Tessa gasps, looking around to see if anyone heard, but luckily they're all too busy schmoozing.

"I don't hear a no," I tease, my hands skimming lower.

Tessa bites her lip, blushing even deeper, but she holds my gaze boldly. "Now that I think about it, I have wanted to see your office," she muses with a saucy smirk. "So I can picture exactly where you are when I'm sending you those dirty texts and getting you hard."

Damn.

I bite back a groan, already pulling her on down the hallway and through the executive floor until we reach the CEO's office, where I've been working these past couple of weeks. The noise from the party is quieter here away from the crowd. "Fancy." Tessa whistles, looking around the luxurious space furnished with a couch, designer chairs, and a massive desk positioned right in front of the incredible view. "The décor leaves something to be desired, though," she adds, holding up a framed photo of my mother.

I take it from her and set it aside. "This is my father's office," I tell her as Tessa grips my collar and pulls me closer, up against the desk.

"And you want to have your wicked way with me right here? You really are the rebel heir."

"What did you call me?" I chuckle, gripping her hips and lifting her to perch on the edge of the polished wooden surface.

"The rebel heir," she repeats, grinning. "That's what they call you around here."

"No," I groan. "Are you serious?"

"Oh yes," she purrs. "And I'm not going to let you hear the end of it."

"I'll just have to find a way to shut you up," I murmur, claiming her lips in a long, slow kiss.

God, I love the way she blossoms under my touch. Tessa's lips part, inviting, and her body seems to melt against me, practically begging to be touched. So I do. Running my hands over her curves, squeezing and caressing where I know it'll make her moan. I palm the ripe swell of her breasts, feeling her gasp against my mouth as I tease at the nubs of her nipples, already stiff in my hands.

Fuck, this woman is incredible. Already my blood is running hot in my veins, craving the tight clench of her pussy, demanding I draw moans of pleasure from her sweet, pliant mouth.

"Saint . . ." she whispers when I finally release her lips.

"I thought I told you to use your words," I scold her playfully, already hitching her skirt higher, running my hands up the insides of her thighs. "Saint, yes? Saint, more? Saint . . . fuck me now?"

"All of the above," she whispers as my fingers find her pussy slick, so fucking wet for me.

"Even with the door open?" I ask, and her eyes flicker over to where it stands a few inches ajar.

"*Especially* with the door open," she whispers, and fuck, the flash of excitement in her eyes undoes me every time.

I circle her swollen clit and then sink one finger inside her tight heat, watching her eyes glaze.

"Christ, you're so ready for me." I bite back a groan, kissing her again instead. This time I slide my tongue deep, wanting to own her mouth, to taste and devour every inch. Tessa throws an arm around my neck, pulling me down to deepen the kiss, hot and hard, as her body bucks against my hand.

"You want some more, baby?" I tease, flexing my finger inside her.

She makes a noise of frustration. "You know I do."

"Then ask nicely . . ." I nip her earlobe, and Tessa shivers.

"Please?"

"Even nicer . . ." I withdraw my finger and circle her clit again, making her whine in frustration. God, I love driving her crazy like this. Making her need me, making the pleasure that much sweeter. It's a rush like no other, the power to make her beg.

But tonight, Tessa isn't in the begging mood. She grips my collar and levels me with a determined gaze. "Give it to me," she demands boldly, cheeks flushed. Fucking perfect. "Fill me up, Saint. Make me come my brains out right here on your father's desk, so every time you're in here, every time he summons you for a lecture, you'll picture me spread and moaning for you."

Oh *fuck*.

I thrust two fingers into her slick cunt and watch her back arch. "Saint—" she starts to cry, but I muffle her, slamming my other hand over her mouth. Her eyes widen in surprise, but I can feel from the sudden clench of her pussy that she's loving the gag, so I muffle her mouth tighter with one hand as I add a third finger below, stretching her as I start to pump.

"Not a word, baby," I order her sternly, nipping on her ear. "You wanted it, remember? Now take it. Clench that pussy real tight for me . . . That's right. That's my good girl."

She whimpers around my hand, eyes rolling back as I flex and thrust inside, and fuck, it's the hottest thing to watch her like this. The way her body trembles and tenses; the way her cunt grips me like a fucking vise as her climax rises.

"There you go," I growl in satisfaction, feeling it take her over.

First her legs shake. Then her sobs turn desperate and her body writhes, almost like she's trying to escape the onslaught of pleasure. But I don't release her, I don't let her go—I flex my fingers deeper, grinding my palm against the swollen ridge of her clit until she can't hold it back anymore.

Tessa climaxes with a muffled cry, falling back on the desk to shake and moan, my fingers still buried in her clenching pussy, coaxing her through the orgasm until she's spent and gasping amongst the paperwork and files.

Dammit, she's right. There's no way I'll ever step foot in this office without getting hard, picturing the sight of her like this. Sprawled and glowing with pleasure.

A fucking goddess.

Slowly, I withdraw my fingers and lick them clean. Delicious. Tessa looks up at me, somehow blushing bashfully, even though she just demanded I finger-fuck her into oblivion. "Hi," she says breathlessly, and I smile, so gone for this woman, even a single word from her makes my heart swell.

My heart, and other things.

"Hello, there." I gently stroke hair from her forehead. "Doing alright, darling?"

She nods, grinning wider. "I do have a question for you," she says softly, beckoning.

I lean closer. "What's that?"

"Why isn't your cock inside me already?"

Lust blazes. Fuck. "My mistake," I growl, reaching for my belt. "One to be rectified immediately."

But I'm just stripping open my pants when the sound of voices comes in the hallway. Getting closer.

In one swift move, I pull Tessa from the desk and set her upright on her feet again. The thrilling risk of discovery is one thing, but turning her into fodder for cheap gossip is something else. Something I'd never subject her to.

"They can't hear us," Tessa protests, looking disappointed.

"They would, the way I plan on fucking you." I smooth down her dress so she's decent again. Well, except from the orgasmic glow in her eyes. "Trust me, baby. Word travels fast in a place like this. Do you want everyone in the building knowing exactly how you take my cock? My parents," I add meaningfully. "Lionel Ambrose? Cyrus Lancaster?"

Her eyes widen. "Good point!" she yelps, frantically patting at her tousled hair.

I pause, watching her collect herself. And even though my erection is painfully hard at this point, and I'm going to have to walk around with my jacket draped strategically over my arm, hiding the situation in my trousers, I can't keep the smile off my face.

Because these moments, when it's just the two of us—no suspect lists and vengeance, no family bullshit and drama—it's the most peaceful I think I've ever felt.

I want it forever.

"Ready?" Tessa beams at me, taking my hand.

"Uh, yes." I clear my throat and put aside that unexpected thought.

I hold open the door for her, and we emerge back into the hallway. There are people nearby, I notice, talking in corners and spilling out of the main party, so it's just as well I put the brakes on our filthy interlude.

Tessa would have screamed the place down.

"There's your brother," Tessa says, nodding across the floor as we draw nearer to the party. Robert is in conversation with my father and Lionel Ambrose, their heads bent together. "Looks serious," she comments, turning to intercept a passing waiter with a tray of hors d'oeuvres.

"Family business always is," I quip dryly.

The three of them look over and see us, so I offer a polite nod and a wave, and Robert quickly leaves the group to come join us. "Good showing, don't you think?" he says brightly, gesturing around.

"It's a lovely party," Tessa says politely. "Saint's been giving me a tour," she adds, shooting me a private smirk. "It's been a *stimulating* evening already."

I try not to choke on a salmon roll. Robert grins, oblivious to her filthy double entendres. "Excellent. You know, I heard you were working with Hugh now over at the Ambrose Foundation?"

Tessa nods. "I'm working on a fundraising project; it's been really interesting."

"She's being modest," I say proudly. "She's been shaking things up over there. Hugh's been singing her praises for weeks."

"And he would know," Robert agrees, sounding admiring. "The man is going places. Like father like son. I wouldn't be surprised if he was in government in a few years, too."

I blink. I forget sometimes that Robert grew up with a healthy dose of hero worship, trailing around after me and my friends. "I'm not so sure Hugh would agree," I say, amused, but Robert seems convinced.

"You should see him in front of a crowd," he insists. "That TED Talk he did in Stockholm last year, people took notice. You should look it up," he adds to Tessa. "It was all about the foundation mission, how to balance positive interventions with local sovereignty. October, I think it was," he says, frowning. "Yes, that's it. He was running lines on us all through the Blackthorn Society party before he jetted off to take the stage. Shitting bricks, if you'll pardon my French," he adds with a grin.

"I'll do that," she replies slowly. There's something in her expression I don't recognize, but I wait until Robert excuses himself and goes to mingle before I check.

"What is it?"

Tessa looks at me, urgent. "You heard him. He said Hugh left the Blackthorn party last year to go give a speech in Sweden."

"Wren," I realize, with no small measure of relief. "She was held that weekend. It couldn't have been him."

"*If* the alibi checks out." Tessa whips out her phone and starts clicking, a fierce look of determination in her eyes. A moment later, she exhales. "Oh."

She shows me her screen. There's a video of Hugh up onstage, looking bashful—but passionate—as he delivers a speech to a packed conference hall. It's date-stamped for the morning after the Blackthorn party. I keep scrolling and find footage of him from a cocktail reception the night before, too. "Look," I show her. "Friday night welcome drinks. He would have had to leave the party early and go straight to the airport to make it in time."

Just like he said.

"And he wouldn't have made it back to England before Saturday afternoon, either. Maybe later," Tessa agrees. "It can't have been him. Which means . . ."

"Max is the only one left on our list," I say slowly. At least, until we start looking beyond the men sharing this tattoo . . .

"It's him," Tessa says grimly. "He's the one."

"We don't know that for certain," I object immediately.

"He's the only one left!"

"Which means we need to pin down his whereabouts, too, and find out exactly what he did that night." I try to calm her. She looks like she wants to go hunt Max down this minute and drag him through the streets. "You said it yourself. We need to be careful so whoever did this doesn't have a chance to cover his tracks."

"Whoever did this . . . ?" Tessa looks up at me, frowning. "You still don't believe it's him, do you? Even when he's the only other person walking around with that tattoo."

I'm about to broach the possibility that Wren's evidence might not be so clear-cut, after all, when someone joins us. And not just anyone, either, but one of the last people I want to see:

Dr. Valerie DeJonge.

I'd prefer to keep my distance from my father's illicit affair partner, but it's too late—she's already greeting Tessa with a kiss on each cheek. "Saint." She gives me a cool nod. "And Tessa, I'm so glad to see you again," she continues, flashing Tessa a much warmer smile. "How have you been? I didn't realize you were so intimately involved with the St. Clair family."

Tessa looks thrown, clearly still processing Hugh's airtight alibi. "It's . . . a recent development," she says. "Dr. DeJonge was Wren's mentor at the lab," Tessa explains to me.

"Valerie, please," the doctor corrects her. "Her sister was a promising scientist," she adds. "We worked closely on the original trials for Ashford's new drug. I was just thinking what a pity it is that she isn't around to see all our dreams come to fruition. That is, if we launch successfully."

"If?" I echo, surprised. "I thought the results were as good as confirmed."

If they aren't, then the entire future of the company hangs in the balance. My father has gone all-in on this miraculous new drug, if the financial projections for the next years are any indication. Every whispered, hopeful conversation in the building is about the incredible trial results, and how this drug launch will change the world—and Ashford's profit margin.

Valerie gives a light laugh. "You know us scientists. We like to check the data a hundred times. You never know what we might find at the last minute . . ." Valerie shoots a glance back towards the party, and I see that my father is standing in the doorway, watching us.

He looks stressed and anxious. I'm not surprised. He's probably wondering if Valerie is spilling secrets about their affair.

Sure enough, he quickly strides over, interrupting us. "Sorry to drag you away, Saint, but it's almost time for my speech. Tessa, so lovely to see you tonight. You're looking marvelous."

My father shoots Valerie a glance but doesn't say a word to her. In fact, the vibe is so chilly, I wonder if he really did break it off, after all.

"Before you go, let me give you my personal number," Valerie insists, holding Tessa back. "I would love to get lunch sometime, discuss Wren's work on the project. Did you know Tessa's sister was part of my research?" she adds to my father, a little pointedly.

He looks panicked, probably by the fact we're all standing around chatting together, despite the massive infidelity elephant in the room. Any moment now, my mother will join us, too. "Small world," he manages.

"Isn't it just."

Valerie hands Tessa her card, with promises to call. "You should join us, Saint," she adds, giving me a cryptic smile. "I gather you're taking a larger role at the company now. I would love to explain more about our research. You should know how the clinical trials work, what this company is capable of."

My father splutters a cough. "We really should be going," he says, gripping my arm tightly and all but dragging me away.

"You're cutting off my circulation," I point out, and he drops it.

"Sorry, son. I suppose the stress of the evening is getting to me." He loosens his collar. Up close, I can see he's still paler than normal, and has lost weight since the heart attack. Probably from the low-fat, low-cholesterol diet my mother has him on. Now he looks around, on edge. "I could use a drink."

"I thought you were under doctor's orders," I point out, and he sighs.

"You sound like your mother."

"Then God help us both." I turn to Tessa, who looks like she wants to be anywhere but here. I can tell she's itching to continue our fight about Max and the tattoo, and the last thing I want is for anyone in this room to know what's going on. "You know, Father, we shouldn't keep you. Enjoy the night—"

"Not so fast." My father stops us, glancing back towards Valerie with a flash of anxiety in his eyes. "I owe you an apology."

I stop, surprised. "Say that again?"

"I've heard excellent reports about the way you've been stepping up here at Ashford. I'm proud of you."

Words I don't think have ever been spoken by my father. At least not in the past ten years. But before I can wonder where exactly this new appreciation is coming from, he hurriedly adds, "In fact, I think you deserve a break. Since you've been going above and beyond here at the office. Why not take some time away to relax? A trip to the house in Provence, perhaps? I'm sure Tessa would love it there," he adds with another anxious glance back at Valerie. She shoots him a smug glare, and I realize:

He wants to get me out of here. Valerie, his secret affair, the financial shenanigans in the Ashford accounts . . .

It turns out, I'm more trouble for him being a dutiful son round the office than gallivanting recklessly out of it.

I open my mouth to turn him down flat, but Tessa speaks up first. "We'd love to!" she exclaims. "What a generous offer."

"Good." My father looks relieved. "You can leave this weekend. And don't worry about rushing back," he adds, slapping my shoulder. "Robert can handle things around here. You go relax and have fun."

The crowd starts to hush and gather as Lionel Ambrose tests a microphone for his speech, so my father gives a nod and makes a beeline for him.

I turn to Tessa. "Want to tell me what that was about?"

"Max is in the South of France," she says, her jaw set. "I'm not waiting around anymore. He's the last name on our list, the only other one with that tattoo. It's time we had a little chat to find out exactly what he knows about Wren."

There it is again: the chilling, determined look in her eyes. The mission that still stands between us—and whatever future I might have with her.

"Alright," I agree, nodding. "We'll go."

A part of me still can't imagine my friend is responsible for such a terrible crime. There has to be some other explanation, some kind of mistake, but either way, I have to know. Because the sooner we put this awful chapter in her life behind her, the sooner Tessa can release her terrible burden. She can be happy. She can be free.

I just don't know how far she'll go to make it happen.

Chapter Fourteen
TESSA

I t's Max.

The thought consumes me now, filling me with a low, boiling rage. It's him. It has to be. He's the only one left on our list. He attended the party that night, has the telltale tattoo inked on his thigh—and I already know he was hanging out with Wren, perhaps even having an illicit fling with her.

Was he the one who suggested she come to the Blackthorn after-party? I wonder, staring at the picture of her from the yearbook, spinning around at the party, easy and carefree. Max could have tempted her with stories about how exclusive and fun it would be. She wouldn't have thought twice, piling in a car out to his family estate, joining in the dancing and merriment. Just another adventure for her dream trip in England. I can picture Max now, casually pressing a spiked drink into her hand as she danced, just out of frame. Wren would have trusted him, enjoying herself, not knowing where the night would lead.

Not imagining for a moment that the charming playboy could be capable of such evil deeds.

I barely sleep a wink, until dawn breaks outside Saint's windows and I slip out of bed, careful not to wake him. I dress quickly in workout gear, then quietly exit the house for a dawn run—and to make a detour that Saint can never know about.

"Are you sure you know what you're doing?" Phillip asks me,

looking nervously around. I texted him to meet me in a discreet corner of Hyde Park, with the morning dew still glistening on the grass and only a few early dog walkers around. "This isn't child's play, Tessa. This stuff can be dangerous in the wrong hands."

"I'll be careful," I promise him. "Did you bring it?"

Phillip sighs, reluctant, then pulls out a small package from his coat. He passes it to me quickly, and I tuck it away, out of sight in the pocket of my hoodie. "Thank you," I say, meaning it. "I'm sorry I can't tell you anything more but . . . know it's for Wren."

"I don't want to know," he says firmly. "Just . . . be careful?"

"I will," I vow. But the only thing I care about now is trapping Max in his wicked lies.

And thanks to the tiny vials in my pocket, I'm going to make it happen.

* * *

BACK AT THE house, I greet Saint like nothing's happened, and we get packed up and start our journey to the St. Clair house in France. But it soon becomes clear that traveling in his world is *very* different to mine.

"Champagne, sir?" The flight attendant offers the bottle, flashing both of us a friendly smile.

"Why not?" Saint replies, relaxing in first class beside me. "Tessa?"

I jerk a nod, my stomach already tied up in knots thinking of the mission I have ahead of me. The attendant pours us both glasses, and sets out a fruit plate, too, before moving on. I can't help remembering my flight to England, before all of this began: a long, cramped trip across the Atlantic, with scowling stewards, crying babies, and stale pretzels. Now I'm reclining in style, after being whisked through the VIP lines at the airport and offered warm towels and fancy snacks at every turn.

It's a shame I'm too tense to enjoy it.

"We're almost there," Saint says, giving me a reassuring smile. "It'll be a smooth landing."

I manage a faint smile. He thinks my nerves are because of flying and has held my hand every step of the way. I haven't told him the truth.

I know he still hopes that we'll be able to clear Max's name somehow.

I understand his loyalty. The men have been friends for years. Nobody wants to think someone they trust is capable of such terrible things. And despite his conflict, Saint has been with me every step of the way: backing me up in all my investigations, willing to destroy his friendships to uncover the truth.

I can see how it's eating him up inside, having to question everything and mistrust the friends he's counted on for years. Even I hated having to suspect Hugh, before his alibi confirmed he's not the man I'm looking for. Saint needs this whole thing to be over just as much as I do.

It's why I have those little vials from Phillip stashed in my makeup bag. I need to be sure.

Sure enough to make Max pay for what he's done.

The plane hits a tiny pocket of turbulence, making me startle. Saint squeezes my hand tightly. "It won't be long now," he reassures me, and he's right.

This trip is make-or-break for me. Soon enough, Max is finally going to answer for his crimes.

* * *

WE LAND IN Marseille and sail through customs. Saint has rented a classic sports car for us to drive, and he relaxes behind the wheel, speeding through the pretty French countryside dotted with farmhouses and historic villages, earth-toned in the October sun.

"My family has had the house since before I was born," Saint says, clearly happy to be here. "I think some of my favorite memories are from the summers we would spend here. My father would work from the European headquarters nearby, and my mother would go hit the shops in Saint-Tropez, so my brothers and I had the place to ourselves. We'd spend all day horsing around in the pool, and walking into the village to flirt with all the French girls who were way out of our league. Well, out of mine and Robert's," he adds with a nostalgic smile. "Edward charmed the pants off them all, of course, even though his French was atrocious."

I smile back, trying to relax, too. Even though my thoughts are racing with my plans for Max, I can appreciate the beauty of our surroundings. In any other situation, I would be trading tales about family summer trips, and asking to stop at one of these adorable villages to sip a glass of wine and sit at a table on the town square.

But this isn't a vacation for me, and fury still burns in my bloodstream, so I just gaze at the beautiful spread of green fields and woodlands, counting down the miles until Saint turns down a long driveway lined with the cool arch of cypress trees.

"Here we are," he says with obvious affection in his voice as we pull up outside a gorgeous château. It's built from sand-colored stone, with red clay roof tiles and large windows framed by shutters painted in a French blue trim.

"It's lovely," I agree, climbing out of the car. "Like something from a postcard."

"I think that's how my parents found it," Saint remarks, grabbing our bags from the trunk and unlocking the front door. Inside, the décor is warm and French, with tiled floors, white walls, and antique furniture in shades of cream and blue. Saint leads me through the large open living room to the big farmhouse kitchen in back, with views over the swimming pool and gardens. "My mother likes to tell the story of how she found a painting in a gallery, an oil painting of this house. She fell in love with it, and so my father surprised her by tracking down the artist, and then buying the house for their anniversary."

I blink—at the lavish gift, and the idea that his ice queen mother could be sentimental about anything. Saint must see my expression, because he chuckles. "I know, I can't believe it either. But I suppose my parents were young and in love, once, anyway." He pauses. "My father's fucking Valerie DeJonge," he says abruptly.

"What?" I gasp.

"Is, or was. He swears he's ending it, but yeah . . . He was paying her off from the Ashford company accounts—that's how I found out." Saint sighs, dragging a hand through his hair, clearly frustrated. "As if I didn't have enough to be dealing with right now. I have to hide his dirty secrets, too."

"I'm so sorry," I say, moving to wrap my arms around his waist. I hold him close, wanting to support him. "That's a terrible position he put you in."

"It's feeling rather familiar these days," Saint says ruefully. I tilt my head up and give him an apologetic smile.

"I'm sorry," I say softly.

He kisses the top of my head. "Don't be. You have nothing to be sorry for."

Saint stands there a moment, just holding me, then finally draws back. "I suppose we should get started with what we came here for," he says, and pulls out his phone. He dials, putting it on speakerphone, so I can hear Max's voice when he answers.

"You'll never guess where Tessa and I just landed," Saint says. "We're in Provence for a break. You still around?"

"Abso-fucking-lutely," Max cheers. "In fact, I'm having a party at mine. The more the merrier." There's noise on the other end, music and laughter, and female voices calling Max's name. Clearly, the party is already underway.

Saint looks to me, raising his eyebrows in a silent question. I nod.

"We're on our way," he says, and notes down the address from Max before hanging up. "Are you sure?" Saint checks, looking at me. "We've been traveling all day. We could get settled in here tonight and meet up with him tomorrow."

"No, I'm good," I insist. "I can't sit around the house, however lovely it is here. I wouldn't be able to relax, anyway."

Besides, if Max has been partying for hours, his inhibitions will be low.

Low enough to reveal the truth about that night—without me having to take any additional measures?

I hope so.

* * *

THE SUN IS sinking lower over the ocean by the time we make it to Max's place on the outskirts of Cannes. As we drive through the streets, I can see that the coastal town is a totally different vibe to the laid-back, picturesque French countryside. Here it's flashy, with loud bars, and glamorous people strutting their way to dinner dressed in fabulous outfits, wealth on obvious display. And when we reach Max's beach house, set high on the cliffs, it's a dramatic, modern building, looming over the bay with walls of glass, and an infinity pool glittering on the edge of the terrace.

The party is in full force when we pull over, music pounding down the street, and the winding road so full of parked Lamborghinis and Mercedes we have to park and hike the last section on foot.

"Typical Max," Saint comments with a smile. "He could have been raging three hours or three days already."

Gorgeous young people spill out of the house onto the terraces, dressed in everything from skintight dresses to streetwear, with one guy walking around in a massive ski jacket and boxers—and nothing else. My trusty black slip dress looks practically demure in this crowd, and I feel a flicker of nerves as we step into the huge, modern foyer. I'm holding Saint's hand tightly.

Everything's at stake now. I can't make a wrong move, and risk not finding the truth.

"Hello, hello!" Max greets us, emerging from the crowd barefoot in linen pants with his shirt unbuttoned to his navel. He's got a bottle of liquor in one hand and a cigar in the other: every inch the playboy heir. "Get yourself a drink, some caviar. We have everything you need right here. Weed, women, wine. My man Gino is around here somewhere, if you're looking for something a little stronger," he adds with a wink. "Make yourselves at home."

I hang back as Saint greets him with a back-slapping hug. Max has always been loud, and louche, but a predator? I didn't think so.

Now I see him through new, wary eyes.

"Tessa, darling, glad you could make it." Max kisses me on both cheeks, and I have to remind myself not to recoil from his touch.

"Great place." I force a friendly smile, looking around. "So this is where you've been hiding?"

"Escaping more like, but shhh, don't tell my father"—Max puts a finger to his lips in an exaggerated whisper—"or he'll drag me back to London to listen to more of Lionel Ambrose's in . . . dominatable speeches. No, that's not right. Indubitable?" he asks, frowning. "Interminable!"

Saint chuckles. "Just how many drinks have you had?"

"Not enough, my friend. Never enough!" Max leads us through to where a huge living room opens out onto the terrace. The pool is full despite the chilled autumn air, with models strutting around in teeny swimwear. "I heard the Ashford wankfest went down a treat," Max adds with a smirk. "Apparently you and Hugh were very good boys, did the family names proud."

"I refrained from bringing scandal on them all, at least. Barely,"

Saint adds, shooting me a private smile. I remember my private tour of his father's office and feel a wistful pang.

Somehow, it was all so much simpler before I knew about Hugh's alibi.

Before I had to face the stark reality that Wren's attacker could be right in front of me, lazily collapsing on a massive white couch and demanding that they change the music with a regal air.

"There you are, darling," Max cries, looking behind us. "See? I told you it wasn't all insipid Eurotrash."

"Oh, Tessa, thank God!" Annabelle launches herself at me with enthusiastic air-kisses. "I am *so* happy to see you. I know zero people here tonight; I don't know where Max finds them!"

"I just send out the Bat Signal, and the cool people appear," Max declares.

"And by *cool*, he means every model, DJ, and wannabe crypto king on the French Riviera." Annabelle giggles, dragging me down onto one of the couches, then fishes in a huge glass bowl filled with ice and cans for matching mini champagne bottles. "Cheers," she beams, and I feel a fresh wave of conflicted guilt.

I've been so focused on Max, I hadn't thought about Annabelle in all of this. She's set to marry him next month; it's supposed to be the dream wedding of the season.

Soon to be a nightmare, if I have my way.

I catch Saint's eye and give him a look. We're not here to kick back and have fun. We're on a mission.

He gives an imperceptible nod.

"So what's next after this jaunt?" Saint asks Max casually, propping an ankle on his other knee and lounging back, like he's just taking in the view. "I heard rumors you're doing time at the *London Weekly* next, prepping for the big time."

"Doing time is right," Max cracks. "Endless editorial meetings, it's enough to drive a man mad. But my father insists I need to spend time on the ground floor before taking my seat on the board at Lancaster."

"He said as much at the Blackthorn party." Saint smiles. "Of course, he kept one eye on you all night, to make sure there wasn't a repeat of last year. Hugh told me about the kerfuffle, with those girls showing up. I'd have loved to see your father's face," he adds, still casual. "Let me guess, he turned that shade of purple and started spraying saliva like when he gets really worked up?"

"Bingo." Max gives a yawn, distracted by a hot model sauntering past.

"What girls?" Annabelle asks, and Max pats her thigh.

"Don't worry. They were Hugh's entertainment, not mine. You kept me on a tight leash, remember? And then that shrimp got me, and I puked my guts out all weekend. Don't mix tequila and buffet seafood, people," he adds with a grimace. "I still can't look at Casa Noble the same way. The doctors said they'd never seen someone vomit in such copious amounts."

"You were in hospital after the party?" I ask, shocked. That doesn't track with my timeline.

"All weekend," Max confirms with a wince. "Getting my stomach pumped by St. Michael's finest. We practically had to donate a wing to make up for the mess. Hey, Gino!" he suddenly calls, and leaps up. "Be right back. Just need to powder my nose," he adds with a wink, and disappears into the crowd.

My heart sinks. An alibi like that would be easy to confirm—there would be patient records, admittance paperwork . . . If Max was lying, surely he wouldn't pick a story that could be disproven so easily?

Could he be telling the truth? And if he is, where does that leave my investigation now?

"I'll be right back," I say, bobbing up from the couch. I need to clear my head. Saint is looking at me with concern—he must know that Max's story tracks—but I don't want to talk about it right now. "Bathroom?"

"Down the hall, to the right." Annabelle beams, getting up as well. "I'll come, too!"

She steers us through the party, gossiping about some of the guests and what she and Max have been up to the past few days. "And the shopping is great, sure, but you can't move for TikTok stars filming their Hermès bag offers. It's out of control."

We step into the bathroom, and I take a deep breath, relieved by the momentary peace. It's a spacious, white-tiled room with its own balcony and expansive views of the ocean. "You alright, babe?" Annabelle asks, disappearing into the walled-off toilet cubicle.

"Fine. Just a bit queasy from the flight still," I lie.

"Oh, was it terribly bumpy?" her voice drifts out. "That's the worst. If you're still feeling under the weather just say the word, and we'll get you a banana bag ASAP. Max's doctor in London can hook you up with someone here. Shit, do you have a tampon?"

"I think so. Let me check." I rummage in my purse and then slide one under the door to her.

"Angel!"

A moment later, Annabelle flushes, and emerges to rinse her hands.

"This may be a stupid question, but what's a banana bag?" I ask, perching by the open window and taking a deep, calming breath of the sea breeze. My head is still spinning from Max's alibi revelation, and I honestly don't know where to go from here. I need distraction—or some of the tequila that sent Max to the emergency room.

"Oh, they're absolute magic!" Annabelle explains. "It's like a liquid IV bag they pump into you, all kinds of yummy vitamins, flushes a bad hangover right out of your system. Max practically has the guy on speed dial. Don't believe a word of his theatrics about that food poisoning incident," she adds, rolling her eyes as she applies lip gloss in the mirror. "I bet you a thousand pounds he just waltzed in, stuck an IV in his arm, and was good to go in an hour. He does it *all* the time. He's such a drama queen."

I manage a laugh, but inside, my heart is pounding again. Because Annabelle might not know it, but she just took a sledgehammer to Max's alibi. He could have easily found a way to drug Wren, stash her somewhere while he went to the hospital and returned in plenty of time to be the man she remembered attacking her.

The Blackthorn Society party was at the Lancaster estate, after all. Who knows what dusty wine cellars or disused basements are in that place? He could have been holding her there, out of sight the whole time, while everyone else partied on, oblivious to the horrors unfolding nearby.

"I better get back before Max finds himself some trouble," Annabelle says with a wry smirk.

"Good luck," I manage, following her back to the party again. But while she makes a beeline through the crowd, I wander blindly around the outskirts of the room, trying to think of my next move. Max is smoothly lying through his teeth; simple questions won't get me what I need.

I didn't want to resort to this, but those little vials from Phillip are going to prove very useful.

If I can play my cards right.

I watch Max, head bobbing by the DJ booth. He notices me looking, so I flutter a flirty little wave and then walk away, being sure to swing my hips as I saunter down the hall and into the kitchen. It's busy with caterers, but I idle there, taking a bottle of water and sipping it slowly, counting down to—

"I swear, you get lovelier every time I see you." Max strolls in and gives me a charming smile. "That Saint better be treating you right. If he isn't, just say the word."

"And you'll do what?" I ask, making my voice breathy and my smile inviting. Any other guy and I'd think he wouldn't break the bro code, but Annabelle said it was all about the conquest with Max. Proving his dominance. And what better way to prove your manly prowess than to go after your buddy's girlfriend?

Sure enough, Max's eyes roam over me hungrily. "Oh, I can think of a few things." He winks, and I giggle.

"You're so bad!" I say, acting all flustered.

"You've not seen the half of it, love." Max moves closer. "The stories I could tell . . ."

"Don't tease a girl," I pout. "You know, everyone said Saint had the wildest reputation, but he's so busy these days with Ashford stuff, all he does is work. It's so boring. He promised me a fun vacation," I say. "But he's going to be tied up touring some lab facility tomorrow. I'll be left all alone at the house with no one to entertain me."

"Now, that's just a crying shame." Max moves closer, trapping me against the counter. He meets my eyes, playful and cocky. "A beautiful woman like you should be kept *entertained* around the clock."

"Thank you! That's what I've been telling him." I roll my eyes, silently apologizing to Saint for the disloyalty. But I have to sell the bored girlfriend act if I want my new plan to work. "I guess I'll just have to lie out by the pool and get a tan."

"I don't see any tan lines," Max teases, tracing his finger across my collarbone. Again, I fight the instinct to recoil; instead, giving him a seductive smirk.

"It's Europe, darling. Everyone goes topless here. And bottomless, too, sometimes."

Max's eyes flash, hungry. "Why don't you give me a call tomorrow then?" he suggests. "Once boring old Saint has gone to work. I can help apply your sunscreen, and keep you entertained . . ."

Got him.

"Sounds like fun." I duck under his arm and playfully dance out of reach. "Discreet, private fun?" I ask, like I'm worried word might get back to Saint.

"You know me, darling. My lips are sealed." Max gives me a wink, and I laugh.

"I'm sure we can think of better things to do with them." I smirk, then waltz away, returning to the party.

Saint is chatting to some people out on the terrace, and I go join him. "Alright?" he asks, sliding an arm around my waist.

"Great," I reply. He's relaxed, clearly at ease now that he thinks Max has an alibi for the attack and is crossed off my list.

I don't tell him otherwise. He'd only try to talk me out of what I have planned, but I'm not stopping now, not for anything.

Those lying lips of Max's won't be sealed for long, not if I have my way.

Chapter Fifteen
TESSA

I don't have to go visit the facility, you know." Saint straightens his tie as I lie out by the pool at the Provence château the morning after Max's beach party. I'm curled on a lounger in sweatpants and a sweater, enjoying the autumn air—and delicious fresh bread and pastries from the bakery in the village nearby. Saint, on the other hand, is dressed smartly, with a thick folder in one hand and his phone in the other. "Robert only mentioned it might be useful to show my face. You know, give a pep talk. I'd much rather stay here and relax with you," he adds, giving me a smoldering grin that would usually make my pulse race.

But not today.

"Isn't it already arranged?" I swallow hard. I still haven't told him about my secret plan to see Max, but I've been counting down all morning, waiting for him to leave. "They probably rolled out the red carpet already," I add lightly. "Laundered all the white lab coats especially for you. You don't want to let them down."

"I suppose." Saint sighs. "Will you be alright here on your own?"

"You mean, with the pool, the sauna, the game room, and a fridge full of the finest French cheeses? Oh, I think I'll manage," I tease, and he laughs.

"Fair enough. I shouldn't be more than a few hours. Then I can show you my favorite little bistro."

"Sounds great."

Saint leans over and gives me a slow, sweet kiss. "Call me if you need me," he says, and saunters into the house.

I feel a pang of guilt watching him go, and it only grows when I hear the front door slam. The sound of his car engine starts and then recedes as he drives away, leaving me alone.

Finally.

I grab my phone and send a text to Max.

Coast is clear ;)

He responds immediately. *On my way.*

I try not to think about what he's told Annabelle—or what I'll tell Saint. Right now, I have to focus.

I'll only get one chance at this. I have to make it count.

* * *

I GO GET ready, changing into a more revealing tank top and figure-hugging yoga pants. I put on some chill electronic music, then check the house, looking for the right place. *Laundry room . . . Library . . .* Then I open a door near the kitchen and find stone stairs leading down to a wine cellar–slash–general storage room.

Jackpot.

I drag a chair down, and then collect the rest of the supplies from the house. I couldn't risk packing anything that might spark Saint's suspicions, but I figured I could find what I needed here, and I was right. I gather laundry line, electrical tape, and grab an old toolbox, too, full of pliers, a hammer, and some ugly rusted nails. I can't imagine ever using them, but Max doesn't have to know that. All that matters is that he knows I mean business.

Once everything's set up, there's nothing left to do but pace, nervously killing time until I hear a car engine roar into the driveway.

My pulse kicks. It hits me for the first time what a big risk I'm taking. I've been so focused on getting Max here, I haven't stopped to think about what it means, but now I'm alone here in the middle of the countryside with a man I already know is capable of violence. *Evil*. If this doesn't go right . . .

There's nobody to save me.

So it just has to go right. I take a deep breath, checking my reflection in a mirror. I tousle my hair and smudge up my eyeliner a little, trying to look seductive, like a bored girlfriend looking to have a few illicit thrills.

The doorbell sounds. *Showtime*.

"You made it," I coo, throwing open the front door. Max is on the front step, looking worse for wear in dark sunglasses and designer jeans. "I was wondering if you chickened out."

"Of what, darling?" Max smirks, stepping inside. "What Saint doesn't know won't hurt him."

"Right." I trill a laugh, forcing myself to lean in and kiss him on the cheek. He's definitely hungover, and still carries the faint scent of booze; his eyes are bloodshot when he removes his Ray-Bans and looks around. "That was a great party last night," I add, leading him deeper into the house. "How late did it end?"

"Who said it ended?" Max grins. "They're still raging, last I checked."

"But you were able to slip away?" I ask. When I turn to glance back at him, his gaze is fixed firmly on my ass.

Charming.

"Annabelle hit the spa today—something about a diamond facial—so you've got me all to yourself . . ."

"Lucky me," I chirp. "Can I get you a drink?"

"How about a little hair of the dog?" he asks, squinting a little. "I've got to hit the head."

"Coming right up!"

Max makes his way down the hallway—he's clearly been here before—so I hurry to the kitchen. Saint mixed us up a pitcher of Bloody Marys this morning. I pour two fresh glasses, adding extra vodka to Max's and garnishing it with some celery so I don't accidentally switch the drinks up.

Then I pull out the vial that Phillip gave me.

It looks so innocent, a tiny dose of clear liquid, it's hard to believe that it could have any effect, but Phillip warned me to calculate Max's weight and use a precise amount to knock him out. I pause, my mind racing. What if he only takes a sip? What if I can't keep the act up, and he guesses something's wrong?

We're here alone. Saint won't be back for hours. And I already know how dangerous Max can be . . .

I dump half the vial into his drink.

"Pity it's cloudy out," Max yawns, strolling into the room. I quickly palm the vial, hiding it from sight. "I guess we'll just have to do that topless sunbathing indoors, hmm?"

"I guess so!" I swirl a spoon around his glass to mix it up, then hand the glass to him. "Extra strong, the way you like it," I add, lifting my own drink with a smile. "Bottoms up!"

I take a sip, watching Max chug practically the whole glass. *Shit.* Is he supposed to consume it that fast? I have no idea, so I force a smile and hope the drugs kick in before Max actually wants to fool around. Because if this monster puts his hands on me . . . I don't think I can fake it, not even for the plan.

"So, where were we?" Max gives me another grin, moving closer. "You know, I had a feeling you were a bad, bad girl," he muses, reaching out to stroke his fingertips up my arm. "I knew it from the moment Saint brought you around."

It takes everything I have not to shove him off me. "Oh, really?" I flutter my eyelashes at him instead. "What gave it away?"

He chuckles. "I've got an instinct. A talent, you might say. I can tell from looking at any woman just how she likes to fuck."

Asshole. I swallow hard. "And what did your instincts say about me?" I coo, silently praying the drugs will kick in fast.

"I'm a gentleman." He smirks. "But let's just say I think you like pushing the limits. Going hard," he adds. "Just like me."

He's right. He just doesn't know how.

"It's a shame I didn't meet you first," I say, then duck under his arm and sashay across the room. I pretend to scroll through the music on my phone, but really I'm buying myself a little longer before he actually wants to deliver on all this flirting. "Sounds like I've been wasting my time on the wrong man," I add.

"Then we better get . . . We better . . ." Max squints, swaying a little on his feet. He swallows, gripping the counter for balance. "Whasgoingon?"

Finally!

"Are you feeling alright?" I ask as he struggles to stay standing.

"I don' . . . feel . . . good . . ."

Max crumples to the ground.

Thank God.

I spring into action. The sedative won't last long, Phillip warned me, just enough to move to Phase Two of my plan. It's not until I'm trying to haul Max to the cellar door that I realize I didn't reckon on single-handedly carrying the full weight of a grown man. It takes forever to even move a few steps, and I pant and strain to support him, then lose my grip halfway down the stairs. Max takes a tumble, hitting the steps and sprawling on the dusty ground.

Shit.

I rush after him. There's no blood, and I don't think he hit his head, so I drag him into the chair and tie him down with the laundry line and tape. I'm sweaty and exhausted by the time he's secured, but there's still one more step to take.

I produce the second vial that Phillip gave me and transfer the contents to a syringe. Sodium pentothal. Phillip said it's as close as you can get to a truth serum. It's supposed to calm the nervous system and make the user more open and suggestible. Less able to keep track of their lies.

I grab Max's arm and inject it all. Then I sink down on the bottom step, breathing hard. I wait there until Max finally stirs.

"Mmmngghhh . . ." He lets out a muffled groan, waking. He's groggy and disoriented, squinting around the dim cellar. "Tessa?" he says, finally noticing me. "What the fuck is going on?"

"What do you think?" I rise to my feet and fold my arms.

Max blinks, and I can see his brain working overtime as he tries to put the pieces together. Bound and trapped in a dark basement, with nobody around—

He brightens. "Is this some kind of kinky sex game?" He tests the bindings on his wrists, chuckling. "Wow, you didn't skimp, did you? Top marks. But just so you know, I'll be returning the favor when it's my turn."

Is he serious?

"We're going to talk," I say coldly. "And you're going to tell the truth this time."

Max's smile slips. He blinks at me in confusion. "What are you talking about? This isn't a game?"

"Was it a game when you kidnapped my sister?" I demand. "Tied her up in a basement like this and did God knows what to her? You're lucky I'm not recreating her whole experience for you, because those are the kind of scars that don't heal."

Max looks bewildered. "I don't know what the fuck you're talking about. Your sister?" He tugs at his restraints. "What does this have to do with Wren?"

"Nice try." I stalk closer, anger pumping hot in my veins. "I know it was you."

"What was?"

"Your alibi doesn't hold up!" My control snaps. "I know it was you. You took her from the Blackthorn party! You hurt her. You . . . you *destroyed* her!"

After all this time searching, questioning, driving myself half-crazy hunting for him, he's finally in my grasp. The rage is dizzying, knowing what he did to her.

The price she paid for his crimes.

Max struggles harder. "You're a fucking psycho," he mutters, looking wildly around. "You need help."

"No. I need answers. And you're going to give them to me."

I check my phone. Ten minutes, that's how long Phillip said it would take for the truth serum to kick in. Surely it should be working by now?

"Seriously, you've had your fun," Max says, his voice quavering a little. "Ha-ha, good one. Let's give Max a proper scare. You're filming this, aren't you?" he adds, looking around again. "Well, you got what you wanted. Now let me go."

I don't reply.

"Let me go, you fucking bitch!" he roars, furious.

There it is, a glimpse of the real Max.

The monster.

"You're not going anywhere," I tell him, fighting to keep control. "I want to hear it all. Everything you planned, everything you did to her. This is it, Max: your reckoning."

"I don't know what you're talking about!" he insists, red-faced and straining. "I didn't do anything to Wren! Did I want to? Sure. She was hot, in that sexy librarian way. But I never got the chance. It didn't happen."

"You're lying!" I yell.

"I'm not, I swear!" Max gulps.

"You lured her to the Blackthorn party." I stab a finger towards him. "You spiked her drink."

"What? No! I invited her. I thought maybe, you know, we could slip away and have some fun, but that's not a crime," Max blurts. "Anyway, it never happened. She blew me off, just disappeared."

"No!" I yell, shaking my head. The drugs are supposed to be working by now. He's supposed to be confessing. This is all wrong. "You're still lying," I scream at him. "You did this. You hurt her, and now you're going to pay!"

"Tessa?"

A shocked voice makes me turn. It's Saint, standing on the cellar stairs, looking at me in total horror.

Chapter Sixteen
TESSA

Oh God.

Time seems to freeze as I watch Saint process the scene, looking from me to Max and back again.

"Saint! Thank fuck." Max sags in relief. "Get her away from me. She's lost it. I don't know what the fuck she's doing."

A look of stony realization settles on Saint's face. "Upstairs," he tells me grimly, before turning on his heel and marching up to the kitchen.

"Saint?" Max calls after him. "No, come back. Let me go!"

I take a deep breath and follow Saint upstairs, emerging into the bright daylight of the kitchen. He's pacing there, dragging a hand through his hair, and the moment I shut the cellar door behind me, he whirls around.

"What the *fuck*, Tessa?!" he explodes.

"He did it, Saint. I know he did!" I blurt.

"But he was in the hospital—"

"We don't know for how long," I interrupt. "Annabelle confirmed he stops in to get IV drips all the time. He could have been out of there in plenty of time. He's the last suspect left," I insist, feeling desperate. My careful plan is spiraling out of control, and I don't know what I'll do if I can't see this through. "It's him, I know it is," I beg Saint. "We just need to get him to confess!"

"By doing what, scaring him out of his mind so he'll say anything you want?" Saint demands. "There's a reason torture doesn't work!"

"No, it's not like that," I insist. "The truth serum should kick in soon."

"The what?" Saint's jaw drops. He looks at me in disbelief. "How long have you been planning this? Have you been lying to me this entire trip?"

I gulp. "I'm sorry, but I knew that if I told you, you would never agree to it."

"Of course I wouldn't!" Saint yells. "You've got a man tied up in the basement, Tessa! What the hell are you thinking? Have you lost your mind?"

"Maybe I have!" I shoot back. "Maybe I am a little crazy. I don't care. All I know is, Max did it, and we need to get the truth from him. No more lies, no more pretending. Everything out in the open, once and for all. Don't you want that, too?" I ask him, and Saint exhales.

"Of course I do, but—"

"But what? The drugs should be working now," I add anxiously. "But they won't last long. Please," I say, my voice breaking with the pressure. "I owe this to Wren. I have to do it. *Please.*"

Saint paces again, back and forth, then stops. "Just questions," he says, looking furious.

Relief hits me. He won't stand in my way. "Sure. Just questions," I agree, already heading for the cellar again.

For now. What happens when I get my answers . . . Well, that's another story.

We descend into the gloom again, where Max is waiting. "What the fuck took you so long?" he demands, looking past me to Saint. "Untie me and get me the hell away from this crazy bitch."

Saint doesn't reply. He moves to lean against the wall and gives me a nod.

"The Blackthorn party," I start, squaring off in front of Max.

"You took Wren. Tell us what happened. Why did you target her?" I demand, keeping my cool this time. Letting my anger turn icy and harsh. "Did she turn you down, is that what happened? You thought you'd teach her a lesson, take what she wouldn't willingly give?"

"For fuck's sake!" Max explodes. "I told you, I did fuck-all to your sister! Saint, you've got to stop this," he begs. "She's lost it, you know she has. *Help me.*"

Saint looks conflicted, but he holds firm. "Just answer her questions."

"You weren't in the hospital all weekend with food poisoning, were you?" I continue, poking holes in his alibi. "You lied about that, didn't you?"

Something flickers on Max's face. The first crack in his denials.

"Tell me." I advance. "You went back to Lancaster Manor, didn't you? You had Wren stashed in a cellar there, so you could take all the time you wanted."

"No." He shakes his head, frowning. "No, it wasn't her."

"Who wasn't?" Saint speaks up, interrupting.

"I wasn't with Wren, I swear," Max blurts. "It's like I told your psycho girlfriend. Wren blew me off, so I went and found someone else to party with."

"Then why lie to everyone?" I demand. "That whole story about food poisoning and the hospital. Why go to such lengths to cover it up if it was just some random hookup?"

Max makes a noise of frustration. "Because I was fucking Annabelle's cousin, OK?!"

There's silence.

Then Saint moves closer. "Keep talking."

"You can't possibly believe him!" I exclaim. "He's just desperate. He'll say anything right now."

"No," Saint corrects me. "He's in a highly compliant state,

thanks to *your* drugs. I don't think he's capable of making something like this up, not right now."

"Thank you!" Max huffs. I snap my head back around to face him.

"Who is this supposed mistress?" I demand, skeptical.

He squirms. "Kitty Aldridge," he says in a mumble, and Saint lets out a bark of disbelief.

"You were screwing Kitty?"

Max nods, and then gives an impish grin. "Girl's got a wild side. Nearly sent me back to the hospital by the time she was done with me."

"Kitty is a socialite," Saint explains. "She's what, seventeen?"

"Eighteen. Come on, man," Max protests. Saint rolls his eyes.

"And she's not just related to Annabelle, either. Her father is the man who heads the government Commission on Media Standards and Broadcasting."

"You see why I couldn't say anything?" Max nods eagerly. "My dad's already threatened to cut off my trust fund if I don't shape up. Marrying Annabelle is the one thing that will make him happy, and if word about this little tryst gets out . . . shit hits the fan, not just for me but for the whole company." He winces. "Bye-bye, new merger plans. Dad would kill me with his bare hands. Nobody can know."

"I'm sorry," Saint says to me quietly.

"I'm not," Max says. "Now, can you please get me out of this fucking cellar?"

I study him, wondering if this is all some triple bluff to throw us off the scent. "Can you prove it?" I demand. "Is there any evidence you were with this Kitty person when you claim you were?"

Max squirms some more, looking seriously uncomfortable now. "Yeah, there's proof. I kind of, may have . . . knocked her up."

"Max!" Saint looks shocked.

"It was an accident!" he blurts, looking like a shamefaced schoolboy. "She said she had it handled. The family thinks it was some local townie. They're keeping it all hush-hush to save face. But she did a DNA test," he adds, looking at me. "The kid's mine, and the dates all match. I had to promise her a life of fucking luxury to get her to sign the NDA." Max whistles ruefully. "Talk about the most expensive weekend of my life."

I sag back, all my precious hopes falling like shattered glass on the dusty cellar floor.

Max is a selfish, careless asshole, but I can see the truth written all over his face.

He's not lying anymore. It wasn't him.

And I'm no closer to the truth.

"Do you have any more sedative?" Saint asks me quietly.

I nod wordlessly and pass him the vial. Saint goes upstairs and returns a moment later with a glass of water.

"Here," he says, and holds it to Max's lips. "This should cool you down while I get started untying you. We'll get you out of here in no time."

Max drinks. "I know the crazy ones are wild in bed, but seriously, she's not worth the fuck," he tells Saint, then drains the glass. Soon he's slumping back, unconscious again.

"I'll get him up to bed," Saint says grimly, starting to loosen the bindings.

"He won't remember much," I offer. "The drugs . . . they'll make everything a blur. We can just tell him he had too much to drink, partied a little too hard."

Saint shoots me a furious glare. "*We* won't do anything," he snaps, hoisting Max's limp body over his shoulder. "*You're* going up to our room and waiting for me there."

His voice tells me it's not a request, but an order.

* * *

I LEAVE SAINT to carry Max up to one of the spare bedroom suites. I make my way to our bedroom and wait there as instructed. Now that my white-hot haze of fury is clear, I realize just how mad Saint is with me. I understand it, too. From the outside, what I did here today seems absolutely psychotic. Luring Max here? Drugging him? Tying him up and interrogating him for answers? It's madness.

But I wouldn't take it back. Not for a minute. Saint has to see that nothing can stand in the way of uncovering the truth.

Footsteps come, and then Saint enters, his jaw set with tension. He doesn't say a word, just strips off his tie and kicks off his dress shoes. He undoes his belt, too, and looks down at it in his hands, giving a sharp huff. "I've half a mind to put you over my knee and give you a spanking," he says, still looking furious. "Except we both know that it won't make a damn bit of difference to you."

I take a tremulous breath. "I'm sorry," I offer, and he just glares. "No, you're not."

"Fine, I'm not," I agree, coming clean. "What do you want me to say? We needed answers, and so I got them."

"*We* needed answers!" Saint roars, his face alight with fury. "You and me. You promised me you wouldn't run around pulling shit like this!"

"What was I supposed to do?" I yell back, standing my ground. "I owe it to Wren; I swore I'd do whatever it took to find her attacker!"

"And you swore to me that you wouldn't go behind my back again!" Saint exclaims. "Christ, Tessa, we're supposed to be a team!"

"You would have backed me up on this?" I ask, disbelieving. "If I'd come to you and said I wanted to drug Max and force him to tell us the truth?"

"Yes."

Saint's simple response makes me stop dead in my tracks. "No." I shake my head.

"Yes," he insists again, closing the distance between us. He takes my face in his hands, and I can see the desperate anger warring inside his eyes. "Don't you get it yet, baby? I'd do anything for you," he vows. "You make me so crazy, I can't see straight sometimes, but I'd fucking burn the world down if you asked me to, if it got us closer to ending this mission you're on. When will you believe it? When will you finally understand I'm with you until the end?"

God . . .

I stare at him, speechless. Saint's face is a picture of torment, and it's no wonder, the things I've put him through. The friendships I've made him break.

The risks he's taken, simply because I said the word.

Emotion burns through me, a tidal wave of desire. I reach for him, practically throwing myself in his arms and kissing him passionately. Wanting to feel him. Needing to show him what his loyalty means to me. Saint groans against my lips, and then he's unleashed too, shoving me back against the wall, claiming my mouth like it's his to take.

Claiming my body like it belongs to him alone.

Because it does. The rough stroke of his hands sends fire racing through me as I cling onto him, already aching to have him inside. He palms me roughly through my tank top, pinching my nipples tightly and making me yelp at the sudden rush of sensation.

"Quiet." He drags his mouth from mine with fury still burning in his eyes. "If the only time you'll take orders is when you're naked, then you'll fucking listen to me this time."

Saint yanks my clothing off, roughly tearing it from my body without hesitation until I'm naked and breathless in his arms. Then he spins me around and shoves me face-first against the wall, bringing my palms flat on either side of my face, and kicking my legs wider, spread to him. At his mercy.

Fuck. My pulse leaps at the steely dominance, but I'm so far gone, it only makes me want it more.

I try to buck back against him, but Saint pins me in place. "Don't move," he growls, and I answer with a moan as he fists my hair in one hand, dragging my head to one side to expose the long column of my throat. "Don't you fucking move."

He licks up my neck, nipping as he goes, the rough graze of teeth on my skin making my skin prickle with an unfamiliar cocktail: pleasure and pain, breathless anticipation edged with just a little dash of fear.

What does he want from me? What is he trying to prove?

"Do you understand what you do to me?" Saint demands, almost frenzied. He thrusts against me from behind, and I can feel the hard ridge of his cock through his pants, grinding against my ass, pinning me to the wall. I struggle in his arms, but he doesn't loosen his fierce grip on me. "Fuck, Tessa . . . I lose my mind when you even walk into the bloody room . . . And when I'm inside that tight cunt . . ." He sounds a tortured groan, thrusting hard against me again. "I could die from the feel of your pussy going off and count myself a happy man."

"So fuck me," I beg, gasping. Aching and desperate for his cock. "Fuck me, Saint. I *need* you."

"Yes, you do," he growls. "You can take a fucking wrecking ball to my life without thinking twice, but when it's just us, baby, you know I'm the one in charge."

Saint suddenly pulls me off the wall and pushes me to my knees. "So follow a fucking order," he demands, stripping open his pants and freeing his thick, straining erection. "Be a good girl for five goddamn minutes and suck my cock."

He doesn't even wait for an answer. He grabs my hair and drags me closer, gripping his cock in his other hand and slapping it against my cheek. My mouth falls open in shock—and lust. *God, yes.* I eagerly open wider and suck his cockhead deep between my lips.

"Fuck, that's it . . ." Saint groans, sinking into my mouth. I barely have time to gasp for air before he's thrusting deeper, *fuck,* so deep I'm almost choking on his cock. I try to pull away, gagging, but he holds me in place with an iron grip on my scalp.

"No baby, you don't get your way this time." Saint's voice is steely, and when I look up, I see his face is set with a new kind of determination; a desperate control, as if he's trying to prove something to himself, not me. "You'll take what I have to give you and say thank you like a good girl."

He thrusts again, deeper, over and over until it's all I can do just to keep my mouth open and let him fuck it, as the heat coils tighter in my belly, *God,* my whole body, until I'm trembling with need and Saint finally pulls me off with a lewd, wet pop.

I gasp for air, reeling. I've never seen him like this before, so forcefully dominant. It makes me so turned on I'm already drenched and sticky between my thighs, aching for a touch.

"What do you say?" Saint reminds me, still gripping my hair tightly.

"Th-thank you," I manage, thrilling at my own submission.

He doesn't reward my obedience, though. He just pulls me to my feet and throws me down face-first on the bed.

"I bet you're already wet for me. Yes, look at you," Saint hisses in satisfaction, gripping each of my ankles and spreading my legs. I whimper into the sheets as he yanks me back to the very edge of the bed and steps between them. "You want me to touch you, baby?" he croons, leaning over me. "You want me to play with that sweet clit of yours until you're whining, maybe lick it a little and show you just how good it can feel?"

"Yes," I sob, lost in the inferno. Writhing, bucking against the sheets just to get some purchase. Anything. "Please, Saint . . ."

"No."

He slams into me without warning, gripping my hips tightly and thrusting balls-deep, until he's buried to the hilt.

I scream, consumed with the friction, split open and somehow clenching for more all at once. "Saint!"

My voice echoes, shockingly desperate, and Saint answers with his own fevered cry.

"Fuck, baby, I know. I know . . ."

He places one hand on my lower back, almost tender, and then fucks into me so hard, I think I'm about to pass out from the glorious force of it.

Holy shit!

I scream into the sheets again, or maybe I didn't stop; everything's a blur to me now. The world falls away. I can't even form words. Nothing matters except the weight of him bearing down on me, and the thick, sweet drive of his cock, over and over, relentlessly sending me to heaven with every grinding thrust.

It's a miracle. A religious experience, being fucked by this man. *Claimed.* And God, I don't want it to end, but already I feel my climax curling deep at the base of my spine, making me writhe and moan aloud.

"Yeah, that's it, baby. You feel that shake, don't you?" Saint lands a stinging slap on my ass. "Your body can't lie to me, can it? Even when your mouth does it so well."

And then he's drawing me up onto my hands and knees, *mounting me*, as he ruts into me from behind; every thick thrust stretching me open, every wild groan sending fire through my blood.

It's too much. Too good.

Fuck.

I break. My orgasm rips through me, shattering what's left of my self-control until I'm screaming, sobbing, shaking in his arms.

And Saint fucks me through it, driving into me with an animalistic passion. His body curls over mine, encircling me, holding me up when I can't take any more; his cock stroking that fire deep inside until another climax rises, unbidden. Roaring towards release.

"Oh God," I throw my head back and whine. "Don't stop!"

"Never," Saint vows with a desperate groan. "Fuck, Tessa, I won't ever stop!"

His movements turn frenzied, and I can't even keep pace anymore. I'm liquid in his arms, limp and gasping, and a captive to the pleasure that breaks over me again, sending me screaming into my next orgasm.

"Fuck!" Saint howls, slamming into my convulsing pussy once, twice more, before he comes into me, exploding with a wild roar.

We collapse together, panting hard.

I'd do anything for you . . .

Saint's words echo in my dazed and blissed-out mind. If I had any doubts that he meant it, he fucked them out of me just now. I'm shaken by the force of his passion—and my pleasure.

There's nothing like it. Nothing could ever come close.

So why can't I let go of this bitter, destructive quest—before it destroys everything that still matters to me in the world?

Why can't I just let myself love him?

Chapter Seventeen
SAINT

How far will I go for this woman?

It's not a hypothetical anymore. She's kidnapped one of my closest friends. Tied him up. Drugged and threatened him.

And what did I do?

I helped her.

Worse still, I don't regret it, not even in the cool morning light of day.

I take a sip of coffee and let out a weary breath, standing on the back terrace, looking out at the calm open fields and woodland. Tessa slept like a lamb; I'm not surprised, after the ravishing I gave her, but I'm the one who lay awake all night, wondering how the fuck I'm going to smooth this over with Max.

Never mind our friendship. Tessa could wind up in prison over the stunt she pulled yesterday. I just have to pray to God that her drugs worked, and Max doesn't remember what happened to him.

What Tessa did—without hesitating for a moment to think of the consequences, for either one of us.

Shit.

I knew she was getting desperate, determined to find Wren's attacker before time ran out. I just didn't think she'd cross the line this far. Or that I'd barrel over it right after her, to hell with the law, or ethics, or anything but giving her everything she wants.

Please, Saint . . .

I'm a strong man. Stubborn, people call me. I don't bend for anyone, but when Tessa looks at me with that desperate expression in her eyes, I can't refuse her. In life. In bed. Buried to the hilt in her sweet cunt, writhing and sobbing for me the way she did last night.

She obeyed me, sure, sinking to her knees and sucking my cock until I was half-crazy; following every furious order of mine, as if somehow that would give me the upper hand again. But I know even making her weep, making her *beg*—legs spread and wet for me, eyes rolled back with pleasure, gorgeous tits shaking with the impact of my thrusts—it's only a momentary dominance. A brief taste of control.

Tessa has been a force to be reckoned with since the first day we met.

It's why I love her so fucking much.

I drain the rest of my coffee and head back inside. I find Max standing in the middle of the kitchen, rubbing his eyes. He looks terrible, despite being passed out for almost twenty-four hours.

I freeze a moment in the doorway, on alert. Does he remember? Is this whole thing about to unravel in epic fashion?

"Christ, my head hurts," Max mumbles. "You got any more of that coffee on?"

"I'll brew a fresh pot," I say carefully, crossing the room. I keep a watchful eye on Max as I set the espresso machine again for him. He leans against the counter, scratching and yawning, reaching for one of the pastries I fetched from the village.

"Fuck, I must be getting old," Max says, shaking his head. "Hangovers never used to kill like this."

A hangover. He doesn't remember.

Thank fuck.

I try to hide my relief and give a sympathetic smile. "You were going pretty hard," I say, resenting the lie, but not seeing another way around it. "We couldn't keep up."

"Yeah . . ." Max trails off, frowning. "Jog my memory, will you? Last night's pretty fuzzy to me."

I laugh again. "What happened to your superhuman partying abilities?" I tease, and Max manages a smile.

"Fuck, I can still drink you under the table any day you choose," he banters back, chewing a pastry. He looks more relaxed now, back to his old self as he wakes up. "Let me guess, you and Tessa quit early to go be boring lovebirds on your own."

"Bingo," I agree, and push a mug of coffee over to him. "But you looked like you were having enough fun for the both of us. Who were those girls?" I add, and he blinks, looking surprised.

"Hell if I know." Max looks around. "I can't even remember how I got over here."

"You drove," I inform him. "Along with a couple of Russian girls. Or maybe they were from Belarus? Anyway, we left you all to it. Looks like they called a car and made their exit before I woke up."

I feel a shot of guilt at the lies, more bracing than the triple espresso, but what can I do? Better that Max thinks he spent the night having a crazy, drug-fueled threesome than tied to a chair in the wine cellar, spilling his secrets on truth serum.

"Now that you mention it, I do remember something like that . . ." Max smirks as Tessa enters the kitchen. She's wet-haired from the shower, wrapped in a fluffy bathrobe. When she sees Max, she freezes, looking to me anxiously.

"I was just telling Max about his partying last night. With the two Russian girls?" I add, giving her a look.

"Right!" she blurts, still on edge. "We couldn't keep up."

"Hey, like I told your man here, you've got to leave it to the experts," Max crows, looking smug now.

"Don't you mean, professionals?" I banter back, relaxing now. He clearly doesn't remember a thing and is buying our story. "Better go check your wallet, mate. Wouldn't be the first time you got a nasty shock come morning."

"Shit, you're right." Max bolts from the room. A moment later, he calls down to us. "All good! My performance must have been reward enough for them."

Tessa hurries closer. "He really doesn't remember?" she asks me quietly.

I shake my head. "Not a thing."

"Thank God," she sighs with clear relief.

"You believe him now, that it wasn't him?" I check. She nods.

"But Saint . . ." Tessa swallows, meeting my eyes. "He was our last suspect. The last of your friends with that tattoo. If he didn't do it, then what happens now?"

I don't have an answer for her. But before I can try and reassure her that we'll figure it out—together—my phone buzzes with a text. And another. And then a call, too.

Tessa frowns as I scoop it up. "What's going on?"

"I don't know. It's from my brother."

I scan the message. For a terrible moment, I wonder if my father has had another heart attack, but then I see it's something else entirely.

"Dr. Valerie DeJonge . . ." I say slowly, staring at the screen.

"What about her?" Tessa asks.

I look up, shaken. "She's dead."

* * *

WE CATCH THE next available flight back to England, arriving at Heathrow in the early afternoon.

"Do you have any more details?" Tessa asks as I check my phone again.

I shake my head. "Robert says it was a car accident. That's all he knows."

"It's all so sudden," she says. "We saw her just a couple of days ago at the Ashford event."

I squeeze her hand. "Are you sure you have to be getting back to Oxford?" I ask, still concerned about how she'll handle the new dead end in our investigation.

But Tessa doesn't mention it. She just sighs, listless. "I can't keep missing tutorials and lectures," she says. "I'll be surprised if my library pass even works anymore. They might already have revoked my access."

"I can call the master of the college. Just say the word. He's a fan," I add.

Which is why I'm still on unofficial leave from my teaching duties, to help out with my family.

Tessa gives a pale smile. "I'll let you know how much trouble I'm in. I might have to take you up on that."

I put her in a car, and then head straight to my parents' London house in Hampstead to find out more. It's a large property near the Heath, with gardens that are my mother's pride and joy. She shows me in, kissing me faintly on the cheek. "It's such a tragedy," she says, outfitted in her usual crisp button-down shirt and wide-legged pants. "And when we're so close to launching the new drug."

"Mother, you can't say that." I blink, surprised by her cool tone about Valerie's death. Could she know about the affair, after all?

"I simply meant it was a shame that she won't see her work come to fruition," my mother says, then furrows her brow. "Why, what did you think I meant?"

"Nothing. Is Dad around?" I ask, changing the subject.

She waves vaguely towards his office at the back of the ground floor. "He's been on the phone all day, trying to reassure investors that this won't disrupt anything. The stress can't be good for him. Remind him to drink his green juice," she adds, calling after me. "And not just pour it in the plant pots like he's been doing all week!"

I head down the hallway and knock on my father's closed door.

"Come in."

I enter and find him wrapping up on a phone call. He nods, gesturing for me to make myself comfortable as he keeps talking, seated in his favorite leather wingback chair.

"No, Lionel, this doesn't change a thing. It's a tragedy, of course, but the research was a team effort. We have an excellent team over there, and we're still right on track for announcement of the trial results . . . Mhmmm . . . Yes, exactly. Give my love to Carole."

He hangs up, meeting my eyes with a sigh. "It's been nonstop all day," he says. "The teams at Ashford, investors, everyone's jumpy about what this means for the company. But I've been telling them everything's fine. She was a talented woman, of course," he adds hurriedly, "but the bulk of her duties were at the start of the project, the Alzheimer's research and drug design. Now that we've completed the trials, there are plenty of other people who can step up and finish the work."

I frown. He's speaking awfully dispassionately about the death of the woman he was sleeping with. The woman he was keeping in luxury, funneling money from the Ashford company accounts.

"So what happened, exactly?" I ask, leaning forwards.

He looks away. "The police said it was an accident. She spun off a wet patch on the road and went straight into a pylon."

It sounds simple enough, but there's something in his expression that makes me pause. "Dad?" I prompt him, and he lets out a sigh.

"She may have been a little . . . emotional. I went over and ended things with her, like you said," he explains. "She turned hysterical, crying and carrying on. I tried to calm her, but she wouldn't listen, so I thought it best that I leave." He sighs again. "I don't know what she was thinking, haring around so late at night. But the police said there were signs she'd been drinking, so . . ." He trails off, and swallows hard. "Tragic. Just tragic."

I sit back. This makes sense, at least. Valerie seemed like a calm, level-headed woman, but if she was angry and distressed, and had been drinking . . . there's no predicting what she might have done.

But still . . . it feels like there's something my father isn't telling me.

He gets up, going to rearrange some papers on his desk. "How was France?" he asks brightly. "Did you and Tessa have a nice break? You shouldn't have cut it short. We've all got things handled here."

The message is clear: subject closed.

"Yes, nice," I reply blandly, getting to my feet. "Thanks."

"Good seeing you, son." He gives a thin smile. "And don't worry about what happened with Valerie. We'll get through it. I promise, nothing's going to spoil this launch."

I show myself out. I shouldn't be surprised by my parents' cool-blooded response to Dr. DeJonge's death. After all, they've put Ashford first my entire life: the family name, our legacy, and the company, too.

Even so, it leaves a bad taste in my mouth. My father looked more relieved than anything else to have Valerie out of the equation again, and all anyone can think about is her death's potential effects on the big new drug announcement. Not the fact that a brilliant woman just passed away too soon, and has probably left a grieving family behind.

But this is the reason I've kept clear of the Ashford business for so long. It has a way of turning you cold inside, making everything second place to what the family needs.

Not me. I know what my first priority is now—and my second and third.

It's Tessa.

Always Tessa.

But as I get on the road and start my drive to Oxford, I remember the desperate fury in her eyes as she interrogated Max—and the way she seemed so defeated this morning, knowing we were back at square one in her investigation. I hate seeing what it's doing to her, this endless battle for the truth. It's tearing her apart inside.

How long can we go on like this?

Chapter Eighteen
TESSA

I wake back in Oxford with a grim weight in the pit of my stomach. I lie there a moment, still half sleeping. The house is quiet, the birds are chirping outside the windows, and cool autumn sun falls through the open drapes. Everything is peaceful and perfect—including the man sleeping beside me with a possessive arm slung over my stomach.

Then it hits me. It's Wren's birthday.

She would have been thirty-one today.

My heart aches.

I see my phone buzzing softly on the bedside table: it's my mom, wanting to video chat. I've been avoiding talking to her for weeks now, just sending breezy messages about how busy I am with studies and having so much fun, but I know today she'll need to talk.

I slip out of bed and into a robe, tiptoeing downstairs to the sunroom. "Hi," I answer, feeling a pang as her familiar face appears on-screen. "You're up late," I add, noting the time difference. "Isn't it midnight there?"

"I couldn't sleep." My mom gives me a warm smile, but I can see the sadness in her eyes. "I thought I'd catch you before you got too busy to talk. How are you?"

I swallow, curling up on the couch. "I don't know yet," I say truthfully. "It just hit me."

"Be kind to yourself today," she says. "The group all tells me it's important to honor your feelings. Don't just try and push through, pretending you're OK."

Her grief group. She started attending it after Wren died, and always tells me how helpful it's been, connecting with other parents who've lost their children. I'm glad she has people to talk to. That she isn't facing this day alone.

"Are you and Dad going to visit her grave today?" I ask. They never found Wren's body. It was lost to the depths of Lake Michigan, but my parents chose a gravestone at the local cemetery all the same, so they could have somewhere to visit her.

Mom nods. "Then we're going to plant a tree for her in the park down the hill. You remember how much you guys loved to play there when you were kids? Well, I talked to the city council, and they approved us planting a memorial tree for her."

I jerk a nod, already feeling the sting of tears welling in the back of my throat. "That's a lovely idea, Mom."

"What about you?" she asks. "You've been so busy. I'm glad. It sounds like you've been having a wonderful time over there."

"Right," I lie, forcing a smile.

"And this man you've been dating, it's going well?" she asks hopefully.

I nod. "It's going great." I haven't told her half of what's happened with Saint, just that I've been dating someone. "He's special, Mom," I add, still feeling that lump in my throat. "He's really been supporting me with everything about Wren."

Interrogating his friends. Hunting down the truth.

But my mom doesn't know just how far Saint's gone for me. She just thinks we're having romantic dinners and snuggling together watching movies at night. "Oh, I'm so glad, sweetie," she exclaims, clearly relieved. "It's a comfort knowing you have someone to lean on. And that you're enjoying your life there, too. I was so worried about you after it happened. I know that you looked up to her so much, but I'm happy to hear that you're building a life of your own."

I swallow hard. What would she think if she knew it was all a lie, that I'm still consumed with Wren's death, chasing her ghost around this city?

"Is Dad there?" I ask instead, and she smiles.

"Oh no, he nodded off hours ago. He's hooked on this new show about a psychic detective. Have you seen it . . . ?"

We chat a while longer about neighborhood gossip and her garden club before she finally yawns and says it's time for her to go to bed. I tell her I love her and say my goodbyes, but after I hang up, I stay sitting there for a while, watching the birds out in the garden.

She's healing.

I can see it in the way she talks, how she's able to share memories and mention Wren without that stricken grief in her eyes. The wound of losing her daughter will never close, but she's finally found a way to put the pieces of her life together and keep going without living in the past.

The way I'm still doing.

There's a tap on the door, and I look over to find Saint standing there, sleep-ruffled in sweatpants and a T-shirt. "Hey," he says softly, and I can see in his eyes that he overheard at least a little of the conversation.

"Hey," I echo.

He sits beside me and puts an arm around my shoulders. I nestle against him, relishing his warm, sturdy embrace. "How's your mum?" he asks softly.

"She's doing OK," I reply, my chest aching. "They're planting a tree today. For Wren."

He squeezes me, supportive. "I can cancel my calls today," he says immediately. "We can stay home or go somewhere. Whatever you want."

I slowly sit up. "It's OK," I say.

Saint gives me a look. "Birthdays are hard. After Edward . . . well, I never knew what to do with myself."

"I don't either," I admit. "That's why I think I should just get through the day. Be normal. I have a ton of lectures, and reading, and I'm late on at least two essays . . ."

Saint frowns. "Are you sure?"

I nod, determined. If I let this grief blossom, even for a moment, I'm worried it'll consume me. "I'll be fine," I lie, giving him a smile. "I'll see you later for dinner. We can talk then."

I get up before he can argue and go to shower and get dressed. He's still looking at me with concern when I return, but luckily, his phone rings, so I just kiss him on the cheek and grab my things before he can say anything. "You should get that. See you later!" I blurt, and bolt from the house.

* * *

It's just a short walk from Saint's place to the center of the city, where the old colleges lie cloistered behind high, ancient walls. I have a nine a.m. lecture on my schedule, so I join the flow of students heading towards the lecture halls.

But something makes me stop.

I stand there at the foot of the steps, watching everyone heading inside. The students are fresh-faced, studious, young and old; gossiping about last night, or anxiously checking for their notes. From the outside, I know I look just like them, with my bag full of books and my college sweatshirt and jeans—but inside, it feels like I'm on the other side of an invisible barrier, watching them all from a distance. The crowd thins out as nine a.m. comes and goes, until only a few last stragglers push past me, rushing to make it on time.

Still, I can't go inside.

What the hell am I even doing here? I came to Oxford for a

reason, to find Wren's attacker, but here I am months later, no closer to the truth.

I've failed her.

I find myself turning and walking away, down the High Street towards the gates of Ashford College. As I enter, my favorite porter, Bates, calls out a greeting, but I barely manage a limp wave, still in a kind of daze. I wander past the lush quad and through the drafty cloisters, out to the back lawns and the path that winds by the river, leading out through the woodland to the very edge of the Ashford grounds.

I've failed her.

All this searching, the risks and betrayals, and I still have nothing to show for it. I upended my life, traveled thousands of miles from home, and enrolled here under false pretenses. And for what? Nothing but false starts, red herrings, and dead ends. The Blackthorn Society clues led me to Saint and his friends, but I've checked out every one of the men who had the crown tattoo, and they all have iron-clad alibis for the weekend Wren was held. Saint was out of the country. Sebastian Wolfe was in New York. Max Lancaster was fucking his fiancée's teenage cousin. Hugh Ambrose was addressing a conference in Stockholm.

None of them took her, and now I have no more leads left to chase. It could have been anyone with that tattoo—if Wren even remembered it right at all through her splintered memories and drugged-up haze.

Where does that leave me?

My phone buzzes in my pocket. It's Saint. "Just checking to see how you're doing," he says, his voice low and steady. "You rushed out of here so fast."

"I'm fine," I reply, except it comes out as a sob.

"Oh, baby," Saint says softly. "It's alright. Where are you?"

I look around, sniffing. "The riverwalk, at Ashford."

"I'll be right there."

I find a shady spot on the riverbank and sink down to wait, leaning against a tree. It's not long before Saint appears and settles beside me, sprawling his long limbs on the leafy ground. "You picked a good spot."

"For my minor meltdown?" I try to joke.

"To remember her," Saint says softly. "I used to walk along here, too. It's peaceful. Edward would always tell me how important it was to meditate and spend time in nature," he adds with an affectionate eye roll.

I smile. "Wren was like that, too. She had her mindfulness podcasts and self-care routines. She would always send me these links about how the brain responds to trees and sunlight, as her subtle way of telling me to get my ass off the couch."

Saint chuckles. "You know, they probably would have gotten along."

"Yes. They would have." I exhale, wistful. "It's such a waste. That they're not here with us. That I can't talk to her anymore."

"Of course you can," Saint says, and I look over in surprise. "You just can't expect her to talk back," he adds with a wry smile. "But I talk to Edward all the time, telling him about what's going on. Imagining what he'd say in response. Usually tell me to shape up and settle down." He grins.

I smile back. "Wren was the opposite," I say softly. "She wanted me to have big adventures. Travel the world, and fall in and out of love, and do amazing, impulsive things."

"You still can," he says, watching me. "You can do anything."

"Except find the man who did this to her," I point out. "The one thing I promised myself I would. I don't know what to do next, Saint," I add, hopeless. "How are we supposed to track him down? I've been searching, used every last piece of information, and I still have nothing!"

"You have me," Saint says immediately, taking my hand. I grip it tightly, like a safety rope keeping me from the undertow. "Look,

I know you've been determined to find answers, and if you want to keep searching, then I'm with you all the way," Saint ventures, concern clear on his chiseled face. "But when do you draw the line? What if there's nothing left here for you to find?"

His question lingers on the riverbank between us, confirming all my secret fears. Ever since Max ruled himself out of the suspect list, I've wondered how I'm supposed to continue the hunt, facing dead ends at every turn. Am I going to search the rest of my life for a monster who may well be long gone?

And if I do end the search, will I be haunted with guilt and regret?

"What would I even do?" I ask, lost at the idea. My quest for justice has been driving me for so long, I can hardly imagine any other way. "Go back to the States?"

Saint shakes his head. "You could stay and build a life here in England."

Again, I try to picture it. "I don't belong here at Oxford," I tell him. "I can't keep up with the work. I don't even want to. I just stood outside my lecture this morning; I couldn't even bring myself to go inside."

"So don't." Saint shrugs. "Quit."

I marvel at his casual tone. "Just like that?"

He smiles. "You were only here at Ashford College to retrace Wren's steps. And I'm only here these days because I want to be close to you. So move in with me, in London. I love you, Tessa," he adds, and my heart swells in surprise at the words. "I want a future with you. But this isn't about me. You deserve a future, too. You already have a great job you love at the Ambrose Foundation, helping people there, making a real difference. You could start fresh," he says, softly cupping my cheek. "Build a life for yourself this time, not just following in Wren's footsteps . . ."

I inhale, hearing the possibility in his words.

"My visa . . ." I start to say, but Saint just smirks.

"That's not a problem. My lawyers can handle it, or the foundation will sponsor you. Either way, you're staying. If you want to . . ."

I do.

I can picture it already, life here, with Saint. Waking up together at his house in Kensington, chatting over morning coffee, before I take the Tube across town to the foundation offices. Working with Priya and the team on meaningful, worthwhile projects, then rendezvousing with Saint for a romantic dinner somewhere. We would spend our weekends exploring London: taking in a movie on Southbank, strolling in Hyde Park, exploring the Portobello market . . . And every night, exploring each other.

No more secrets or hidden agendas; no more searching the world with suspicion, haunted by the past. A fresh start, like he said. Just the two of us.

I want it all. The longing rolls through me with a sudden, bone-deep ache.

"I need to think about it," I blurt, feeling overwhelmed, and Saint gives me a smile.

"Of course. I'll just have to do my best to convince you," he adds, the smile turning playful. "Show off all the perks you'd be getting as part of the deal."

"I like the sound of that," I tease, snuggling against him. "Breakfast in bed?"

"Always."

"What about foot rubs?"

"I'll need an excuse to keep my hands *off* you."

* * *

WE SIT A while longer by the riverbank, watching the sunlight play on the water and the ducks gliding by. Saint doesn't mention his proposition again, just asks me about Wren and some of my favorite memories with her, and listens while I talk. It helps, talking like this. I know he understands what I'm going through, trying to navigate the path between honoring someone I loved and releasing the past to be able to move on.

When it finally gets too chilly to stay, we walk home hand in hand on the cobbled streets. Oxford already looks a little more magical, and with every step, I can feel the weight that's been anchored around my heart start to ease.

Starting to let me go.

"Are you hungry?" Saint asks as we arrive at the house. "I could rustle up some lunch. We've got the leftovers from the roast chicken, and—"

I cut him off with a kiss.

After all this talking, I just want to feel close to him. To be with him in a way that isn't about distraction or escape, but about *us*. The future he's offered me; the one my heart already aches to accept.

So I kiss him. Both arms wrap around his neck, my body pressing closer, my mouth trying to tell him all the things I haven't yet found a way to say.

He knows.

Saint wraps his arms around me, holding me tightly, deepening the kiss until my head is spinning and I'm gasping for more. He pulls back then and takes my hand, leading me upstairs to the bedroom without a word.

He undresses me slowly, unhurried in the afternoon light. I savor every touch, running my hands over the broad planes of his body, peeling away every layer between us until we're both naked, my breath quickening as the heat starts to curl inside, wanting. *Needing him.*

Still, we take our time.

Saint lays me on the bed, covering my whole body in a trail of featherlight kisses, licking and teasing my breasts and stomach; trailing hot breath over the inside of my thighs, worshipping every inch of me until I'm trembling with desire. I moan, reveling in the slow, sweet caresses, arching up in pleasure as his mouth finally suckles at my core.

"Saint . . ." I gasp as his tongue laps over me, soft and insistent, lavishing my clit until I feel my body start to rise. I grip his shoulder, pulling him up. "You," I moan, already sliding my hands over him, finding the sculpted curve of his ass and pulling him into the cradle of my hips. I'm wet, aching, so ready for his cock. "I need all of you."

"You have me." Saint settles between my thighs, bracing himself above me with his eyes fixed on mine.

He sinks into me slowly, inch by devastating inch.

Oh my God . . .

I moan in sheer pleasure, arching up to meet him; take him all the way inside. It feels different this time. Deeper. *More intense.* Our eyes stay locked on each other, and the intimacy takes my breath away. I can see the fierce passion burning in his eyes, the aching tenderness in every motion as he bears down, sheathing himself to the hilt.

I clench around him, and he growls, low and ragged. "Christ, baby . . ."

It's bliss. Saint starts to move, grinding his cock inside me in slow, luxurious strokes, and it's all I can do to hold on for dear life, sobbing with pleasure in his arms. Fuck, I've never felt like this before: So connected. So perfect.

I love you.

It's only when Saint's eyes flash in wonder that I realize I've said it out loud.

"I love you too, baby," he murmurs, dropping kisses on my mouth as his cock drives me wild. "Fuck, Tessa, there's nobody else . . . I'm yours."

Mine.

I hold him tighter, wrapping myself around him, losing myself in the slick thrust of our bodies and the race of my heartbeat; the pure white-hot pleasure rising up, blotting out the world.

"Saint," I gasp, shaking, strung out on the edge of the drop.

"I've got you, baby," he vows, plunging into me again, never breaking pace, taking me those final glorious inches to oblivion. "You can let go. Let it all go for me. *Come.*"

His ragged order shatters through me, and I break apart with a cry. My orgasm sweeps through me as Saint finds his climax; bright like sunlight in my veins, it chases all the shadows and darkness away, flooding my body with a pure, perfect radiance until I'm left gasping in his arms. Golden and glowing.

Cleansed.

I look over at Saint, collapsed on the bed beside me. His eyes are shut, eyelashes thick on his cheeks under damp, tousled hair. He always looks one step away from sin, but right now his smile is so wide, there's no mistaking his happiness.

God, I love this man.

And just like that, the future seems so simple. "Yes," I whisper, nestling closer.

"Give me five minutes, darling," he replies with a smirk.

I laugh. "Yes to moving in with you."

Saint's eyes fly open. He turns his head, searching my face. "Are you sure?"

I nod. "I'm sure about us," I whisper, lacing my fingers through his and placing our hands together over his heart. "I want to make a future with you. I want to be happy." I take a deep breath.

"It's time I let Wren go."

Chapter Nineteen
TESSA

O nce my decision is made, everything falls into place. I sit
down with the administrator at Ashford and tell them
about my decision to leave, saying just that the academic pressure is too much for me, and I don't want to waste anyone's
time.

Not surprisingly, nobody asks me to reconsider.

I don't have much stuff, and most of my clothes are still at
Saint's place in London, so I barely have a couple of bags to pack
before Saint loads up his car and we make our drive down to
London, watching the dreaming spires of the city recede in the
rearview mirror for the last time. It's a crisp, blue-skied day when
we arrive, and I take it as a good omen.

It's the start of a brand-new chapter—one where I can hopefully leave the anger and bitterness of the past behind, forging a
new future for myself.

For us.

"What do you think?" Saint asks on Saturday, showing me the
space he's made in the walk-in closet. "If it's not enough room,
you can use the bedroom down the hall as a dressing room."

"For what?" I protest, laughing. I'm dressing for the dinner
party he's throwing tonight—I mean, *we're* throwing. Guests
will be arriving soon, but Saint distracted me in the shower long

enough that we're both running late now. "I barely have enough stuff to fill a single rail."

"Yet," Saint says with a mischievous smirk. "I bet one more trip to Bond Street with Imogen will take care of that."

"You're not buying me more clothes," I warn him as I shimmy into a pair of jeans and a drapey cashmere sweater. "You've already been way too generous . . ."

The free rent. All my expenses. Not to mention the lawyer to deal with my British visa.

"I don't know what you're talking about." Saint tries to look innocent. He's dressed down tonight, in dark jeans and a casual sweater, but with his tousled hair damp and his eyes sparkling with mischief, innocent is a long way off. "Besides, you're the one with the steady job now," he reminds me. "I'm just a former professor, mooching off my trust fund."

"Because future dukes really mooch," I tease, laughing.

"In a long tradition," Saint assures me. "It's what we do best."

He draws me into a kiss, slow and heated. "I forget where we were up to," he muses, moving to nuzzle at my neck as his hands skim lower. "The guest bathroom? The stairs?"

He insisted we christen every room in the house to celebrate me moving in.

"We already did the stairs," I remind him, breathless from his teasing caress. "Twice."

"You know what they say." Saint reaches for my zipper. "Third time's the charm—"

We're interrupted by the doorbell. "Later," I promise, dancing out of reach. "Go play host, while I try and make my hair look like you weren't just doing unspeakable things to me up against the shower wall!"

* * *

I PULL MYSELF together and go join Saint downstairs as more people arrive. Before long, the small garden is filled with chat and laughter, lit up with twinkling tea lights and candles as we enjoy a lavish spread of food and wine.

"Catered, I hope?" Imogen teases Saint, and he groans.

"Tell them, Tessa. I'm a perfectly capable chef."

"Capable of spending four hours assembling this lasagna?" I tease him lightly.

He grins, slipping an arm around my shoulder. "OK, maybe I do have better things to do with my time . . ."

I smile. It's just a small group—Imogen, Annabelle and Max, Hugh and his date, plus a few new faces besides—but I feel right at home, sitting beside Saint, stealing food from his plate. It's a relief to look around the table and not have to view anyone with wariness and doubt; see everyone here as friends, not suspects, now that I've confirmed everyone's alibis.

"Time for a toast for our guest of honor!" Annabelle announces, beaming. "I'm so excited for you and Saint . . . and for you to join my bachelorette party!"

There's a chorus of groans. "Not everything is about the wedding," Imogen comments, looking amused.

"I just mean, I'm excited for us to be friends," Annabelle protests. "But Tessa, seriously, this is perfect timing. My friend from boarding school just broke her ankle, and that cast would have *ruined* the photos, but now you can take her place! We have the girls' tea, the spa trip, then our glam squad run-through—"

"The happiest day of your life, they said," Max interrupts, sardonic. "More like the most mind-numbing six months of your life!"

"Aww, you love me really," Annabelle coos, leaning over and kissing him on the lips.

"I suppose I do." Max makes a show of rolling his eyes and smirking, draping an arm around her shoulder.

I feel a twinge of guilt. Thanks to that truth serum, I now

know Max's dirty little secret. It's the last thread from my investigations still holding me back, and I'm still not sure if I should say anything to Annabelle about it.

"But back to Tessa." Hugh takes up the toast. "I think I speak for everyone here when I say I never thought this day would come. Anthony St. Clair, in a stable, committed relationship." Saint laughs easily beside me at the cheers, raising his glass. "But we're so glad you came along and brought him to his knees."

"Hear hear!"

I laugh along, giving Saint a mischievous smile. "Did you hear that?" I murmur softly, so only he can hear. "They know you like it on your knees . . ."

He grins back. "Only for you, darling. Just say the word."

His fingertips graze soft circles on the nape of my neck, and I shiver with delicious anticipation.

"Time for a bathroom break," Annabelle announces, bobbing to her feet. "Come on, Tessa, I want to tell you about an amazing interior designer I know. She would work wonders with this place."

"Not so fast," Saint protests. "What's wrong with my house?"

"Nothing, except it's so masculine and dreary."

"You mean classic."

Annabelle waves a hand, dismissing him. "You'll learn soon enough to just agree on these things. It's so much easier when they don't put up a fight," she adds.

"But much less fun," Saint says, shooting me a smoldering look. He pinned me down over the arm of the couch this morning, and teased my clit relentlessly until I was spitting mad and ready to claw his eyes out—and then I came so hard, I swear I almost passed out.

I clear my throat, blushing, and follow Annabelle into the house, but she must have caught the look, because she grins. "The honeymoon phase is the best, when you just can't keep your hands off each other."

"It's . . . nice," I agree. Understatement of the year. "Especially living together now, we can really just relax and enjoy each other without it feeling so temporary."

"If you want permanent, just wait until he puts a rock on it!"

I blush again. "I don't know about that."

"Well, I do, and that man is smitten as a kitten."

I pause, idly clearing some glassware in the kitchen as Annabelle ducks into one of the bathrooms downstairs. I'm trying to think of a way to broach what I found out from Max—or if I even should. I know that if our positions were traded, I would want to know he had a secret child stashed away before I walked down the aisle and said "I do." But Annabelle has always seemed to have a different kind of view on things.

Would I be sticking my nose in where it's not wanted?

I wait until she reemerges and browses Saint's wine collection to select another bottle. "It was fun hanging out in France," I say casually. "Maybe a little too much fun."

Annabelle trills a laugh. "Max needs to let off steam from time to time, that's all. No harm, no foul. Isn't that what you Americans say?"

I wouldn't exactly call a love child no foul, but before I can think of how to raise the subject, Annabelle looks over. "Did I tell you my father and Cyrus Lancaster are in business together?"

I blink. "No, you didn't."

"Daddy's business was going under last year, and Cyrus bailed him out with a big investment. They're thick as thieves now, can't wait for the wedding. It's the title, you see." She smirks. "As much as Cyrus likes to make a to-do about being a self-made man, he's simply gaga at the thought that his grandchildren will be in line for the English throne. That's why I know I can depend on Max never to embarrass me," she adds, giving me a pointed look. "He'll always do whatever it takes to clean up his messes and keep his father happy. Which keeps me happy. Ooh, a '97 Dom!"

Before I can process her words, she brandishes a bottle, all smiles. "We should get back," she says, sunny. "Heaven knows what they're up to without us."

She links her arm through mine and steers me back out to the garden. They've moved to the couches by the firepit, and I slide into a spot beside Saint, relishing the warmth of his embrace.

"Everything alright?" he asks, checking in.

I nod, because it is. Annabelle's made it clear in her own way that she knows Max has some scandals hidden in the closet—and she doesn't want them dragged into the light of day. I don't really understand it, but I have to respect her choice. And feel a wave of relief that the last unfinished business hanging over me can be set aside.

The future feels wide-open.

"It's supposed to rain tomorrow," I tell Saint, nestling closer. I think of snug afternoons by the fire, and walking by the river, bundled up against the wind. "What do you want to do?"

"You," he murmurs, giving me a smoldering look. I laugh.

"All day?"

"All week. All year," he says, tilting my face up and claiming a kiss, making my head spin. The others hoot and jeer good-naturedly.

"I'd say get a room, but you already did," Hugh teases when we finally surface again.

"You're right. Get out, the lot of you." Saint rises to his feet. "Party's over!"

I think he's joking, until he suddenly hoists me over his shoulder in a fireman's lift and strides towards the house. "Show yourselves out!" he calls behind us. "We're otherwise occupied!"

"Saint!" I laugh in protest, swinging upside down as he carries me inside. "We can't just leave our own party!"

"Why not?" Saint climbs the stairs and sets me down in the guest room, right-way up. "We can do whatever we damn well like."

In an instant, he's got me backed up against the wall, my wrists pinned by my sides and my body trapped against his. My pulse kicks, desire igniting in my blood. "They'll all know that you're . . . you know . . ." I blush deeper.

"Going to rip your panties off and lick that delicious pussy until you're screaming?"

Saint sinks to his knees, already undoing my jeans. *Dear God*, he looks unspeakably hot undressing me. I sink back against the wall, my legs turning weak. The bedroom door is still wide-open, and I can hear everyone's voices in the garden below through the open window, getting ready to leave.

They'll know . . .

The knowledge is hot and thrilling, and I can't help but give a whimper as Saint yanks my panties down and dips his fingers between my legs, finding me wet and aching for him.

"That's right . . ." He looks up, giving me a smirk that makes my stomach curl. "You like having an audience, don't you, baby? If you moan nice and loud, they'll all hear exactly how much you love my tongue in your cunt."

He sets his mouth to me, licking and suckling, and *fuck*, I have to shove a fist in my mouth to keep from crying out in pleasure.

It's too good. The feel of his tongue probing into me, the heady risk of that open door . . . Excitement glitters like a drug in my bloodstream, and soon I'm clutching his hair, gripping tightly, bucking shamelessly against his mouth as I chase the incredible high, stifling my whimpers until I can't hold back anymore, and I come—*fuck*—I come screaming his name, not caring who hears me.

Not caring about anything but the pleasure shattering through me, a high I'll never match.

"That's my good girl . . ." Saint licks me through it, until I'm just about ready to collapse in his arms. He gets to his feet and throws me down on the bed, already tearing off his clothes. I can't hear anything from the garden anymore, and I pray to God everyone's left by now, because the look in Saint's eyes can only be described as ravenous as he frees his cock and fists the hard length.

"But that was only the warm-up," he says, advancing. "And when I tell you I want the whole fucking neighborhood to hear you take this cock, I mean it. Spread those legs and scream for me, baby."

So I do.

* * *

TWO HOURS AND five wild orgasms later, I'm surprised nobody's called the cops with a noise complaint. "Your neighbors are going to hate me," I laugh breathlessly, naked and sweaty in his arms.

"Are you kidding? They're all jerking off to the sound of you," Saint replies, lazily stroking circles on my spine.

I shiver at the idea, and he chuckles. "Oh, really?" He rolls over, facing me with a smirk. "You like that, huh?"

"Maybe . . ." I smile back, loving how in tune he is with all my secret desires.

"I'll have to keep that in mind," Saint says slowly, and I can already see his filthy, magnificent mind working overtime. "I'm sure something could be arranged at the club . . ."

I let out a sigh of satisfaction, which turns into a yawn.

"Go to sleep," he says, dropping a tender kiss on my forehead. "It's been a long day."

"But all the mess downstairs . . ."

"I'll deal with it in the morning."

"Shit," I realize, looking around. "I left my phone outside."

"I'll get it," Saint offers, but I slip out of bed.

"I need to grab some water, too. I'll be right back."

I grab a robe, then pad barefoot downstairs. Some organized angel—Imogen, probably—brought in most of the dishes and glassware and stacked them in the kitchen. I blush again, remembering our unceremonious exit from the party, but my body is still humming with such satisfaction, I can't find it in myself to feel ashamed.

They're probably used to Saint's wild antics by now.

Outside, the garden is dark, and I wish I knew where the light panel is as I hunt around in the shadows for my phone. Wasn't it somewhere here by the firepit—

There's a sudden rattling noise from the far end of the garden. I freeze.

It's pitch-black, and I can't see anything but shadows. My skin prickles, an icy trickle of awareness running down my spine.

Then another noise comes, the thud of someone knocking into something—and the skitter of hurried footsteps.

Somebody's here.

My heart races.

"Hello?" I call out, trying to stay calm. "Is anyone there?"

There's no reply as I edge closer, peering into the dark. Maybe an animal's trapped, or has built some kind of nest—

"Shhh, don't scream."

A voice emerges from the dark, so familiar that I swear I'm hearing things.

It can't be . . .

Then the intruder steps out of the shadows, and my heart stops beating in my chest.

"No . . ." I whisper, standing there in total disbelief.

"Yes. It's me, Tessa," the ghost replies.

But somehow, it's not a ghost. It's not a dream. Because the woman I'm staring at, I've known since the first day I drew breath. I would recognize her anywhere, even skulking in the shadows with dyed hair and anxious eyes, a year after I wept at her funeral and said goodbye for the last time.

Not dead. Not gone. Here.

Wren.

Acknowledgments

A huge thanks to Alessandra Roche and May Chen, and everyone at Avon. To my team standing on business: Gary Ungar, Tanya Mallean, Anthony Colletti, and Sue Carls, Berni Vann, and the team at CAA.

To my cheerleaders and confidantes, Elizabeth L, Ava H, Ally C, Elisabeth D, Riann S, Ann M, Zach A.

And finally, to everyone in the BookTok community for championing these books. I love your smutty minds.

TO BE CONTINUED . . .

What happens next? Check out this sneak
peek of the explosive conclusion of Tessa
and Saint's thrilling love story in

Seal My Fate

the final book in the Oxford Legacy trilogy,
coming in April 2025!

Chapter One
TESSA

"Where the hell are you?" I mutter, searching the dark garden for my cellphone. I'm naked beneath my robe, with a hot man waiting for me in bed; the last thing I want is to be on my hands and knees, hunting around the patio furniture.

Not when I could be on my hands and knees for him . . .

I smile, unable to keep the delighted beam off my face. Moving in with Saint is a major step, but already, it feels like home here, with him. And after everything we've been through in the past months—all the suspicion and doubt—it's a relief to finally be able to breathe easy and know everything is finally settled and—

There's a sudden rattling noise from the far end of the garden, then the skitter of footsteps. I freeze.

Somebody's there.

"Hello?" I call out, trying to stay calm.

There's no reply as I edge closer, peering into the dark. Maybe an animal's trapped there, or has built some kind of nest—

"Shhh, don't scream."

A voice emerges from the dark, so familiar that I swear I'm hearing things.

It can't be . . .

Then the intruder steps out of the shadows, and my heart stops beating in my chest.

"No . . ." I whisper, standing there in total disbelief.

"Yes. Tessa, it's me," the ghost replies.

But somehow, it's not a ghost. It's not a dream. Because the woman I'm staring at I've known since the first day I drew breath. I would recognize her anywhere, even skulking in the shadows with dyed hair and anxious eyes, a year after I wept at her funeral and said goodbye for the last time.

Not dead. Not gone. Here.

My sister.

"Wren?" I gasp, frozen in place. Blood pounds in my ears, and I feel like I'm going to pass out. "How? How is this possible—"

"Shh!" She grabs my hand and yanks me into the shadows, sending a fearful look towards the house. "Keep your voice down. We don't have long."

"But . . . I don't understand . . ."

I stare at her, still not sure this is real. *How can this be real?* "You're dead," I blurt, gripping her arm. I clutch her, my legs weak. "You died, Wren. You walked into the water and left a note and never came back. What are you doing here? How could you—"

"I said quiet!" Wren hushes me again. "We can't talk here," she says, already pulling away from me. "I'm sorry, I know this is a lot, but there isn't time to explain. Meet me tomorrow."

"What? Wren, no—" I try to hold on to her, like this is a dream that I'll wake from, but Wren wrenches back.

"I'm sorry, Tessa, but you have to trust me," she says, glancing around again. Skittish. *Afraid.* "Tomorrow, two o'clock. There's a pub in Hackney called the Two Hearts. I'll be there. I'll explain everything, I swear."

I stare at her, open-mouthed, still numb with shock.

"But, Tessa, you can't tell anyone," Wren whispers urgently. "Not even Saint. *Especially* not Saint. Promise me."

I shake my head dumbly. "Wren, no. This is crazy. Just come inside. We can talk—"

"No!" Her eyes flare with panic. She grips me by my shoulders and stares into my eyes, desperate. "You can't tell. Promise me! *Please.*"

I stutter. I've never seen her like this before, even in the worst of her downward spiral, when she was self-destructing and barely keeping it together. There's something raw and wild in her eyes, like a caged animal willing to do whatever it takes to save itself.

"Trust me, Tessie." Her gaze turns pleading. "For old time's sake. I swear, I'll explain everything. You just have to trust me on this. Pinky swear?"

She holds up her little finger, the way we always did when we were kids. It was a sister thing, rare and precious, and only meant for the most important kind of promises. Like when I wanted to sneak out with my friends to a rock show in the next town, or Wren accidentally scraped the paint on our parents' old Honda.

It seems absurd to be doing it here, in the dark shadows of Saint's garden, when my sister has just come back from the dead. But the old gesture pierces through my shock and confusion, and I can't help holding my own pinky up to link with hers.

"Promise," I echo, still stunned.

"Good." Relief flashes across her face, and then she's backing away, into the shadows. "Tomorrow," she whispers. "It'll all make sense."

And then she's melting into the dark as if she'd never been there at all, leaving me standing there in the middle of the yard, my head spinning with a thousand questions as I struggle to process the impossible.

She's back. Wren's alive. As if my prayers have all been answered. All year I've been wracked with guilt, tormented by grief; I would have done anything to have my sister back again . . .

And now I do.

So why is she so scared? What—or *who*—has she been hiding from?

What the hell is going on?

Chapter Two
TESSA

I lay in bed awake all night, unable to sleep for even a second. My mind is still reeling, and my emotions ricochet from joy to anger and back again a thousand times over.

What happened to you, Wren? What the hell have you put us through?

The minute dawn breaks outside the windows, I slip out of bed and into the bathroom, but even the sharp shock of an ice-cold shower can't snap me out of my confusion. Wren hid from me. She lied. We grieved her, all of us, Mom and Dad and—God, do they know? How could she do this to them? Why would she torment us all like this, when all the while, she's been alive?

When all this time, I've been trying to avenge her death.

"Morning, sunshine," Saint greets me as I reenter the bedroom. He's sprawled in bed, looking sleepy and handsome with his dark hair rumpled and his plush mouth curled in a grin. As he sees me, wet from the shower and wrapped only in a towel, his smile grows. "Damn, if I knew what moving in with you would be like, I'd have done it eons ago."

I muster a faint smile. "You didn't know me eons ago," I correct him lightly. "And asking me to live with you the first day we met wouldn't exactly have played too great. We're moving fast enough as it is," I add.

Saint searches my face, as if intuiting my mood. "No morning-after regrets, I hope?"

"No," I say immediately, crossing to the bed. I lean over and drop a kiss on his lips. "No, I'm happy to be here."

At least I had been, up until the moment last night when Wren turned my whole world upside down.

"Good." Saint gives me a lazy grin and reaches up to stroke my damp skin. "Because I'm not hauling any more boxes for you, baby. So it looks like you're stuck with me."

"What boxes?" I tease. "I had all of two suitcases, thank you very much. I travel light."

"Not anymore." Saint suddenly pulls me into his lap and wraps his arms around me. "You travel with me now," he promises, his mouth humming against the sensitive point right above my collarbone. "First class all the way."

He pulls my towel open, already skimming his hands over my curves as his mouth moves to claim mine in a slow, heated kiss. My body reacts to him in an instant, the way it always does, but my mind is a million miles away, still fixed on Wren's cryptic comments.

You can't tell anyone . . . especially not Saint.

What did she mean? Why can't anyone know she's really alive? How can I keep this from him?

Luckily, his phone buzzes loudly on the nightstand, interrupting us. "You should get that!" I blurt, slipping out of his embrace.

Saint gives a rueful laugh, checking the screen. "It's work. Hold that thought," he adds as he answers. I quickly move to the massive walk-in closet and dress for the day in good jeans and a button-down. By the time I emerge, he's just finishing up.

"Be there soon."

"Ashford emergency?" I ask lightly, as he gets out of bed and stretches. Even in my anxious state, I can't help but admire the sight of his body, lean and powerful, carved like one of Rodin's finest masterpieces—and capable of bringing me to the height of pleasure over and over again.

"It's all an emergency these days," Saint replies, playfully rolling his eyes. He catches me for another quick kiss, before grabbing some clothing for himself. "All hands on deck," he reports, dressing. "Apparently, the peer review results for the Alzheimer's drug trials are publishing in a matter of days. And our sources on the review board say it's good news."

"That's huge," I blink. Wren worked on an early phase of the drug trials, and I know that Saint's family company, Ashford Pharmaceuticals, has everything riding on their success.

"Huge? It's going to change the face of modern medicine," Saint enthuses. "I mean, not just for the millions of families who won't have to watch their loved ones slip away from them, but beyond that, the roads it opens up for treating other neurological diseases . . ." He looks thrilled. "You know, all this time I've been pushing back so hard against my family legacy, resisting being the dutiful son and heir, but now . . . now I feel proud that Ashford could be making a difference like this. Actually doing good. And, of course, making a stinking great profit, as I'm sure my father would remind me," he adds with a wry smile.

"Can't forget about that part," I agree. It's amazing news, and I wish I could be more present to celebrate with him, but a part of me is already anxiously eyeing the clock, counting down to my meeting with Wren.

"You want to get lunch?" he asks. "I'm sure I could sneak away long enough to toast with you."

"I, umm . . ." I rack my brains for an excuse, still distracted.

Saint notices. He steps closer and tenderly cups my cheek, searching my face. "Are you OK?" he asks, concerned. "You've been quiet since the party last night. Not too overwhelming, I hope? Everyone was just teasing, talking about boring domesticity," he adds. "I promise there'll be nothing boring about our living together."

I quickly force a laugh. "I know. I'm fine," I lie, glancing away. "There have just been a lot of big changes for me recently. I'm still catching up. Dropping out of my studies at Oxford, moving in here with you, starting full-time at the Ambrose Foundation . . ."

"And giving up on your quest to avenge Wren," Saint finishes softly.

I jerk a nod, feeling guiltier than ever for keeping this from him. The whole reason Wren spiraled—the whole reason I thought she'd killed herself—was because of a brutal, twisted attack that happened last year in Oxford. I swore I would find who was responsible, and Saint has been by my side every step of the way in my search for Wren's attacker. He's risked it all to investigate his friends and help me bring about justice for her death.

And now she's not dead. Everything in me wants to tell him.

But I promised her. Pinky swore.

And until I know what's going on—how this impossible situation has come to be—I owe her my loyalty, even if it's eating me up inside.

"I'll settle in soon," I tell Saint brightly, and he must be reassured by my act because he smiles, and releases me.

"How about we go shopping this weekend?" he suggests, buttoning his shirt. "We can pick out some furniture and things for this place together."

I frown. "But it's already furnished," I say, looking around. Saint's mews house in Kensington is the height of understated luxury, full of artistic, vintage pieces and gorgeous textiles.

"I want you to feel at home." He smiles over at me. "Like it's *our* home, not just mine."

"Even if I want to paint the living room bubblegum pink and replace your beloved record player with a pinball machine?" I manage to tease, touched by his determination to open his life to me. Saint was a wild and reckless playboy for long enough; I'm guessing he's never thought about a woman's design preferences in his life.

He laughs. "Whatever you want, darling. Chicken coop in the back garden. Sex swing in the library. Now, on second thought, that last one sounds like a must-have for us . . ." he adds with a smolder, and I can't help but smile.

"I love you," I say softly, even as guilt curls in my gut.

"Good," Saint says with a playful smirk.

I laugh. "Arrogant, much?" I smack him lightly on the arm as he sweeps me into a hug.

"Grateful. Very, very grateful . . ." Saint kisses me slowly, until my legs are jelly and my heart is beating fast. "And I plan on showing you just how much tonight," he adds with a low rasp. "Hint—it involves those silk ties I absolutely refuse to wear to the office. Because I think they'd suit you far better, tied down and spread wide on that bed like a good girl, while I make that tight pussy clench until you see God."

* * *

I SEE SAINT off to the office with a final breathless kiss, and then look around the house, feeling restless. I still have hours to kill before the meeting with Wren, and I know I'll go crazy if I stay cooped up here with all my questions, so I grab my jacket and laptop, and take the Tube over to Shoreditch, where the Ambrose Foundation headquarters is based.

"Tessa, good to see you." My boss in the fundraising department, Priya, greets me with a smile as I step into the converted warehouse, which buzzes with energy and chatter. "I hear we'll be seeing a lot more of you, too."

I nod. I've been working part-time, mostly remote while I juggled my studies in Oxford. But now that I'm living full-time in

London with Saint, the plan is to become a full-time employee, too. "I hope that's OK."

"Of course!" Priya smiles warmly. "Your influencer campaign is shaping up so well. We're all so excited to launch it in the new year. And I have a number of other projects where I'd love your input. I'm just about to jump on a call, but how about I swing by your office later to discuss?"

"Maybe yours would work better," I reply. "Mine's a little hectic." I nod to the desk in the middle of the open-plan floor where I've been working. Except today, someone else is sitting there. I pause.

"Oh, didn't Hugh tell you?" Priya laughs. "You have your own office now."

"I do?" I gasp in excitement.

"Right this way." Priya shows me to a cool, funky room on the second floor, filled with a desk, potted plants, and a window overlooking the bustling street below. "Vik is spending the next few months in Islamabad, overseeing our education programs there," she explains. "So this is all yours. On one condition—you keep the plants alive," she adds with a grin.

"Of course!" I beam, looking around. "Thank you. This is great."

Priya checks her watch. "I'll find you later," she says, and bustles off, leaving me to take in the cool, private space. There's a comfy couch in the corner, colorful artwork on the walls, plus photos of various Ambrose Foundation staff around the world, working on their projects. I smile, pleased to be a part of the team and hopefully contributing to our impact, too.

I settle in with my laptop, determined to focus and get some work done.

But that focus lasts all of five minutes. No matter what I do, my thoughts keep going back to Wren.

How is this even possible?

In the first days after her disappearance, my—er, *our* parents and me clung to the desperate hope that she might still be alive. She left a suicide note, which they found with her purse and shoes on the beach, along with an empty bottle of prescription pills. But even after the coast guard searched the waters nearby, they didn't find a body.

So maybe, somehow, she survived.

But as the days turned into weeks, our hopes faded. Nobody had seen or heard from her. Not one single clue to suggest she'd made it off that beach alive. She'd been erratic and suicidal before, and it was clear the police thought she'd done it again—and was successful this time. They called off the search, closed the case file, and soon, we all accepted the heartbreaking truth.

She was gone.

Now I sit there, trying to make sense of this new reality, the one where Wren has been alive all this time. Was she in hiding? How did she disappear so thoroughly? Why would she stay away so long?

What could have driven her to such a drastic act in the first place?

No matter how many times I turn it over in my mind, I can't make sense of it—or why she would suddenly appear in Saint's garden last night, revealing herself to me after all this time. She was scared. In trouble, somehow? But why the secrecy, the wig and disguise? And on top of it, demanding that I keep her return a secret—from Saint, in particular?

I shiver, chilled. The Wren I knew would never have put her family through this traumatic ordeal, so clearly I don't know Wren half as well as I thought I did.

What does she want from me?

"Knock, knock." There's a tap at my door, then Hugh enters. "How are you settling into your new digs?"

"Great!" I exclaim loudly, trying to shove the thoughts of Wren aside. "I love it in here. But are you sure someone else shouldn't be getting this office? Someone more important."

Hugh chuckles. "Believe me, with the way this influencer campaign of yours is shaping up, you're the VIP around here."

"Don't." I roll my eyes, blushing, but he insists.

"No, really. Priya showed me the plan for the rollout and some of the names you have signed up to participate. It's impressive stuff," he adds. "Of course, I don't know who on earth Lady-JaneLocks or BeastMode are, but I'm told they're quite the celebs with the younger crowd."

I smile, relaxing. It's so much easier to chat with Hugh now that I've crossed him off the list of suspects who might have been behind Wren's attack. He'd been safely in Stockholm, giving a TED Talk that weekend, so I don't have to keep my defenses up or view him with suspicion anymore.

"LadyJane is a hair influencer," I explain. "She has two million followers on Instagram and TikTok. And BeastMode is a gamer, he's huge on Twitch. I saw he posted a bunch about his dog, so I figured he would be a good fit for one of the animal protection campaigns."

"Twitch, Beasts . . . You ever feel old before your time?" Hugh asks with a grin.

I laugh. "Constantly. These influencers are still teenagers, and they have more of a platform than most big sports stars, or Beyoncé." I pause. "OK, well not Beyoncé."

"And since we can't sign her up to promote the foundation's projects, I'd say you're doing just fine with this list," Hugh agrees. "Coffee?"

"I'd love some."

We stroll downstairs to the kitchenette area, chatting about some of the foundation's upcoming projects. "I've been itching for us to expand," Hugh confides as he sets the expensive espresso machine humming. "And not just in scale, but also the kind of projects we support. It may be unseemly to say, but it's easier to get people to donate money for starving orphans in some far-flung nation than it is to get them to pay attention to problems right here at home. I'm hoping in the years ahead, we can focus on issues right here in England—drug rehabilitation, food banks, the less sexy charity goals."

"And how does your father feel about that?" I ask before I can stop myself. Hugh's father, Lionel Ambrose, is in the running to become the next British prime minister—and seems to have the votes sewn up, if the polls are anything to go by. "I just mean, he likes to paint a rosier picture of the country, that's all. At least, judging by his campaign speeches."

I remember meeting him at the Ashford Pharma event, seeing how he charmed and worked the room, every inch the trustworthy politician.

Hugh gives a wry smile. "My father and I have very different priorities," he replies, thankfully not seeming offended by my comment. "But we are alike in one way—we have a vision for the future. For this country. That mission is all that matters."

I blink, surprised by his grim tone. Then he flashes a grin. "And if BeastMode and Lady Jane will make it happen, then I say, I'm all in," he adds. "Even if they make me feel about a hundred years old."

I laugh, relaxing again. "I'll get one of the interns to make you a cheat card," I suggest. "So you don't mix up your GroJo with your GoPro. He's a gardening influencer," I add. "Big on Lawn-Tok."

"I'll need it." Hugh sets the espresso to drip, then expertly adds steamed milk in a swirl. "And *voilà*. If all this fails, I can always run off to Rome and become a barista," he adds with a grin.

"I'm impressed." I take a sip. "Wow, this really is good."

"Annabelle begged me to train the staff for her wedding breakfast," Hugh says, looking amused. "Apparently, she wants her and Max's initials swirled into all the foam on every cup."

I laugh. "That sounds like Annabelle."

"Did you get the itinerary?" he asks.

"Itinerary?"

"For the wedding events. They kick off next week, you know, and it's scheduled down to the minute." Hugh looks mock serious. "I think she even put the bathroom breaks in."

"I'll have to check with Saint," I say, amused. Then I pause. "You don't really think Annabelle meant it when she said I would be a bridesmaid, do you?"

Hugh smirks. "Not only did she mean it, but I would wager you a hundred pounds she's already having the bridesmaid dress altered and is making a personalized flower crown for you. Or rather, one of her poor minions is."

"Oh dear." I laugh. "Isn't that kind of weird, me being a part of the wedding? I just met you all!"

"But you're part of the family now, aren't you?" he asks. "I mean, Saint's like a brother to us, and if he's happy, then we are, too."

I smile back, touched. "He should be happy," I crack, and then realize that came out sounding dirtier than I meant. "I just mean, with everything going smoothly at Ashford," I add quickly, and Hugh laughs.

"Yeah, I heard some whispers about that. I'm glad. A lot of people have a lot riding on the Ashford Pharma fortunes, including the Foundation here."

"How do you mean?" I ask, puzzled.

"Our endowment is invested in the markets," Hugh explains. "I don't follow the details, but since it was all set up before I took the reins, I'm guessing a tidy sum is tied up in Ashford shares. My father likes to keep his friends close and their profits closer."

"Oh." I blink, not sure how to process that. Just another example of how tightly all these powerful families' fates are intertwined. But before I can respond properly, my phone buzzes with an alarm. It's 1:30 already. I need to go meet Wren!

"Hot date?" Hugh asks as I quickly rinse my coffee cup in the sink.

"I'm meeting with another influencer," I lie quickly. "Not sure if they're a good fit, so I thought I'd sit down face-to-face and check the vibe before I mentioned anything."

"Great work." Hugh grins. "Let me know if it all pans out. We're rooting for you."

* * *

I escape back to my office to grab my things, then head out. Shoreditch is on the east side of London, about a twenty-minute walk from the address Wren gave me, and I walk fast, my nerves twisting tighter with every step.

Why the cloak-and-dagger routine? Couldn't she just have sat down and talked last night? She was on edge. *Scared.* Acting like she could have been discovered at any moment. I wonder now if she thought she was being followed.

I walk a little faster, glancing around me, but the streets are busy and nobody is paying me any attention. My surroundings turn from the newer hipster coffee shops and boutiques to a slightly seedier side of London, the East End of disheveled diners, mini-marts, and boarded-up shops. It's definitely far from the glamorous hot spots Saint and his friends frequent. Nobody I know would expect to find me way out here.

But clearly, that's the point.

The Two Hearts pub is on the corner, a dingy local spot with faded carpet and a weary-looking barmaid on duty behind the bar. Early in the afternoon, the place is quiet, with just a few drinkers alone at the bar, or heads bent over the horse-racing scores.

And Wren. Already cloistered in a booth in the back, half-hidden from the room but with a clear view of the door.

I make my way over, relieved she turned up at all. If she slipped away from me again. I would have no way of finding her. No way to even prove she'd shown her face at all.

"Wren," I greet her, smiling despite everything. Just seeing her face fills me with emotion, even if it is drawn and tired. Her eyes jump nervously around the room.

"Don't call me that, not so loud," she says hurriedly, pulling me down in the seat across from her. She's nursing a soda, and has one waiting for me, too. "Did you tell anyone you were meeting me?"

"No."

"No one?" Wren demands, grabbing my hand. "Not even Saint?"

"I told you that I wouldn't." I pull my hand away. She's scaring me now, so sharp and intense, but this meeting isn't making any sense so far. "I hated lying, but I made you a promise, and I've kept to it. Now it's your turn to keep your side of the bargain," I continue, leveling her with a stare. "Tell me what's going on. Wren . . . I want answers. I deserve to know the truth!"

Wren exhales. She glances around the room again, but nobody's paying us any attention. Finally, her posture relaxes. She gives me a nod. "You're right. I'm sorry for all the sneaking around, but you'll see, I'm only trying to protect you. All of it was to protect you."

I shiver. "What are you talking about? Start at the beginning," I say, needing to make sense of this. "Faking your death, the suicide note . . . you planned it? It was all an act? You never meant to kill yourself?"

Wren slowly nods. "I didn't see any other way. You see, a few weeks after I got back from Oxford, I started getting threatening letters."

"What kind of threats?" I ask, confused.

"They said I needed to keep quiet, that bad things would happen. Not just to me, but to Mom and Dad, and to you." Wren swallows, fear flicking across her face. "They had photos, Tessa. Surveillance of you, at that nonprofit job you were working. Out running in the mornings. They drew a bull's-eye on the photo."

"Oh my God," I breathe. "Who was doing it? What did they want?"

"I didn't see any other way out," Wren continues desperately, not answering my question. "Everything was falling apart, you were already so worried about me, and I . . . I was losing my grip. I didn't know what to do. I thought if I could just disappear, then they wouldn't care about you guys anymore. You could be safe."

"Who?" I demand again. "Who were these people? What did they want with you?"

Wren swallows hard. "There's something I didn't tell you, something that happened when I was in Oxford . . ."

"Connected to the attack?" I ask.

She shakes her head. "Something else. Something big . . ."

She trails off, clearly still terrified by whatever it is she knows that made these people come after her.

I lean forward. "You can trust me, Wren," I promise her. "I won't let anyone hurt you again."

She gives me a faint smile, and for a moment, I see a spark of the old Wren in her eyes again. My beloved sister. My closest friend. "What are you going to do, beat them with your tennis racquet, the way you did with Marcy Littleton when she called me a stuck-up nerd at camp?" she jokes softly.

"If that's what it takes," I vow. I take her hand and squeeze it. "We're in this together now. Please, Wren, whatever's going on, you don't have to deal with it alone anymore."

She squeezes back. "I know. I hate to bring you into this, but I can't stay silent, not when you're with him now."

Him? Does she mean Saint?

"I tried to warn you to stop digging," she adds. "I sent you that note . . ."

"That was you? But why?"

I'm frowning at Wren in confusion when she takes a deep breath and continues. "It was my research, at Ashford Pharma. I stumbled across something I should never have seen. It's the Alzheimer's drug, Tessa," she says, looking stricken. "The results from the trials were all faked. The drugs don't work."

"No . . ." I gasp, stunned.

She nods. "That's what they were threatening me about, to keep me quiet. They said . . ." Wren's voice breaks, but she soldiers on, urgent. "They said that if I ever revealed the truth, then they'd get to you. They would show you the inside of that cell, the way they did to me. And they wouldn't use the drugs, either. They'd make sure you remembered every single moment."

About the Author

ROXY SLOANE was born and raised in England, and got her bachelor's degree at the University of Oxford, where she absolutely did not attend any scandalous parties or secret society events. Not at all. She currently lives in Los Angeles, where she enjoys recklessly writing spicy scenes in public places.

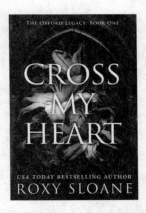